Oddball. Misfit. Lunatic.

Obsessed from his childhood with Jonathan Swift's story of Lemuel Gulliver's travels, Arthur C. Gulliver is committed to an asylum for his pestiferous soliciting to raise funds for an insane voyage to the fictitious land of Lilliput. But, with the aid of two other inmates, he manages to realize his dream and sail to Lilliput.

The Lilliput Arthur finds in the mid 1930s is much different than Lemuel Gulliver's. The monarchy is gone. Lilliputians zoom across land and sea in spheres of transparent steel. Spanking is the Lilliputian method of formal greeting. Drunkenness is required by law. Skyscrapers hang gracefully suspended in mid-air. Politicians pay voters directly and openly for their votes. The military wields a fantastic paralytic ray. Nights in the city are lit by small artificial suns created by great beams of light. And, a mysterious third chamber in the tricameral legislature dominates Lilliputian government.

The people and customs of Arthur's Lilliput seem bizarre at first. But the closer we look, the more we see the politics, economics, and society of 21st century America; the more we see ourselves.

Very peculiar indeed.

Welcome to the new Lilliput!

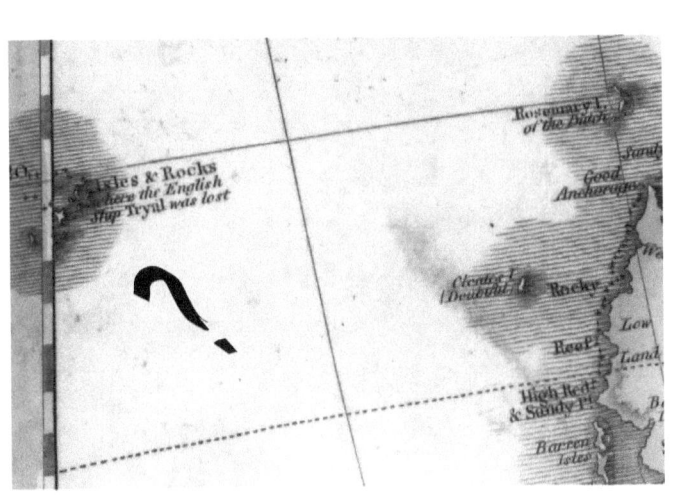

There's a New Shuffle in Lilliput

The Story of Arthur C. Gulliver's Travels

Created by Joseph Martin Cunningham

Edited by Barry Cunningham

Mount Laurel Press
Cleveland Heights, Ohio

There's a New Shuffle in Lilliput
The Story of Arthur C. Gulliver's Travels

Original manuscript by Joseph Martin Cunningham circa 1936. Edited and revised, with Introduction and Afterword added, by Barry Cunningham.

Book design by Barry Cunningham.

Proofread by Karen Beck.

ISBN 978-0-9827420-0-6

Library of Congress Control Number: 2010929155

Library of Congress Subject Headings:
Fantasy.
Imaginary societies–Fiction.
Satire–American.
Swift, Jonathan, 1667-1745.–Fiction.
Swift, Jonathan, 1667-1745.–Gulliver's Travels.
Travelers–Fiction.
Voyages and travels–Fiction.
Voyages, Imaginary–Fiction
Voyages, Imaginary–Humor.

Published by Mount Laurel Press, Cleveland Heights, Ohio.
www.mountlaurelpress.com

Version 1.1

Introduction

THE FIRST TIME I completely read the manuscript copy of **There's a New Shuffle in Lilliput** I was surprised at how topical it was. I had heard about it and read pieces of it when I was young, but the first time I actually read it from start to finish was in the Fall of 2004, when I retyped and edited it as part of a web site I created to celebrate the 100th anniversary of my father's birth. In that election season, just prior to George W. Bush's reelection, it seemed uniquely topical. As I write this introduction in early 2010, following the financial meltdown of 2008-2009 that may presage more serious economic and political turmoil, it still seems topical, but for somewhat different reasons.

★   ★   ★

The story is supposed to have been written by Arthur C. Gulliver in early 1936. Arthur is the son of a poor farmer, who becomes obsessed with the idea of going to Lilliput after he encounters Jonathan Swift's **Gulliver's Travels** in his early youth. This obsession becomes Arthur's undoing during his senior year at college: he is expelled for his pestiferous soliciting to raise money for a trip to Lilliput and committed to an insane asylum. However, it is there that Arthur meets two inmates that help him realize his dream. After a harrowing voyage, Arthur arrives alone in Lilliput.

Arthur finds a Lilliput that has changed enormously since Lemuel Gulliver's day two centuries earlier. In some fields they are more technologically advanced than the outside world. Indeed, Arthur is struck by a formidable paralytic ray in his first encounter with the Lilliputians. But other inventions from Arthur's world, like moving pictures, are completely unknown to them. The political landscape too is completely altered. The monarchy is gone, replaced by a tricameral legislature and an executive branch headed by the **Donkgop**.[1] Lemuel Gulliver, who had fled Lilliput after being condemned as a traitor, had since been elevated to the status of a national hero.

---

[1] A little bipartisan satire first pointed out to me by my wife: a combination of donkey and G.O.P.

So Arthur, enthusiastically welcomed by the Lilliputians, sets about learning everything he can about Lilliputian culture and society.

The Lilliput that Arthur discovers is sort of a miniaturized *Bizarro*[2] world. Instead of shaking hands as a formal greeting, Lilliputians spank each other. Drunkenness is required by law and the drinking requirements are tripled on election days. This theme echoes much of my father's poetry from the early 1930s, before the repeal of Prohibition, which could be characterized as anti-Prohibition satire.

The Lilliputians have made being injured into a criminal offense rather than a grounds for suit. While there are definite parallels with the laws regarding disease in Samuel Butler's **Erewhon**, the Lilliputian legal reasoning on the subject is really quite different.

As Arthur delves into the workings of the Lilliputian economy and government, the more the descriptions seem to be torn out of today's headlines.

The *suckorities* described in Chapter XIV bear more than a passing resemblance to derivatives, collateralized debt obligations, asset backed securities, and credit default swaps of the recent financial crisis.

The scene of confused ship building in Chapter XV forcefully recalls Arthur C. Clarke's classic short story *Superiority*,[3] written over a decade later.

It is hard to believe that the descriptions of the legislative processes in Chapter XVI were not based on current events rather than the Congress during Franklin D. Roosevelt's first term. The Lilliputians' reconciliation conference committee practices seem little different from those current in the U.S. Congress. The hearings on the Stang-Hinstool scandal could be a parody of congressional hearings on Lehman Brothers, Goldman Sachs, Enron, or innumerable other recent financial scandals. Finally, the description of the third branch of the legislature, the *paynetakit*, and the *estibelobs*[4] pulls back the veil on the real power controlling government, which,

---

[2] *Bizarro* is a fictional character first introduced in *Superboy* #68 by D.C. Comics. Originally he was created as an imperfect copy of Superboy, but in the later evolution of his story he inhabits a world governed by the Bizarro Code, "Us do the opposite of all Earthly things."

[3] Arthur C. Clarke, *Superiority*, ©1951 by Fantasy House, Inc., reprinted in **Fantasia Mathematica**, edited by Clifton Fadiman, Simon and Schuster, 1958.

[4] A near anagram for **lobbyist**.

through its control of mass media, distracts us from the real issues and tells us, "Pay no attention to the man behind the curtain."

★   ★   ★

Most of my father's poetry and short stories can be easily dated using notes on or accompanying the manuscripts. Dating the manuscript for this book is a little harder.

The only explicit date in the book is that of Arthur Gulliver's foreword: January, 1936. I think that this is about the right date for the composition of the novel for three reasons. First, my half-sister Tanya recalled it from her childhood. She was born in 1930, but her mother and our father were divorced sometime between 1942 and 1944. Second, Chapter XVI could have been composed no earlier than 1935 because it contains a parody of Franklin D. Roosevelt's Postmaster General James Farley in the character of Stang Swarly. It alludes to the small scandal in the stamp collecting world referred to a "Farley's Follies" that led to the special printings of the imperforate National Parks stamps and some other souvenir sheets in 1935.[5] The third reason is more circumstantial, but the lack of any clear reference to the prelude to World War II leads me to believe that my father must have finished it prior to 1938.[6]

Barry W. Cunningham
Cleveland Heights, Ohio
May, 2010

---

[5]As Postmaster General, Farley had reprints made of some current stamps without perforations which he presented to President Franklin D. Roosevelt and Interior Secretary Harold Ickes, who were both stamp collectors. When ordinary stamp collectors learned of the reprints, they complained. The stamps were reissued as special printings without gum and sold to the general public at the Philatelic Agency in Washington, D.C. from March 15 to June 15, 1935.

[6]Arguably, the Scanezi military buildup against Lilliput mentioned in Chapters XV and XIX may be a reference the Nazi rearmament of Germany during the 1930s.

There's a New Shuffle in Lilliput

by

Arthur C. Gulliver

Dedicated to the memory

of

Professor Isaac Eliminom

whose

faith, service, and devotion

made this book possible.

... for my purpose holds
to sail beyond the sunset ...

Tennyson, *Ulysses*

Contents

Contents

Foreword

IT IS WITH MUCH HESITANCY and many misgivings that I have undertaken to write the history here presented. First of all, the voyage and sojourn abroad, an account of which occupies a chief part of this narrative, was not intended, had my plans been carried out, to produce the material for a book either literary or historical in character; that would have been the work of others to follow me better qualified in those fields.

My dear friend Spaddle's purpose was missionary; mine was scientific, or merely curious. His efforts ended in tragedy, and mine led to a complete fiasco. Had I been left entirely to my own judgment in the matter, I should have been content to let the matter rest there, since a book written about a fiasco by the one who produced it is more than likely to be one itself, especially if the author is deficient in literary qualifications.

However, a recent acquaintance of mine, who dwells in the same institution as I (I hope only temporarily) has been very insistent in his repeated assertions that I should embody in a book the stories I told him, whether they are true or not. (That is the heart-rending part about it — nobody *believes* me.) While my friend has been very persuasive, I am persuaded only enough to have undertaken this book with much doubt. As I write, my bitter experience shrieks the words back at me. It all seems so futile. I have told my story time and time again, only to be silenced with the maddening stare of incredulous eyes. Perhaps, I should not wish more than that some may find a short-lived enjoyment in these pages; but how my whole being *hopes, hopes, hopes* that some kindred spirit will read and will *believe*.

Although the meaning of each Lilliputian word is given when the word is introduced into the text, a glossary has been appended to the end of this work for the benefit of those who may like to know how various names and words are pronounced as well as to reinform the reader of their meanings, if by chance they should be forgotten.

Spoop Sanitorium
January, 1936   Arthur C. Gulliver

Prologue

SMALL CIRCUMSTANCES can indeed, have prodigious effects upon the life of a man. When I look back over the events of my life and analyze the substance of those events, I am almost startled by the trivial things without which I should never have set out upon, nor experienced, some of the most interesting adventures that ever fell to the lot of man. For instance, what but the merest chance, a spin of the wheel of fate, determined that my surname should be Gulliver? Why not Jones, or Smith, or McNutt? What but the rarest coincidence could account for the fact that I, a son of a dry farmer, dwelling on a homestead in one of the bleakest territories in the United States, away from the usual educational facilities available to the youth of our country, should ever have come upon that famous book of travels written (as I have since learned) by my illustrious ancestor, Mr. Lemuel Gulliver? By chance though, I did come upon **Gulliver's Travels** while yet a small boy. A vendor of patent medicines traveling about the country, plying his quackery in the towns and villages, happened by reason of a broken axle to stop near my father's shack long enough for him and my father to repair the damaged part of the wagon. My mother had taken great pains to teach me to read and write. The Bible, Bunyan's **Pilgrim's Progress**, and a dog-eared copy of simple Bible Stories comprised our whole library, and until **Gulliver's Travels** was added to them, served as the only text books for my early education.

Notwithstanding his questionable calling, the old vendor proved to be a kindly man. He allowed me to range through his wagon to examine the curiosities he had collected. It was there I found **Gulliver's Travels**. At once I became so absorbed in the adventures narrated in that book that when the axle was at last repaired, I asked our departing guest if I might not keep it, taking care that my mother or father should not hear me. The medicine vendor readily granted my request. Although my father's later inquiries as to how I had obtained the book forced me to own that it had been by my asking, the punishment he gave me I considered, and still do consider, a small price to pay for such a treasure. It has been more than a treasure to me; it has been a foundation and cornerstone of my whole career. Without it my life would have lacked a prime motivating power which eventually led to a certain success and achievement of purpose through veritable walls of obstacles ranging from a mere lack of sympathy upon the part of friends who looked upon me as a "nut" to those forcible and unfriendly acts of others which at times have been instrumental in limiting my travels to the confines of an insane asylum.

It is no exaggeration to say that I read **Gulliver's Travels** hundreds upon hundreds of times. I would never permit myself to memorize it, for that would have spoiled the next reading. I remember having told my mother soon after I had completed reading the famous chronicle for the first time that I was going on a voyage to Lilliput. She smiled and accepted my statement as a bit of childish make-believe until the time came when I had mentioned the fact so often that the fixity of the idea in my thought began to attract her special attention. At last the effect of **Gulliver's Travels** upon me came to the notice of my father. While I do not attempt to justify any of my boyish shortcomings, I will state that my father showed toward me considerable harshness and quite an absence of understanding as to what was taking place in my mind upon the occasions about which I am now to write.

One exceedingly hot day while I should have been hoeing young corn, which, already stunted from drought, was drooping in the intense heat, I so far neglected my duty as to retire to the shade of a dry arroyo, there to peruse again Gulliver's account of his extraordinary adventures. My father came upon me while I was thus mis occupied and his anger was quick to chastise me with a sound thrashing. The book was taken from me, and flung into the cornfield from whence I retrieved it upon my first opportunity.

This drought of which I write had a fortunate effect upon my life. It continued unbroken throughout the summer. Nothing upon the plowed face of that broad prairie, which so lately had been range land for cattle, could possibly grow in the unrelenting, dry, blistering heat. In September, my father, with tears in his eyes, packed the few belongings we had into our only wagon, and with my mother and me set out for Boston, the city of his birth.

At that time both my mother and father were of the opinion that (to put it mildly) my reason was somewhat impaired. During the long, tiresome journey eastward, I had more time for conversation with my father than I ever have had either before or since. It was during this journey I first noticed the peculiarity of my parents' attitude toward me – an attitude of tolerance toward my talk concerning Lilliput – which had not before been part of their demeanor. Now it is quite evident to me that my father had hit upon the scheme of trying to reason me away from what he considered a fixed idea which rendered me mentally unbalanced. I remember his saying after listening again to a fresh vow of mine to visit Lilliput, "Son, there is no such place, and there never was. That book, **Gulliver's Travels**, is only fiction – a story which is not true. It was written many years ago by a man named Jonathan Swift, and he made up the whole business. There is not truth in it. See this name here," he added, thumbing the title page and pointing to the name – JONATHAN SWIFT.

With all due deference and respect to my father, I must here observe that he made the mistake of meeting me upon my own ground. Turning to the opening page, I pointed to the note of the publisher, *Richard Sympson*, concerning the author, Lemuel Gulliver.

"This man, Sympson, knew Gulliver," I replied. "He tells all about him. And if I could get the part he says he cut out of Gulliver's book, I could easily get to Lilliput. All the directions about getting there are in that part."

"But son, Mr. Swift wrote that note, too. That was just to make the story seem more real."

"But it is signed by Richard Sympson, and Gulliver wrote a letter to him, too. He was Gulliver's cousin. Gulliver says so."

Facing me with a firm countenance, my father made one more thrust in an attempt to pierce through the cloud he imagined befuddled my reason.

"Why is Mr. Swift's name on the book, if he did not write it?"

It was then that something miraculous and inexplicable happened to me. I knew the answer and I knew what I must do. Although I have no sons, I will set down for any I may later have this wonderful thing I experienced when my father asked me that question, for I probably will not find time from my future travels in which to write letters to my sons.

I knew that Jonathan Swift had stolen Gulliver's book for the mere profit that would accrue to him from it, and this was the answer I gave my father.

"I know," I continued, "that there is a Lilliput. I know that Gulliver went there, and I know that I am going there. I am sure of these things."

The almost imperceptible shake of his head as my father looked at my mother did not escape me. His pity for me was not pleasant to bear, though nothing I could then do or say would shake his belief concerning my mental condition. My sons, although it is not possible for me to say how I knew, I knew there was a Lilliput. I knew I knew. Something in me told me. I could no more fail to respond to those inner urges to find Lilliput than I could have voluntarily failed to breathe. Insanity? Was Columbus insane because he knew the world was round? Faith lights the way where paths of reason are yet untrod, and so, my sons, I knew there was a Lilliput!

Chapter I

Wherein the author is expelled from college and sent to Spoop Sanitorium where he meets Professor Eliminom and Glykus Spaddle; and wherein the author receives proof of his descent from Lemuel Gulliver, with aid of his new friends successfully lays plans for a voyage to Lilliput, and gets started.

WELL, I DID GO TO LILLIPUT, and knowing as I do that the reader is more interested in that distant country and its inhabitants than in the events of my early life, I will hasten to that part of my story. However, before I can carry the reader with me to Lilliput I must first mention a few incidents preliminary thereto, even though by so doing I run the risk of presuming too far upon kind patience; otherwise things would happen without explanation in an unrelated sequence thereby covering the narrative over with an atmosphere of a dream rather than that of reality. In as far as my poor ability will permit of such a thing, I wish my writing to seem as real and truthful as the facts to which it relates. Nothing could be more real than those facts.

Upon arriving in Boston my father soon was able to gain a livelihood in his old trade as a tinsmith and for a number of years my parents and I led the normal life of an average American family. To be sure, I continued to be embarrassed by opinions of people who regarded me as a young man with a complex, but as the years passed I became gradually more accustomed to the feeling of loneliness engendered by the adverse judgment of men.

In 19-- my father acquired a small fortune left to him by his only living relative, an old man, one John Simpson, whom our family befriended in Boston during the last years of his life. I had entered college that same year, and my father, with his new wealth, was able to see me comfortably through three years. In my senior year I ran afoul of the college regulations, described by a physician who accompanied me to another institution as "persistent begging and solicitation of funds both in and out of classes for a voyage to Lilliput."

At first I took my dismissal stoically enough, for in all fairness I must state that the prexy had solemnly warned me to stop my "pestiferous" solicitation of funds, and I had deliberately violated that order out of loyalty to my set purpose. The other institution heretofore mentioned, I discovered a few days after my incarceration therein, was a Sanitorium for nervous and mental cases. To be taken to such a place was, indeed, a humiliation from which I thought for a time I should not recover. Could I really be crazy? No, I could not. My confidence in myself soon returned, and not long after my arrival at the Sanitorium I began to forget my feeling of resentment against a world that would treat me so unjustly. People and things in my new environment began to attract my attention. Since I was permitted to roam at large every day through the beautiful grounds of my temporary home, good fortune again came to me in these circumstances which at first I had been unable to recognize as anything but an almost intolerable adversity. About the seventh or eighth day after I took up my new abode, I came upon an elderly man, also an inmate, who had suffered this isolation from the world quite as unjustly as I had. I soon learned that he was a former professor of mathematics imbued with the peculiar idea that the brain of man functioned according to a mathematical formula. According to the theory of this gentleman, Professor Isaac Eliminom, if a mathematician were able to take notes on the exact utterances of any person for a period of several days, it would be possible from this data to forecast exactly what that person would think or utter at any particular time in the future. The gist of his theory was that the curve of normal distribution of the words a person uttered could be determined by a study of the things he had said or written already. Then by following the scheme of the individual curve as accurately determined, modifying it according to the rate of acquisition of new ideas, also determined from the data of previous utterances, plus a very slight deviation computed by the law of averages as governing accidents normally shifting the course of an individual life, my friend was positive that he could predict the future utterances of any individual. My mathematical knowledge being very deficient, the explanation I have given of the Professor's theory must perforce be only an inadequate layman's explanation, but I have done my best to set forth the general import of it as I understood it at the time.

Upon first hearing the Professor expound this theory, I was inclined to be not greatly surprised at finding him in our then mutual environment, though very shortly I was ashamed of this hasty and faulty impression.

Upon learning that I was Arthur Gulliver, my new friend evinced a keen interest in me.

"Are you by any chance a descendant of the famous Lemuel Gulliver, who made the only voyage ever made to Lilliput and Brobdingnag?"

In answer to this question I confessed that I had always thought I was descended from Lemuel Gulliver, although I had never been able to establish the fact by actual proof.

"By Jove," exclaimed the old man, "My old friend, Doctor Seabury Allbright of London, is a genealogist *par excellence*! If anybody in the world can trace your ancestry to Lemuel Gulliver, he can. I will write to him about the matter at once."

My friendship for Professor Eliminom grew rapidly, which was no more than what was to be expected, since he was the first person I had ever met who, without any effort of persuasion on my part, shared my belief in the veracity of **Gulliver's Travels**. I soon found that he was well acquainted with the book; so well, in fact, that he had at one time worked out some interesting computations on the velocity of Lilliputian arrows as shot from bows made of various woods at varying angles in assumed winds.

A very few days after I met Professor Eliminom he introduced me to Mr. Glykus Spaddle, a young man who studied at some theological college during those intervals when he was not sojourning at the Spoop Sanitorium, which was the name of the institution in which I was detained. The reason for young Spaddle's detention in such a place he never revealed to us. Neither the Professor nor I were ever able to see any trace of mental unsoundness in him. For all the world, he seemed to be a studious young fellow, deeply interested in religious studies and fired with a worthy ambition. Spaddle would have liked to have seen the whole world, especially the Hebrews, converted to Christianity. He was quite zealous about it, but as for having a complex on that subject, nothing could ever convince me he had a complex on that or any other subject.

These two friends, Eliminom and Spaddle, had a profound influence on my life and fortune. About three months after I met the Professor he presented me with positive proof from Doctor Allbright that I was a direct descendant of Lemuel Gulliver. My elation over this news I cannot describe; yet, it was weighted down with a despair arising out of hopelessness.

My one consuming desire was to go to Lilliput, but even though I could establish my identity as a descendant of the great Lemuel Gulliver, how could this ever help to get me there? Two obstacles of gigantic magnitude, in view of the world's harsh judgment of me, were to be overcome. First, how could I raise funds for my projected voyage? Second, how could I find my way there? I had long since concluded that the publisher, Richard Sympson, had not preserved the portions of **Gulliver's Travels** which he struck out before publishing the manuscript, for I had been in correspondence at one time or another with every major repository of knowledge throughout the world, and none of them gave me any hope. No man ever committed a more careless act than thoughtless Richard Sympson. Those lines through which he drew his pen undoubtedly gave full and accurate directions by which one could locate some of the most interesting and instructive nations in the universe. His unparalleled act of vandalism lost for the rest of the world the countries of Lilliput, Brobdingnag, and Houghnhnm Land for more than two centuries! How his soul must have writhed in purgatory for that crime!

For long sleepless hours one night I had brooded upon my thwarted life until the early hours of the morning, when suddenly like a brilliant flash of lightning an idea came to me. So simple was it in its details and so certain was it to enable me to get to Lilliput that for a time I really was in doubt concerning my sanity for not having thought of it before. I could not wait for the morning attendant to free me from my room, so anxious was I to present my idea to Professor Eliminom and Glykus Spaddle.

Briefly, the idea was to enlist the Professor's mathematics in overcoming one of my obstacles, and Spaddle's missionary zeal in overcoming the other. If the former could predict a man's future utterances by analysis of his past utterances, obviously he could supply the deleted parts of **Gulliver's Travels** by the simple expedient of analyzing the first chapters of that book and applying his theory. By the information so obtained one could sail directly to Lilliput. As for Spaddle, he could aid in as large a way as the Professor. In spite of the fact that I had tried unsuccessfully a thousand times to raise money to finance the trip, I had never thought of making a missionary expedition out of it. Gulliver made no assertion that the Lilliputians were Christians. If some of their barbaric customs had not died out with the passing of centuries, I could conceive of no other field in which Spaddle might exercise his high calling with so much spiritual accomplishment and benefit to look forward to.

When I greeted my friends early in the morning after my sleepless night and presented my plan to them they seized upon it with an enthusiasm exceeding even my highest hopes. Professor Eliminom's face brightened with joy and it was not ten minutes before he was busy with a copy of **Gulliver's Travels** in one hand and a pencil in the other, rapidly tabulating a strange jumble of words and figures upon a sheaf of papers. Spaddle immediately wrote letters to every one of his former theological student friends, many of whom were then ministers in churches having some of the largest congregations in the country. By what I suppose was the usual means, though I never discovered what the usual means were, Spaddle three days later obtained another of his frequent furloughs from Spoop Sanitorium. He was gone for a period of three weeks, during which time Professor Eliminom pieced together all of the missing parts of **Gulliver's Travels**. That voluminous and valuable work I must leave for the Professor himself, to hand down to posterity. It being totally his work and property, it would verge upon fraud for me to present any verbatim portion of it here. However, that generous old gentleman granted me the right to use it as a guide to Lilliput. It suffices to say here that it proved to be a most accurate and comprehensive guide which led me to the island I had so long wished to visit.

When Spaddle returned he had amassed a sum of currency and credits well above a million dollars. I think I have never been so filled with ecstasy as I was the afternoon the three of us met in the garden to lay definite plans for the glorious adventure. Professor Eliminom would not go, pleading old age and the wish to complete his mathematical research ere death put an end to his labors. But many were the helpful suggestions this old man gave to us. Neither Spaddle nor I ever ceased to count him as the finest friend we ever had. We laid plans for going to New Orleans and there acquiring a staunch little vessel. After loading her with provisions to last us for a period of two to three years, we planned to sail away. Of course, there were numerous details to settle which would not be of interest if related here. It is enough to state that we laid our plans carefully in order that there could not be the least setback or delay once we had set about their execution.

One thing yet troubled me somewhat. The fact remained that both Spaddle and I were inmates of Spoop Sanitorium. I, at least, had not been allowed to pass beyond its confines since my arrival. This cloud, like the others, was soon dispelled. Again did our grand old friend, the Professor, come to our aid. By a series of mathematical operations much too intricate for me even to attempt to follow he foretold that on the night of March 6th, 19--, the guard by the north gate would fall asleep through over-drinking, that he would have dropped the key to that gate on a spot nine feet from the north wall, six inches from the edge of the path skirting the wall, and four yards from the gate itself. His calculations also revealed that the attendant on the floor where Spaddle and I each had a room kept a duplicate master key in the right pocket of his extra pair of trousers hanging in the closet of his quarters, and that he never locked the door to his own room.

While I never had any experience in the art of sneak thievery and could not boast a special relish for it, Spaddle's scruples were such that I knew he would never steal the attendant's key, so I had that task to perform myself. On the afternoon of the last day we planned to remain at the Spoop Institution, Spaddle and I bade Professor Eliminom goodbye. He put so much feeling into his farewell that he could not hide the tears which appeared in his eyes. His wishes for our good fortune, and his praises for our undertaking of an enterprise which should add so much to the world's store of knowledge, were so warm and sincere that I felt considerably chagrined upon parting with the old man. When looking at the frail and aged frame of this princely old fellow, the best friend I ever had, I was especially saddened by the thought that in all likelihood I should never again see him alive. Glykus must have shared something of this feeling, for I noticed him swallowing hard as he pressed the Professor's hand in bidding him goodbye.

All went as planned. I obtained the attendant's pass-key and Spaddle picked up the north gate key exactly where the Professor's calculations indicated it would be. The night guard propped in a spraddle-legged sitting position in a drunken stupor against the north wall, took no notice of our exit. In two hours Spaddle and I were on a fast night train speeding toward New Orleans. In less than a month from that date we were sailing in a trim little schooner-yacht, the **Night-Hawk**, bound for Lilliput with enough provisions aboard to last for two years or more.

Chapter II

Wherein storm and death strike heavy blows upon the
Night-Hawk; and wherein the author, in spite of great
difficulties, reaches Lilliput and is warmly greeted by a
man-of-war.

AN ACCOUNT OF THE VOYAGE from New Orleans to Lilliput, although filled with adventure interesting enough in itself, I will
not put down here at length, for to do so would only further delay my coming to the matters I set out to chronicle in these pages.
It must suffice to say that misfortune seemed to glide in the wake
of our vessel from the time we set sail. The trip around the Horn
was a terrible one. In one of the bad blows in the South Pacific our
two seamen were washed overboard and drowned, leaving only the
cook, Spaddle and myself aboard. Some of the cabin furniture was
damaged by salt water, and, worst of all, our sending and receiving
wireless apparatus was put totally out of commission, though, after
the loss of our sailors, I do not know what use we could have made
of it, for neither Spaddle nor I knew anything whatsoever about operating it. Out of necessity we were both obliged to man our small
vessel, and, out of the same necessity, our practical nautical education proceeded at a rapid pace, notwithstanding we had no better
master than a seamen's cook.

After many days and nights of fearful ordeal in a storm which
seemed to have no ending, we hauled out of the affected area under
the power of our gasoline motors, which we had hoped not to use,
owing to the fact that we carried only a scant store of fuel. Our good
fortune at last in encountering calm seas was of short duration, for
two days later the grim spectre of death again trod our decks. This
time his hand stilled the brave heart of my dear friend "Glyk" as I
had learned to call him. Spaddle was seized suddenly with a strange
illness. Whether it was a disease with which I am not familiar or
poisoning, I do not know. He was to have relieved me at the helm
at eight bells in the evening. When I had waited for some minutes
after the end of my watch for him to appear, I locked the wheel
and went to look for him in the cabin, thinking as I did so, that

he must have overslept, for he was weary unto death, as were we all. There I found him in a mad, agonizing convulsion, writhing upon the floor. In a very few moments the attack was over and his distorted purple face gradually blanched to the color of chalk. With this change, his limbs relaxed. I felt his pulse which was at first rapid, violent, and irregular, but quite soon slowed down and weakened very perceptibly. He never became conscious again. Before morning that splendid young man was dead.

As the cook and I pieced together a winding-sheet from a torn stay-sail, I could not hold back my tears. Weariness and sorrow gripped my soul — weariness from trying toil and lack of sleep through a long furious storm — sorrow at the death of a congenial, steadfast, loyal friend. For some reason I could not help but think I had brought "Glyk" and the two faithful seamen to their untimely deaths. But for my besetting zeal to sail to Lilliput the three of them would in all likelihood still have been living. Why my despondency did not lead me to leap into the sea when at last the remains of Spaddle were in the sheet and dropped overboard, I cannot say, unless it was that I was too tired even for that. I remember having had such an impulse while reading a passage from the Bible in a last rite over the body in the winding-sheet. Together the cook and I lifted it on a plank to the railing and silently it slipped into the sea. A stinging spray of salt water on the wings of a sudden breeze struck me in the face. I remember nothing further until I awakened some time later in a moonlit night, stiff and chilled from having lain asleep on the open deck. One by one my senses returned while the events which took place immediately preceding my sleep began to form and take their proper sequence in my clearing memory. I stumbled to the cabin and there, finding a flask of brandy, gulped down a generous draught, which, with a change to dry clothing, soon served to restore in my half-paralyzed body something approximating normal circulation.

I had yet another terrible blow to experience. A search of the whole vessel that night and again after daylight failed to reveal even a trace of the cook. He, the only living soul aboard, had vanished utterly, whence I knew not. In spite of this latest adverse thrust of destiny, my despondency had given way to a certain clear-headedness which stood me in good stead. Unless death prevented me, I would go on to Lilliput, come what might. I reasoned rather blindly that I must be somewhere near the Coast of Australia, although I had lost all track of the exact location of the vessel, which had been adrift

ever since the death of Spaddle. The following day I was able to ver-
ify this belief after having repaired to the cabin long enough to learn
from nautical books there the use of a sextant with which I "shot"
the sun.

Within a fortnight I succeeded in reaching what I knew unmistak-
ably to be Queen's Channel, off the coast of Australia. From there I
got my bearing fully. Then with the aid of what sail I could man alone
and Professor Eliminom's excellent reconstruction of the deleted portions of **Gulliver's Travels**, I sailed for another six days until I came
in sight of land which, owing to one peculiar characteristic, I soon
recognized with certainty to be Lilliput. The island, along with that
of *Blefuscu* (as the reader has never been informed), consists of one
floating piece. The submerged land in the channel between Lilliput
and Blefuscu connects these two islands and floats as do the islands
proper. This oddity was prophesied by Professor Eliminom and is
here mentioned to explain my immediate recognition of my objective. Owing to the fact that it floats, ocean currents move it in an
approximate circle having a radius of about one hundred miles. The
entire circle is far off any regular steamer lane. A scientific explanation of so queer a phenomenon as a floating island must make its
way into another book, for it is not only complicated but lengthy.
The important thing here is that watching through a fixed telescope
for twenty minutes after I had dropped anchor showed conclusively
that the land ahead of me was drifting rapidly and that my goal was
reached! To keep Lilliput in sight and not have it drift away into the
darkness, I had to weigh anchor, and run the hazard of going upon
the rocks by sailing near enough to the shore to drop my anchor in
a submerged part of the moving land itself. This feat I accomplished
without mishap, whereupon I no longer could contain myself. In my
great happiness, I fear I let my feelings lead me through a course
of hysterics. I sang, shouted, and wept sometimes separately, sometimes all at once, and the sound of my voice was muffled even in my
own ears by the splash — splash — splash of the waves on the shores
of the long-sought land.

When at last I had conquered my rampant emotions enough to
permit calm reflection, I set about making plans for my visit. While
it is true that the Lilliputians are small people physically, nothing
but foolhardiness would drive one to their settlements without first
taking some very definite precautions. I could not overlook the fact
that nearly two-hundred years before my arrival upon the shores

of their country, armed soldiers had poisoned arrows which could quickly bring about the death of even so large a creature as me. Nor did I overlook the account of my ancestor's departure from that land. He left in the role of a fugitive under solemn sentence to have his eyes put out for treason. Would that event have any effect upon the kind of reception the modern Lilliputians would accord me? Would they be inclined to put me out of the way as soon as possible, or had time so changed the temper of the people that they would welcome my visit? Of course, I held no key to the answer of either question. In fact, I could not even be sure that the small peoples still dwelt upon the island, but common prudence dictated that I proceed with the utmost precaution. The question as to what particular precautions were necessary was a difficult one. What contingencies had I to guard against? Was Lilliput still a bow-and-arrow nation, or had it during the past two centuries progressed to the gunpowder stage? Could I, so large a creature, manage to observe these small peoples while remaining unobserved to obtain data for my future course of action?

Quite soon it became plain to me that I could not answer these questions. I had nothing to go upon. Therefore I resolved to stay on board and pursue a course of watchful waiting. If my presence there became known to the Lilliputians, I would have an opportunity to learn in comparative safety what kind of a reception I might expect.

The next morning broke brilliant, warm, and beautiful. The sea had stilled to a placid lake with only tiny ripples washing the shores of Lilliput. From early dawn I lay upon a heap of folded sail gazing landward through my telescope. Far to the inland, once the sun had risen, I could discern regular splotches of bush-like greenery, with here and there gray block-like structures towering thirty to forty feet into the air. The sides of these blocks sparkled with innumerable spots of reflected sunlight, and as the red morning sun became more brilliant the dazzling effect of these spots became greater. "This must be a great Lilliputian City," I thought; but during two hours of watching I saw no sign of life on the whole island.

As hazardous as it might have been, I could hardly overcome the impulse to land, so anxious and impatient was I to see the curiosities I knew were to be found upon the shores only a short distance away. By eleven o'clock in the morning I still had observed no movement on the land. Therefore, I resolved to do something to attract attention to myself. In the cabin hung a large mirror which I used to send flashing reflections of the sun into what I supposed to be a Lilliputian city. Even this brought forth no sign of life upon the island. But when I finally decided to arise from the pile of canvas upon which I knelt while manipulating the mirror, a strange paralysis seemed to have possessed my lower extremities. I could move neither leg. Twisting my body around from the waist, I noticed a broad ray of bluish-green light impinging upon my stricken limbs. Upon letting my line of vision follow the ray to its source, my eyes came to rest upon a vessel somewhat larger than a life-boat lying off the stern of my yacht. Upon the deck of this boat were Lilliputian sailors grouped around a mechanical device which emitted the ray responsible for my partial paralysis! By a quick twist of my torso I was able to roll off the canvas, whereupon the use of my legs, much to my relief, returned. I must confess that the experience made me quite nervous, so that immediately I crept to refuge behind a lifeboat and set up a cry for truce in the most fitting Lilliputian words I had learned from **Gulliver's Travels**. Peeping around the bow of the boat, I observed that the commander of the man-of-war (for very plainly now I discerned it to be such) evidently heard and understood me, badly as I had expressed myself through nervousness and lack of mastery in the language. The bluish-green ray was turned off as the warship cautiously approached, but the crew stood by to man the device should another occasion for its use arise. It was then I noticed that more than twenty guns of about three-quarters of an inch diameter across the muzzles were trained against me. At once I decided that there was but one proper thing for me to do — to make a brave and friendly gesture. Accordingly I arose to my full height and shouted a halloo to the approaching ship. In return I heard a few terse commands, then very distinctly a thousand small voices shouting in unison — "Gulliver! — Gulliver! — Gulliver!"

The man-of-war approached rapidly, albeit with considerable caution, its heavy guns and peculiar ray machine still being pointed toward me. Further to assure these diminutive sailors of my friendliness, I tossed over a rope to which was attached a large wicker basket. I invited them to climb into it and made motions to indicate that I would draw them aboard. There was considerable hesitancy, but eventually through difficult conversation and the making of signs, I made them understand my friendly intentions. However, as was befitting a navy, no man on that steel sea-dog (or should it be said more fittingly — sea-puppy) ever once relaxed his attitude

of strict vigilance, and every one of them stood in readiness for any
eventuality. The ship came to a stop about twenty yards to my starboard. In a few minutes I saw about ten sailors being lowered in
a row-boat about four times the size of a Dutch wooden shoe and
so oddly shaped as to resemble one. Not long afterward I hoisted
them aboard, and they stood rigidly at strict attention before me.
The bravery of these staunch little fellows was remarkable indeed.
At the command of their leader they marched to a point within two
feet of the spot where I was standing. My astonishment at their bravery was exceeded only by my astonishment of the leader's voice as
he addressed me in a language which I immediately recognized as
English, rather good English at that! (It will be remembered that
the search of my illustrious ancestor two hundred years earlier had
relieved him of a packet of letters. When I arrived in Lilliput it was
explained to me that these letters had been deciphered and studied
by Lilliputian scholars so painstakingly and carefully that they had
been able to compose an English grammar from them. For over a
hundred years the erudite among them had studied and mastered
the classic language of English.) Soon we fell into a conversation in
which I explained the purpose of my visit to them. The leader assured me he knew I would receive a great welcome, but being as he
was, only a *Chalbrig* (*petty naval officer*) the invitation must come
from somebody higher in authority. He further informed me that he
would carry a report of my wishes to his Admiral. Whereupon I inquired if it would be possible for him to carry a message of salutation
to His Majesty, the King of Lilliput. A look of consternation passed
over his face. Apparently he did not understand me. I repeated my
question. The leader still looking perplexed, one of the men who at
my request had been ordered to rest (out of strict formation) stepped
forward and said to the leader: "*Digrug fallertz ontz haba unto port
out Kanutz,*" which does not lend itself to exact translation, but is
about the equivalent of the American expression — "Aw nertz, Sir,
he does't know we haven't a King."

It was then explained to me that my message would be carried by
the Admiral, if he saw fit, to the head of the Lilliputian government.
The name of the officer highest in the government was the *Donkgop*,
but what sort of an office it was, the sailors had neither the time nor
the vocabulary to explain to me.

After the sailors departed, the Admiral himself paid me the courtesy of coming aboard accompanied by an escort of forty well disci-

plined seamen. His stature was somewhat above six inches, nearly an inch taller than the petty officer, who first boarded my vessel. The members of the escort were of about the same height. What a flashy little group they were in their red, yellow and purple uniforms, hung with long strands of silver and gold tinsel, and each crowned with a heavy feathered hat made from the hollowed upper portion of the skull of some great blackbird! The upper bill was left attached to this peculiar head-dress in such a way that it served excellently to shade the eyes from the sun. The Admiral did not speak English, having long since forgotten all he ever knew of it, but one of his escort did. Therefore, through him as an interpreter, we were able to communicate with each other quite well. At last it was arranged that word of my request to visit Lilliput, as well as of my arrival, would be taken forthwith to the Donkgop and word from him returned to me on the morrow. With a grand salute which consisted of three pistol shots fired in rapid succession overhead, the Admiral and his escort departed to board their ship, which had now drawn up very near to the **Night-Hawk**. The forty pistols together scarcely made the noise of one small Chinese fire-cracker, but the efficacy of those tiny weapons is by no means to be measured by the noise they make, as I later learned.

Chapter III

*Wherein the author is formally received in Mildendo —
and is warmly greeted; brief historical account of events
on the island soon after Lemuel Gulliver's departure;
insult by a working man; the first banquet feast; accident
in which Onk Watwil narrowly escapes injury.*

THE SECOND DAY after the visit of the Lilliputian sailors, I set out
at about a quarter to ten in the morning to land on the shores
of Lilliput. Word had been sent to me the previous day that the
Donkgop and Officers of State would be awaiting me outside the
capital city, **Mildendo**. Before embarking shoreward in my row-boat,
I took special pains with my toilet, being careful to shave closely, and
to don my newest, best-pressed, cheviot[1] suit. For a time I was in a
quandary, debating with myself whether or not to go armed. Such
an act would not exactly be a friendly gesture, yet, after all, I was a
lone man in a strange land, the inhabitants of which might or might
not prove friendly. Although I am not exactly a coward, I must admit
neither am I a man given to an unthinking, headlong, heroic conduct
in the face of danger. Safety first, I have always considered, is not a
bad rule. Consequently I carried with me a revolver concealed in a
shoulder holster under my coat.

When I had beached my row-boat, a mounted cavalry company
met me and saluted me with sabres flashing in the white sunlight,
then led me to the gates of the city some two-hundred yards from
the beach. The city was walled to a height of about five and one
half or six feet and heavily fortified. The tops of the wall were lined
with hundreds of people, men, women and children. On the ground,
immediately outside the wide gate opening into the city, were vast
contingents of the armed forces of the country. The naval forces
I recognized by the uniforms I had already had the pleasure of seeing; the army, lined in precise motionless formation, was resplendent
in bright orange uniforms highly ornamented with silver trappings
which glittered in the sunlight. But the colorful dress of the civilian population made the strongest impression of all upon me. Every

---

[1] A type of fine woolen tweed.

color of the rainbow plus others of which even the rainbow cannot boast could be seen in the throng atop the walls. Clothing styles of every conceivable kind and combination in both men and women's dress were represented in that crowd. Silks, satins, sackcloth; cotton, linen, cheesecloth; leather, frogskin and even feathers were visible. In fact, as I later learned, style to the Lilliputian civilian population consists not in likeness of cut or design, but in cuts and designs entirely different from the type of clothing worn by any other person. While it is true that with my people there is a tendency among the more sensitive to discard clothing the exact replica of which one sees another person wearing, the tendency is not carried to the extreme it is in Lilliput. Though a banker may discard a necktie the replica of which he sees the janitor wearing, and Mrs. Smith will avoid wearing a dress exactly like Mrs. Jones's, there are modes and styles which everybody follows, such as length of skirt, or cut of suit. Even certain colors seasonally predominate. Not so in Lilliput. Except in the lower and poorer class, no person dressed like any other in any respect. In all the world there is no greater ingenuity expended upon the matter of clothing than in Lilliput. To create an utterly new mode for every customer is a task beyond the power of any but Lilliputian tailors and modistes.

Several paces from the entrance to the city was a marble statuary figure of a man chiseled in proportions about equal to mine. (I later learned that this was a statue of my ancestor, Lemuel Gulliver, who, in the eyes of modern Lilliputians, has become the greatest hero of all time.) Beneath this statue there had been erected a great table-like platform, about the height of my waist, to the top of which a stairway led from the ground. Assembled on the platform were about forty gentlemen in white suits of various designs, whom I took to be the dignitaries of State. At the head of them was a large corpulent man with a ruddy face. His demeanor was even more solemn than that of the others on the platform, all of whom were, at my first approach, solemn enough indeed. As I drew nearer I could feel a tenseness in the atmosphere. Every eye was upon me; not a sound could be heard in the whole waiting multitude — only the soft click of horses hoofs on the hard earth as the cavalry company led me nearer. A brave little people are the Lilliputians. Not a soul displayed any sign of the fear many of them must have felt at seeing such a mammoth creature as I. The company of horsemen marched under the platform, wheeled around, and came to a halt facing me.

I stopped within three feet of them and made a bow to the Donkgop.

He returned my bow just as a flourish of tiny trumpets sounded, after which he began reading a proclamation to me in English. One of the dignitaries turned in the opposite direction and interpreted for the people as the Donkgop read:

> To Gulliver, Son of Gulliver, Hero of the Universe, Father of our Greatness, Greeting:
>
> The Donkgop, *Medid Wherding*, Donkgop of Lilliput, and all the Lilliputians, greet and welcome the one we have so long awaited, and the Donkgop Medid Wherding of Lilliput does hereby, herewith, herein, and by these presents say, proclaim, affirm, and announce that we do greet and welcome Gulliver; that we welcome his greatness to our shores; that we are happy to have him with us; that we are honored by his presence; that we are glad he is here; that we are fortunate; that we greet him, and will be pleased, honored, elated, delighted, and completely overjoyed to show him our capital city, Mildendo, on the island of Lilliput in Mid-Ocean.
>
> Greeting — Greeting — Greeting!

When the Donkgop had finished reading, briefly I replied, thanking him and his people for their kindness, and stating that it was my desire to make a complete study of the country, its people, and their customs, as far as I might be permitted. After I had finished my reply the whole throng of civilians broke into a wild raucous booing. I could distinguish my name pronounced with a thousand different accents and intonations. The Donkgop filed down the stairway followed by the men of State. Upon reaching the ground he showed me his right hand which I perceived to be bound thickly in bandages. He also turned around to show me a pillow strapped to that part of his anatomy with which nature has provided man primarily for sitting. Then he faced me again and requested me to lie prone upon the ground. To say the least, I was considerably at sea and undetermined whether to comply with his request. Finally, two cavalry officers dismounted and by their antics and explanations made me understand what was desired of me.

The Lilliputians have a queer custom which they follow upon being introduced to a stranger, or greeting a friend. When one wishes to greet a person or to bid him goodbye, the custom requires that one or more slaps should be delivered to the person, much in the manner we would use in spanking. In all truth, a sound spanking *is* the warmest, friendliest kind of gesture among the Lilliputians.

When at last I understood what was wanted of me, I lay down laughing heartily at this strange custom. Later the Donkgop had his turn at laughing when I told him we used the Lilliputian salutation as a means of chastising children, but my laughter caused some hesitancy and misgivings on his part at the moment. Had I known what was in store for me I would not have been in such a laughing mood.

The Donkgop, having a very sore right hand and even a more tender hinder portion from having greeted and received greetings from a large agrarian delegation which had called upon him the previous day, was unable to deliver my salutation in person. Besides, the officers of State who served as a Board of Etiquette, had decided that a strictly Lilliputian slap would be disrespectful to so large a person as I, therefore had arranged with one of their foundries for the casting of a handle about four feet long. With this contrivance forty or more people could greet me at once and with sufficient force to make the gesture a truly friendly one. The ceremony lasted long enough for one hundred twenty thousand persons to take an active part in it, consequently the Donkgop was not the only person who needed a pillow to sit upon when the business was finished. To escape the labor of returning the sign of esteem to the many who welcomed me so warmly I pleaded danger of injuring some should I attempt to thump them where custom demanded I must. This plea put at ease many a mind which had entertained the very apprehension which I expressed, and it proved highly pleasing to the Donkgop. However, I am far from being certain that my decision was a good one. I am not sure but what the relays of small people who delivered me "*Lilliputian handshakes*" did so with more thoroughness and gusto than they would have employed, had they known the affair was to have been reciprocal. The rites lasted for more than three hours, during which time I became very stiff from lying upon the ground as well as smarting and bruised in a southern locality. When the last comer, man, woman and child had fittingly given me their best regards, the Donkgop commanded me to rise and turn again to the platform where, during the ceremony, a large chair suitable for me had been carried on a huge army wagon (as I afterward ascertained). A hundred small barbecue fires were ablaze just outside the city wall and more than half of the Lilliputian army was engaged in carting the dressed carcasses of cattle, sheep, deer, and other meats to the fires, or in turning them upon the spits. Hundreds upon hundreds of casks about the size of water tumblers were piled in long rows by the wall, while fifty or more vintners were busy knocking out the bungs and inserting spigots.

It was at this juncture that an inebriated workman among the rabble on the wall shouted at me something which caused me a deep humiliation. Although he shouted in his native tongue, he repeated so often what he had to say, unused as I was to the language, I was unfortunate enough to understand him only too plainly. The story of Lemuel Gulliver's visit to Lilliput is well recorded in histories and legends even in the minutest details, and at this particular moment the vulgar drunkard happened to recall one of the great Gulliver's most astonishing feats. "Let's see you make water!" he shouted, over and over. Before that vast crowd I blushed as I had not blushed since I was a young boy. I have never known such painful embarrassment in all my life. After what seemed an eternity to me, two men who appeared from a distance to be men of high office, accosted the inebriate in a manner which was successful in silencing him, but which by its inappropriateness was exceedingly shocking to me. Instead of forthwith hustling the fellow off to jail or starting him homeward, the two white-clad officials bowed and scraped to the ruffian much as they would have done had they been paying their respects to some high plenipotentiary of all that is heavenly and earthly. This deference toward the hooligan was then quite incomprehensible to me and I fear I would have lost my temper over it if the Donkgop had not at that time apologized for the insult I had received. I repressed my desire to ask at once why my insulter was not being given the punishment he deserved, being glad to accept a proffered invitation to be seated before the platform and begin the feast, thereby calming in some degree my enraged feelings.

If it had not been for the discomfort I encountered in sitting, the occasion would have been one of the happiest I have ever experienced. Upon the platform was set a long banquet table at which sat the Donkgop and other dignitaries. Food was served by an endless line of soldiers who filed up the stairway, and past my place each carrying a heavy burden of roast meats, vegetables, hors d'oeuvres, and delicacies of such quantity and variety that they defy description. Three large casks of wine were hoisted on block and tackle and opened before me. Each was of such delicate flavor and aroma that no country in the whole world has anything even remotely comparable to it. Each cask contained a different variety, and each cask I drank tasted better than the last.

My plate, which was of hammered silver, was equal in size to those with which the reader is familiar. Around the edge of it was engraved in large letters — LEMUEL GULLIVER. The history of that plate as related to me by the Donkgop is interesting in itself. After Gulliver's departure from Blefuscu a long war broke out between that country and Lilliput in which Lilliput for a time was on the verge of complete rout and defeat. But gradually the course of the war was turned, largely through new sciences which never would have been mastered if Gulliver had not made his famous voyage to Lilliput. Using the pistol taken from Gulliver, careful smiths were able to make guns, then unknown to Blefuscudians and other small peoples. Lilliputian chemists were finally able to make gunpowder by taking that left by Gulliver, analyzing it and then producing it from its known constituents. It was gunpowder that brought Blefuscu to its Waterloo. The world's finest archers quailed, broke, and fled before hot lead. Thus it was that Lemuel Gulliver, who left Lilliput a fugitive convicted of treason, was now looked upon almost as a god, whose name reverberates in national legend, poetry, and song, and whose life-size statue — twenty years work of fifty best sculptors — stands before the principal gates leading into the great capital city of Lilliput.

In my conversation with the Donkgop I learned that even the downfall of *Golbasto Momarem Evlame Gurdilo Shefin Mully Ully Gue*, the last King of Lilliput, was indirectly attributable to Gulliver. After the eventual defeat of Blefuscu the near-worship of Gulliver turned to a hate for the monarch under whom he had been convicted of treason. First the enmity of the people grew toward *Skyresh Bolgolam*, the great enemy of Gulliver, who during the war had fallen under some suspicion of misappropriating money entrusted to him for the buying of naval provisions. An unknown assassin shot him with a poisoned arrow. Then in rapid succession, *Flimnap*, the High Treasurer, Lalcon, the Chamberlain, Limtoc, the General, and Balmuff, the Grand Justiciary, the men who had brought the articles of impeachment against Gulliver, were assassinated. Before the last of these was dead the whole nation had been fanned into a state of anarchy. Open threats were to be heard against the Emperor. When the army and navy revolted against him, the poor, unfortunate man fled to the island he had so recently conquered — Blefuscu. But he lived to spend only a few unhappy days. Poison reached him through his food and caused his death, although a thousand precautions had been taken by a few faithful servants to guard his Majesty from all harm. The date of his death is a great holiday in Lilliput. It marks the founding of a new era. No man since that time has been strong enough to establish himself as a monarch. Their government became what we would regard as a republic, though in many respects it is unlike any other national government in the whole world. The history of transition from monarchy to republic in Lilliput is a long tapestry woven in threads of glory and threads of human misery, encarmined over with much spilt blood. I was later to study in detail the history of the Lilliputian people, but that is too long to be reproduced in these pages.

So far I have not named any of the important people to whom I was introduced on the day of my reception by the Donkgop. First there were the nine members of the Nitpoopo. Translated the word *Nitpoopo* means *Footlickers*. The *Nitpooperlers*, as the individual members are called, are the Donkgop's chief officers, each heading some department of governmental activity. *Nitpooperler Flebrow*, a pompous, fat, ruddy-faced little man, was the High Civil Officer of Elections and Politics. *Nitpooperler Garnite*, the Head of the Bureau of Garbage Disposal, Onion Culture and Sandburr Conservation, was perhaps the most dignified Lilliputian I have ever known. His straight slender build, his long white beard, his stern eye are unforgettable. The High Officer of Health, Happiness, Disease, and Mortality was *Nitpooperler Gravinap*, another stern greybeard. *General Ossdoc*, the High Commander of the Army, and *Admiral Spraygrees* were also members of the Nitpoopo. *Barrister Bittzzora* was a young man who occupied a very important Lilliputian office as head of the Department of Prisons, Crime, Injustice and Liquor Consumption. It was his duty to prosecute criminals, supervise prison, collect delinquent taxes, enforce the drinking laws, and attend to one-thousand other things which appertained to his great office. The High Nitpooperler of Education, Labor and Cockroach Extermination was a very able person, one *Wickdomp Ooick*. While the office of Money, Change, Currency, Cash, and Corruption was filled by a very wealthy man named *Tomatocumber*. *Nitpooperler Hirear* occupied the great office as Head of the Department of Gambling, Recreation, Amusement and Public Works.

Through the cooperation of these officers and their subordinates I was enabled to make a study of life as it is lived in Lilliput. Each one upon request of the Donkgop put at my disposal all of the facilities of his Department. It was arranged that on the second day after my reception I was to visit the capital city, after notice of my intended entry had been spread among all the inhabitants warning them to stay indoors for sake of safety.

After the feast was over I departed shoreward from the city gates amid great booing and fanfare. I was escorted to the beach by the same cavalry company that had led me to the Donkgop that morning. While on my way back to my boat a very unfortunate thing occurred which might have cost the life of a high cavalry officer, but luckily did not, much to my relief, for indirectly I would have been to blame. I have always been fond of chewing-gum and that morning I disposed of a chewed pellet of that substance on the beach near my boat. One of the horses got its forefeet stuck in this, and fell heavily upon its rider. But for the softness of the sand the officer undoubtedly would have been crushed. I apologized to the whole company for having been the cause of such an accident. Outwardly the apology was accepted, but later I fully learned of the resentment which the fallen rider, **Onk Watwil**, harbored against me.

Chapter IV

Wherein the author makes an excursion through the city;
adventure with the blackbirds; the marvelous mechanical
advances made in Lilliput since Lemuel Gulliver's time;
accident resulting in the author's injury and arrest.

NITPOOPERLER OXMUT HIREAR, the Head of the Department of Gambling, Recreation, Amusement, and Public Works, was commissioned by the Donkgop to take me through the principal parts of the capital metropolis on the day designated for that adventure. Until I reached the gate early in the morning I, as previously stated, expected to wander through the city while the populace remained within doors, but I soon learned that only the civilian populace had been forbidden to go out-of-doors. The Army, Navy and Police contingents met me at the gates. Much to my disappointment, my visit was made quite a formal affair, including a repetition of the greeting I had submitted to on the occasion of my first reception. The Army and Navy delivered me a salute such as they give only to the Donkgop and ranking officers. It seemed a strange salute to me but the solemnity of it totally dispelled any suggestion of the humorous in it. In a long line extending for about twenty yards the Army, Navy, and Police swung into a circle around me, and after coming to a halt in that formation each man lifted his right foot off the ground and held that position while pinching his nose between the thumb and forefinger of his left hand, and at the same time emitting a snoring noise from his puckered mouth.

Somewhat more than two hours were spent in the ceremonies attendant upon my entry into the city, after which the police marched away to take up their posts, the navy to **Sizez Harbor**, the naval headquarters, and the army to its encampment some distance away. At last I was left with Nitpooperler Hirear, and I must say that the Lilliputians can be as informal as they can be formal. Once the ceremonies of the morning were completed, my companion relaxed his official mien to become one of the most talkative and entertaining little fellows imaginable.

Before going on to describe the wonders of the city, I must relate for the reader one unexpected and very trying experience. Nearly all of the creatures of Lilliput (not all of them) are proportionate to the size of the Lilliputians. However, there are in Lilliput both a diminutive Lilliputian variety of birds and many larger species familiar elsewhere, which from time to time find their way there. Of course, birds from the outside world are very large and formidable creatures to the Lilliputians. I was informed that blackbirds, sea-gulls, hawks, and eagles once were a terrible scourge to the entire nation. When they descended in great numbers, scores and even hundreds of people met violent death by being attacked much as rabbits and other small game are attacked by some of our birds of prey. At the time of my visit the danger from great birds had been scientifically removed by means of paralytic rays which are cast into the skies in such a way as to form a pyramidical canopy over the whole of Lilliput, thus protecting the nation by a light screen through which birds cannot pass.

The small Lilliputian birds with which I had my adventure live under the canopy of light, being unable ever to venture beyond it. Native Lilliputian blackbirds are about the size of ordinary houseflies, but possessed of beaks as hard and sharp as steel needle points. I had no sooner started down the broad boulevard leading to the central part of the city than hundreds of tiny pecking blackbirds began to buzz around me, alighting upon my head, ears, nose, and shoulders, and pecking me viciously wherever the bare skin presented itself. So afraid for the safety of my eyes did I become that immediately I flung myself upon the ground and pressed my face tightly into the curve of my arm to prevent the loss of my eyes. In a few moments Nitpooperler Hirear standing near my left ear informed me that the birds had been driven off and would be held helpless within the ray of a paralytic lamp shining on them from the top of one of the tallest buildings, whereupon I arose and proceeded on my way accompanied by the Nitpooperler, who at his own request rode standing up with his head peering out of my right coat pocket.

The Lilliputian city known to Lemuel Gulliver is no more. Fires, along with the march of time and progress, have almost totally effaced the old city. A few of the landmarks described by him still remain. The edifice in which Gulliver lodged stands almost in the center, preserved as a historic shrine and temple. I was not permitted to enter it owing to the fact that it housed relics of Gulliver: his pistols, wearing apparel, snuff-box, bed, purse, and many other things bearing historical significance in connection with his visit. Although I was naturally curious, even had I been granted leave to enter the Gulliver Shrine, I would have hesitated, so highly did the Lilliputians prize the treasures hoarded there, and so great was the risk that I, because of my bulk and clumsiness, might damage some.

But it was not the houses of antiquity in the capital city of Lilliput which most caught my interest during the first day of inspection. Perhaps the reader will remember it is stated in **Gulliver's Travels** that the inhabitants of Lilliput, even in the eighteenth century when my illustrious ancestor visited them, had acquired great proficiency in mathematics and mechanics. This aptitude, especially as exemplified by their prodigious advance in engineering science through all of its branches, has grown into a ripe perfection with the passage of years. There are in the capital several buildings towering well over a hundred feet into the sky. This fact alone would not have been startling, for relatively such buildings considered in the matter of height were comparable to our own skyscrapers in New York City. But New York is not built on a floating island as is Lilliput. During heavy weather the twisting, rocking motion, like that of a great boat, is more than merely perceptible; it is at times startlingly evident. Low buildings, such as those common in Lilliput at the time of Lemuel Gulliver's visit to the island, seldom if ever incurred any damage as a result of the swaying motion of the earth upon which they rested. In truth, the early inhabitants of the island, having never experienced the solid immobility of land such as people in the other parts of the world take for granted, were, for many centuries, quite unaware of the earth's movement. Rattling of dishes, swaying of trees, and other phenomena directly attributable to the motion of the island were accepted by the Lilliputians as manifestations of the inherent character of the object affected. It, they reasoned, was the nature of dishes to rattle occasionally, for trees to sway now and then, even for walls and floors to creak.

My guide, Nitpooperler Hirear, as he informed me, was an engineer of some repute, and as I walked down the broad streets, which varied in width from some ten to twenty-five feet, he sitting upon my shoulder, poured forth quite volubly interesting facts from his immense store of information. The building of the first *zingpup* (which translated literally means *moon-scratcher*) led to a great catastrophe in the city. In about the year 1885, as nearly as I am able to transpose Lilliputian time measurement to our own calendar, a government building was erected to the height of one hundred one feet, and three inches (one thousand and twenty Lilliputian *scandunks*). The entire project progressed rapidly and was completed within twenty-eight days. All might have gone well except for the land movement, of which as already stated, the people, and engineers as well, were not aware. Except for its greater bulk, anchorage, and strength, the foundation used for the new zingpup was like those employed in the structure of ordinary houses.

Two weeks after the government offices had been moved into the great building a storm arose, and, at ten thirty o'clock the morning of the storm, the upper stories of the zingpup began to crack and crumble. Becoming alarmed, the occupants flew into a panic and raced for the elevators and firemen's poles, very common in Lilliputian buildings, and used by nearly everyone for rapid descent from upper to lower stories. Many of them were trampled and crushed from this cause alone. At ten-thirty-five o'clock, the rocking of the island caused the top-heavy structure to snap off its foundation. In toppling downward with a mighty crash, like a fresh felled forest giant, not only were all of the people imprisoned therein brought to a sudden death, but the great tower fell across some thirty lesser buildings, shops, dwellings, and stores, killing and maiming many hundreds who were not at the time in the zingpup. Like so many misfortunes which befall a people, this experience, terrible in itself, indirectly led to the great discovery — the fact that Lilliput is a floating island, to which further reference will be made later.

Unfortunately, the discovery did not come early enough to enlighten or be of aid to the architect **Scan Zinpan**, who drew the plans for the zingpup, or to aid his unfortunate Chief Engineer, **Manzupe Orflatz**. These two were hastily charged in the criminal courts, tried, convicted of multiple murders, and sentenced to be eaten alive by starving lizards. Of this example of Lilliputian justice the people are not proud, so Nitpooperler Hirear has hastened to inform me, and, as I was later to learn, justice in the new Lilliput is not so revoltingly barbaric.

After the death of Scan Zinpan and Manzupe Orflatz, some of the more inquiring minds among the Lilliputian scientists were not satisfied that defects in structure of the zingpup had caused its collapse. Minute examinations of the fallen giant under the direction of **Stinglot Ampspamps** led to the conclusion that earth movements producing a horizontal stress were the only plausible explanation for the disaster. Subsequent tests and calculations, the mathematical nature of which is too intricate to be set forth here even should reader interest warrant so doing, finally established the fact, knowledge of which in the future would prevent, and has prevented, a recurrence of such a calamity as the fall of the first zingpup. Following the discovery, some of the greatest advances in the science of metallurgy were made. The Lilliputian mastery of this science is amazing. Glass has been made with all the tensile strength of the finest American steel, and steel has been made with all the transparency of glass. Metal alloys of every weight, color, and consistency are used for nearly every object used in their daily lives. Wood is still plentiful on the island, while the long-since conquered island of Blefuscu has been transformed into one great cultivated forest, so wood as a building material is still in great use, but metal is rapidly replacing it.

As Nitpooperler Hirear and I drew near the most populous part of the city where most of the zingpups tower overhead, my attention was arrested by scores of what I at first took to be rainbows looping by threes and fours in various intricate geometrical designs over each of the tallest buildings. These variegated colored spans running from the ground upward over the center of each building were, as I soon learned, steel tripods or quadripods used to support the zingpups, underneath each of which was suspended like a plummet in the midst of the strong, graceful girders. It was explained to me that no zingpup in the city had a foundation. In fact, after having it called to my attention, it could be readily seen that none had a foundation, that none even touched the ground. Movable and unattached metal steps led to the doorways, thus permitting easy access to the first floor while the building itself swung free. This peculiar system of building from the top down and dangling the edifice from steel supports overhead entirely removed the danger from rocking earth movements on the floating island. The floors would always maintain a level horizontal plane by reason of the direct pull of gravity and the movable joint in the attachments between roof and tripod; the walls would always remain exactly perpendicular regardless of the movement of the earth and supporting steel arches. The utility of the great arches is fully equaled by their ornamental character. Such colorful bows of long curving steel anchored in the ground and swinging heavenward could not be adequately described other than as magnificently beautiful, especially when the sun shines brilliantly upon them.

After a leisurely stroll through the main thoroughfares of the city during which I took great pleasure in gazing upon the many interesting sights – buildings, parks, dwellings, highways, and tiny gardens, I turned down the **Stang Lob** (*State Street* – the principal street of the city). All the while, Nitpooperler Hirear had kept up a fluent conversation being at all times very obliging in answering my questions. Many of the things I asked him must to him have seemed simple to the verge of being child-like.

As I turned eastward toward the gate opening upon the beach, the sun had sunk very near the western horizon, and long before I had traversed the entire length of the street the deep gray twilight peculiar to Lilliput had descended. Without warning a blaze of light flooded the city making it lighter than it had been even during the brightest part of the day. The sudden brilliance of the light almost frightened me. My courteous companion, again having descended from my shoulder to the safer depths of my coat pocket, must have sensed my consternation, for immediately he launched upon an explanation of the city's lighting system. Indeed, an explanation was necessary. The silvery illumination in which the whole city and countryside basked seemed to be generated in a ball of fire, white as a magnesium flare, high in the sky above the city. Converging toward this ball from four different spots on the ground around the city thin piercing shafts from searchlights speared their way into the sky. Those blades of light, according to Hirear were so-called **zangnuts** (or *mirror rays*), an electric ray generated in a lamp only recently invented. Unlike an ordinary beam of light, these beams, upon impinging, failed to penetrate each other, but were mutually reflected with a considerable diffusion much in the manner that a mirror reflects a light directed upon it. Four powerful lamps directing their concentrated rays at right angles to each other to a fixed point overhead were able to illuminate the entire city in a soft though marvelously clear flood of light.

The arching rainbow tripods over the zingpups in the artificial light were even more arresting than in the light of day, and, if it had not been for an odd mishap which forced my attention into other channels, I suppose I would have lingered a long while that evening to thrill at their beauty.

Abruptly there appeared a transparent ball in size somewhat between a medicine ball and a basket-ball racing at a terrific rate of speed down the street. When scarcely ten paces from me it veered crazily to the left, screeched loudly into a curbstone, rebounded high into the air, and smashed in my hat with a glancing blow. It was quite a blow.

When my dazed senses finally permitted me to perceive things other than exploding stars, I was lying flat upon the pavement. A corps of firemen was training a stream of water from a fire hose upon my face while a cordon of police were holding back the populace who by that time were no longer obliged by the decree of the Donk-gop to remain indoors. Nitpooperler Hirear was standing upon my breast swabbing my face with a mop. Without further ado I placed Hirear gently upon the ground and staggered to my feet. A piping blast from a whistle blown by a policeman near my feet halted me where upon it was made known that a police surgeon must examine my skull. My first impulse was not agreeable to such a demand, but the throbbing ache in my head made me realize there was something very attractive about lying down again for a few minutes, so I complied. The examination lasted only a moment and revealed nothing more than a bump about the size of a horse chestnut on the right side of my cranium.

For a time I was scarcely interested, though I was soon informed that I had been struck by the common vehicle of Lilliput, a hollow sphere propelled by alcohol exploding in a turbine. The driver of the particular vehicle which struck me was uproariously drunk, and, after having been so informed, I was then much more interested in venting my spleen upon that careless individual than I was in learning the mechanical principle underlying the construction of this "glass canon-ball" masquerading as an instrument of transportation. However, Hirear proceeded to describe at great length the working mechanism of the spherical vehicle.

Usually my temper is under control, but my aching head precipitated me into a mood out of which I then viewed Hirear as a talkative, impertinent, little windbag, although he was speaking on a subject that should, and ordinarily would have, interested me, for, of course, a spherical vehicle was something entirely new in my experience. In a niggardly way, I displayed my irritation by hurriedly plucking the dignified Hirear from my shoulder and setting him upon the pavement in a manner not calculated to add anything to his dignity. Moving rapidly, though carefully, as I did not wish to injure any of the inhabitants by stepping upon them, I strode up to the gate at the end of the street. A guard dressed in a coat so shiny that it appeared luminous informed me in a loud voice that I was invited and commanded to attend a banquet with Donkgop Medid, the Officers of State, and their ladies then being arranged for me just outside the gate where on a previous day ceremonies already described took place.

Since I had already begun to repent my show of bad temper, I did not obey my first impulse to refuse to attend the social function, although my head was still aching as though it would burst, and I looked forward to the evening with little enthusiasm. A crack upon the head can certainly bring out the meanness in a man. The guard further informed me that I could not yet pass through the gate, for complete arrangements were not yet made, and there was danger of my injuring some of the workmen if I were to appear amongst them before they were ready for my reception.

At this moment, Nitpooperler Hirear appeared and addressed me with dignity in a way which, if he bore any ill will toward me, certainly did not reveal the fact.

"Man Mountain Gulliver," he said just as though nothing had happened, "I was outlining for you the mechanical principles utilized in the construction of the *scazpop*, the Lilliputian vehicle which, I believe, you erroneously called a *damn* when one struck you. In the first place, the spherical body is made of transparent steel, as you have observed, while the interior mechanism rests upon three cross-bars which may be described as the axes running parallel to the faces of a cube. The ends of each of these cross bars is fitted with a roller driven by a shaft from the alcohol turbine which is fastened to the frame in the exact center of the sphere where the bars cross. The bar running vertically, that is in the direction of the gravitational pull, is heavily weighted on the downward end to maintain the skeleton within the hollow body in the same position at all times regardless of how the shell may move and spin. The operator sits in a seat suspended from one of the horizontal cross-bars. Before him is a set of six keys each of which controls the power applied at the end of a cross-bar. With practice, skill in manipulating these keys, alone and in proper concert, can be attained. Properly controlled, this vehicle is remarkably mobile and travels almost anywhere owing to the fact that it can be made to respond quickly and move in any direction.

"Perhaps you would also be interested in the *schipidtpot*, a machine —"

"Pardon me," I said, "if I am to attend a banquet tonight I would like very much to wash my hands."

"Oh, that is quite all right, Man Mountain Gulliver. You were thoroughly washed by the fire department a short while ago."

Thus, through an over-fastidiousness on my part and the failure of Nitpooperler Hirear to clearly understand my meaning, I was condemned to bear not only a bursting head for some time longer.

Chapter V

The banquet wherein the author receives an introduction to Lilliputian life and politics.

JUST AS A MESSENGER left word with the guard that I might pass through the gate, a corps of police in scazpops whizzed down the street and surrounded me. After emerging from a door of his "glass cage", an officer, who appeared to be the captain, addressed me thus: "You, Man Mountain Gulliver, are by zhe — hic — expressh order of the Top Magistrate, the *Skork* of all the Skorks, and the law of the land plached under arrest for having been struck contrary to zhe law by a scazpop while it wash being driven by an honorable Skork in hish most honorable moments. We, zhe polich, the mighty arm of the law, command your submission to being tied in chains under pain of paralysis by the ray even though it cause your death."

As kindly as I felt toward my new Lilliputian friends, the sight of the little drunken popinjay of a police captain heaping insult upon injury was too much not to set my blood boiling. My face must have swollen purple with righteous anger, but even so, prudence has always been the better part of my valor, rage or no rage. Consequently, although I might have forcibly resisted many dozens of Lilliputians for a time much to their injury, having once experienced the power of the paralytic ray and not knowing what other contrivances these clever little people might turn loose upon me, I meekly submitted myself, apologizing for any offense I might have committed, laying the blame on my ignorance of the country. What a maddening experience to be arrested by a drunken policeman scarcely six inches high for having had my head nearly broken by a steel ball propelled by another drunkard of no larger stature!

While the police captain was conferring in undertones with several of his fellow officers, doubtlessly discussing ways and means of maintaining in custody so large a creature as I, Nitpooperler Hirear came forward on my behalf and demanded that the police delay execution of their project until Donkgop Medid had been consulted upon the matter. Whereupon a haughty little red-nosed fellow, dressed in a floppy suit of material resembling overlapping pansy petals, stepped out of his crystalline vehicle and stated to Hirear that, although he had no objection to consulting the Donkgop, the legal principles involved clearly precluded that officer from offering me any assistance, for it was the law of Lilliput that the high executive could pardon only an offense not yet committed, whereas I had already been struck by a scazpop, contrary to, and in violation of, the criminal law.

"But my dear **Buzknut**," (*prosecuting attorney*) Hirear replied, "you will admit that our admirable guest, the Man Mountain Gulliver, could scarcely be expected to be acquainted with Lilliputian law the third day after his arrival among us."

The Buzknut's eyes became two sharp black pin-points.

"You, Nitpooperler Oxmut Hirear, appeal to a principle unknown to any people in any age excepting the barbaric Blefuscudians. Ignorance of the law is no excuse in Lilliput! Would you run the peril of uttering treason in defending this criminal upon a contrary, not to say, unsound, pernicious, and damnable principle?"

"No, your cherry-beaked Honor, I would not run the peril of uttering treason, but this man is a guest of Lilliput, and the recent matter upon which he stands charged seems to have in it at least as much of the unfortunate as of the illegal. We will, with your permission, await the arrival of the Donkgop."

The reference to the "cherry-beak" I took to be a lighted fuse leading to a bomb of trouble, though much to my surprise the Buzknut appeared flattered by it, as indeed he was, for, as I later learned, to be recognized as "cherry-beak" in Lilliput is considered a very high compliment.

At that moment the gate swung open and several new "glass balls" rolled in through the crowd. From the leading one stepped the Donkgop resplendent in a golden suit cut in a manner suggesting a cross between an old-fashioned nightgown and a hula-hula skirt. He addressed me courteously and requested my lying prone in order that he might administer the usual Lilliputian "handshake", which he proceeded to do in person very gently with his sore hand, and without the aid of any mechanical device, much to my relief. Then, after a rather lengthy confab with the captain of the police and the Buzknut, he turned again to me abruptly and said: "Great guest of Lilliput, it is my advice that you immediately obtain the services of a lawyer."

"But, your Excellency — "

I could not say anything further. A shrieking wail arose from every Lilliputian within hearing of my voice, and that must have included one-quarter of the population of the city. When the noise died down, the captain of the police shouted: "You are under a second arrest for addressing the Donkgop with the nomenclature of royalty!"

Only the value I place upon my person kept my patience from cracking to splinters. I had attempted to state that I knew no lawyer and knew no way of obtaining one without some assistance. It would have been better had I saved my breath, because at this juncture there appeared a conveyance larger than any I had yet seen containing three persons in beds and obviously bound for a hospital. Out of it there sprang seven men, each of whom accosted me stating his name and informing me that he was a member of the legal profession. I was afraid to open my mouth for fear of committing another crime. Again the only true friend I seemed to have made in Lilliput came to my rescue. Nitpooperler Hirear beckoned me to lift him to my ear that he might whisper to me. In this matter I complied and he advised me to engage **Blaptrap Fuzzlebeanz**, one of the seven attorneys. This I did at once, calling Fuzzlebeanz from among the others. A thin, bony, little creature with a wrinkled face and bleary eyes came forth and addressed me in a squeaky voice.

"Have you any money?" he asked.

"Yes," I answered.

"Then," said he, "your troubles are nearly over. Give me half of it; give one-sixth of it to the **Degrethre** (*captain of the police*), one-sixth to the Buzknut, one-sixth to the **Grafnix** (*Top Magistrate*) and you shall go free. The law demands no more."

Nitpooperler Hirear pinched my shoulder and whispered surreptitiously, "You need not give all — give some."

Luckily I had some pennies loose in my pockets. Carefully feeling out six of them I dropped three at the feet of Fuzzlebeanz, and in so doing showered him with a cloud of dust. Then I tossed one to the Degrethre, one to the Buzknut, and with the third I inadvertently bowled over a policeman as I flipped it saying, "Take this to the Grafnix."

Several minutes later I had with considerable difficulty signed some twenty-eight tiny papers which Fuzzlebeanz had pulled from his portfolio, advising me it was necessary to sign such papers to make the settlement completely legal. This having at last been accomplished, the crowd dispersed, and the police yanked away their unfortunate and loudly protesting member who had been struck by the penny, which offense then and there resulted in his arrest.

This strange adventure having been thus happily concluded, I felt as though a great load had been lifted from my spirit. I would have been in a mood for rejoicing had I not been apprehensive lest I soon be arrested again — this time for bribery, since I could not see how my payment to the police, the prosecuting attorney, and even a magistrate could be viewed in the same light as the payment of a fine. Upon my confiding this fear to Hirear, he hastened to relieve my apprehensions by asserting that no such crime as bribery was known in Lilliput, having ceased to be such more than three-quarters of a century ago. I had, so he stated, gone through a well settled legal procedure and my crimes were entirely requited.

So to the evening's entertainment. The great banquet was not in my especial honor, but was in observance of the eve before the national Lilliputian election. Outside the city gate, in the area where I had been first formally welcomed to Lilliput, were arranged perhaps a hundred tables of a size suitable for Lilliputians on either side of the high platform from which I had once previously partaken of native hospitality. Each of the small tables would accommodate about sixteen persons. When I, accompanied by Nitpooperler Hirear and the Donkgop, each riding comfortably in one of my coat pockets, came upon the scene of the festival, a crowd was already gathering. The whole area was artistically lighted by a battery of reflector-ray machines, much smaller and less powerful than the four which lighted the city. An effect, very pleasing indeed, like that of silvery moonlight blended with green, blue, and red starlight, was produced by these globes in a white magnesium light, others glowing warm and red like brilliant embers, and still others gleaming with cold blue and greenish lights.

All of the officials of state, including those I had previously met, along with many whom I then saw for the first time, were gathering around two very long banquet tables placed on top of the platform which was to serve as my table. A happier arrangement could not have been made, for it gave me a close-up view of the cream of Lilliputian leaders of state and men of affairs. Of course, as the reader will surmise, though I will not again presume upon his patience by rendering a full account of it, the greetings and introductions were inescapable. First the entire judiciary pummeled me (on what by this time was the most sensitive portion of my physical person) with the sturdy symbols of their office — small steel hands intricately fitted on the palm side with needle-like points, the sharpness of which is unequaled by any instrument produced elsewhere in the world. Following this I was obliged to endure greetings by directors of bureaus, etc., etc., the lesser lights of officialdom. When it came to the turn of the ladies, I must confess my gratefulness for the happy circumstance of my bulk, which made it necessary to lie face downward not only because it enabled me to hide in the crook of my arm the embarrassment I actually did experience, but also because it precluded the arousal of certain emotions which inevitably would have arisen in me had my size been normal in relation to that of those dainty Lilliputian women.

Finally the preliminary business was ended, and I, pleading a desire to retire some distance toward the beach to brush from my clothes the dust (of which there was none, the ground being quite clean, hard, and smooth), obtained permission from the Donkgop, Medid Wherding, whereupon I hastened down the shore and gave strict attention to a matter which, if it had not been soon accomplished, might have led me into some unpleasant embarrassment, if not into further difficulty with the law. I recollected that my illustrious ancestor, Lemuel Gulliver, incurred the displeasure of the Queen over just such a little matter and he was never done with the trouble it occasioned.

Upon returning to the gathering I was a much happier and more comfortable man than I had been five minutes before in spite of the tender soreness of either extremity. Everyone was seated except the Donkgop, who was standing ready to deliver a speech. His first words startled me with their loud clarity. Small as he was, he was speaking in a voice fully as loud and strong as mine. I looked for something resembling a public address system, but nothing of that nature was to be seen. I could only sit listening to this strange loud voice booming forth from so tiny a man, all the while itchingly curious to know how his naturally high piping voice could have become thus suddenly transformed. In a few moments my attention was entirely fastened upon the substance of the Donkgop's speech, while I found, somewhat to my surprise, my understanding of the Lilliputian language was steadily becoming more nearly perfect as the evening progressed. I began to comprehend almost everything that was said.

"Fellow countrymen and women, citizens all, we are met here tonight to observe the great national elections which fall on the morrow," began the high executive. "In observance of the national law and support of the national constitution, it is fitting that we open the ceremonies of the evening in drinking three **ruquats** of that most exhilarating liquor, **thgbainbut**; also it is highly appropriate that the honorable gentleman who drafted the noble law requiring the citizens of this land to drink at least four ruquats daily should, on such an occasion as this, offer the toast to which we may drink in unison. Ladies and gentlemen, the Honorable **Randew Olvedts**."

As a puffy-eyed, cherry-beaked little fellow staggered to his feet, the air filled with a strange wailing whistle to the great volume of which everyone present contributed. At first, I thought this to be the Lilliputian equivalent of a "Bronx Cheer", since it was difficult to see how those present could be sincere in showing respect to such an obviously dissolute and dissipated individual. In this I was mistaken. The peculiar wailing to which I have alluded was the approved method of applause employed in that country.

"Sfellow cshitizens, it is with great spleasure I ashk you to trink to the successh of our leader, the worth Donkgop Medish Wherdong, and to the continuance and further successh of the great guzzshel law. Lesh ush trink and pe merry for tomorrow we may go dry."

Following suit of the weaving gentleman who offered the toast, every person present lifted a cup as large as half an egg shell and drained the contents thereof. These bowls were so large that all but the strongest of those people present employed both hands in lifting them to their lips. A glance from Nitpooperler Hirear, who occupied a place at the Donkgop's table immediately before me, indicated clearly that I was expected to take part in the drinking of the toast. Fortunately for me, especially since the toast was not completed until everybody had drained three bowls, I was supplied with a Lilliputian bowl for this purpose, and not with one proportionate to my size. Even as it was, so strong was the liquor that my ears soon rang, and I felt somewhat dizzy. Lilliputians are certainly persons of no mean or trivial alcoholic capacity, else I do not see how any of them could remain conscious after such prodigious draughts. Banquet customs of Lilliput, though as boresome as our own, differ from them in several minor respects. For instance, it is the custom in that country to do all the speaking before the food is served, which has numerous advantages. Not only does the speaker gain in this order of things by reason of the fact that he has the ears of his listeners before they have become torpid with gluttony or stupefied with drink, but the listeners gain in that they know they at least have something to look forward to, in that they will eventually get something to eat, if only they have patience.

After the toast by the venerable Randew Olvedts, the assembly, which remained standing while performing the rite, were seated, and the Donkgop commenced the principal speech of the evening.

"Fellow Skorks and Patriots, we are on the eve of a great event. Not only does a national election occur on the morrow, but there occurs a contest between two irreconcilably opposed schools of political thought. You are aware that throughout the whole of this fair land, cross currents of dissension, strife, and bigotry are fanning a spark of discontent. There are abroad persons, who, though undeserving of the name, we must still call citizens, going around broadcasting the absurd proposition that the government must feed them for no other reason than they are hungry. Our party has always held, and as leader of that party I still hold, that the right to food is not concomitant with the need of it, that just because a man is hungry is no reason he has to eat, and that, above all, even assuming as he does, that being hungry, he must eat, it by no means follows that the burden of supplying him with food properly falls upon the government. Our great party has always, excepting rare misfortune, been able, through economy and astute business management, to pay the highest prices for the citizen's vote. How unfaithful and despicable a man or woman is, who, having in the past partaken of our bounty at election time, now deserts our cause and bolts to the opposition merely because my opponent offers him a handful of dry peas to gratify the vague and lowly cravings of his belly — — "

At this juncture a long loud wailing burst forth from the crowd in approval of the Donkgop's words. When at last the noise had subsided, he continued: "Without wishing to appear immodest in taking credit to myself, I feel nevertheless impelled to point out that our party under my leadership has, during this administration, been able to accomplish many things for which we may feel justly proud. We have, as stated, been able to offer the highest price for votes, and, having been elected, have been most diligent and assiduous in scaling down our payments for those votes, thus saving money for the public treasury. During our administration taxes have mounted greatly, much to the glory of our nation, for with the money so acquired we have been able to hire hundreds of unemployed in hundreds of new bureaus under our various departments — and this in spite of the fact that those bureaus are neither utilized nor useful, and we higher officials might, instead of pouring public moneys into so worthy a use, have pocketed it ourselves. We have subsidized great industries, which had it been otherwise might have had to spend their own moneys in increasing their various businesses; we have let down the bars to merger and combination that business might prosper; we have withstood the bombardment of many small businesses who have incessantly demanded aid, and this properly so since *ix nertz oink blutz* (a maxim in a dead language studied in Lilliput which loosely rendered is nearly the equivalent of the Latin — *De minimis non curat lex*[1]); we have paid the linen grower to plow under his linen, the grain producer to rot his grain, the silk manufacturer to poison his worms, in order that fewer and fewer people might obtain these commodities at higher and higher prices; we have been unrelenting in cramming into the gaols the ever increasing hordes of **nitzbutz** (*persons who refuse to observe the laws relevant to intoxicating liquors and in violation thereof persist in abstinence and sobriety*); we have cut the cost of public education to a point consistent with the needs of a people as well governed as our people are, for it is a fact that none can gainsay that our great government now operates under and by the advice of the mightiest brains in the nation — the most pedantic of the pedagogues. Whatever defects there are in our government, if defects there be, we are prepared to cure with an infallible remedy — a well rounded series of new laws which for the sake of brevity we will refer to as the *a-b-c-d-e-f-g-h-i-j-k-l-m-n-o-p-q-r-s-t-u-v-w-x-y-z* laws. Once these enactments are, by the aid of our legislative and judicial workmen, superimposed over the inscriptions on the great marble cornerstone supporting our governmental structure, our troubles will be over. The opposition has directed upon us the criticism that in superimposing these new laws upon the cornerstone, our chisels must necessarily destroy the ancient inscriptions already upon it, as well as knock off some of the corners. In answer, my fellow citizens, I ask: What of it? Do not the **a-b-c-d-e-f-g-h-i-j-k-l-m-n-o-p-q-r-s-t-u-v-w-x-y-z** laws embrace the whole alphabet, and therefore necessarily embrace every possible remedy which can, by human ingenuity be devised out of that alphabet? What of it, if the old cornerstone be marred so long as the remedy wrought in so doing is so patently infallible?

"In closing, friends, let me reiterate that a vote for our ticket

---

[1] The law does not concern itself with trifles.

will bring the voter his highest price — that with the ballots today mailed to each and every voter throughout the land went a forty-five *schrunk* note (a schrunk relatively speaking in terms of purchasing power is equal to about twenty-five cents, though formerly of a greater value), which will be validated at the polls when the voter deposits his ballot. Had we nothing else to offer the voter in return for his vote, this, we know, is a hundred-fold more than the opposition can offer. To the continued success and glory of our administration, may we all offer up a cheer!"

As the Donkgop finished and sat down not a person opened his mouth, but a long, ripping, noisome sound ran throughout the assembly in response to the request for a cheer. This mode of cheering could not be other than offensive to my foreign ears, and I will not dwell longer upon it. Following the cheer a long applause ensued, after which the Donkgop again rose to his feet, introduced me to the gathering, and called upon me for a speech.

My cheeks burned with the sudden flush of humiliation. Never in all my life have I been able to make a speech in public. Try as I will no thought will ever enter my head, and my tongue always becomes completely paralyzed. In spite of this shortcoming, I arose to my feet on this occasion, and, after gazing dumbfoundedly at my audience for a moment that seemed an eternity, I inadvertently emitted, whether by reason of the stress of my emotions, or of a certain lamentable defect in my self-control I have always had, a loud, reverberating Lilliputian cheer after which, faint with embarrassment, I slumped into my seat. There arose such an applause as I would have believed impossible for these small folk to make. They wailed for nearly ten minutes, setting up a din fit to wake the dead. Some of the more excited amongst them even pelted me with dishes and silverware. It was not until Nitpooperler Hirear ran up near my face and shouted for me to make a bow to the people in acknowledgment of their of their applause that I realized I had not insulted them. Indeed, so far were they from thinking this that many of them afterward complimented me on my great eloquence on this, the most humiliating occasion of my life. I bowed as advised, and did well at it, having already witnessed a Lilliputian bow which consists of pointing the chin high in the air and making "goo-goo" eyes much in the manner of an American "broad" drumming up trade.

There was more speech-making, and much more drinking — so much more that long before the food was served I was as crocked as a bedbug in a cider jug. Although I am unaccustomed to drinking, I dared not run chances of coming afoul of the law again, consequently imbibed much too heavily. At last, when I became so hungry that further delay before eating would have been nearly unbearable, the banquet was served, and here again the Lilliputians have a custom which, although perhaps not laudable with respect to delicacy, is none the less highly gratifying after listening to speech-making for five hours, and that is the custom of serving all of the food to be served at one time rather than in courses as is our custom. This has the advantage of permitting each guest to choose the order in which he will eat the various foods set before him, instead of compelling him to follow the strict, though often capricious, order dictated by the caterer, and being, all the while he may be eating one thing set before him, in the dark as to what may be coming next. Heaped before me on large silver platters especially hammered out for the occasion by ninety-five silversmiths were hundreds of very small roast ducks, geese, blackbirds, sheep, swine, steers and other meats including cockroaches, grasshoppers, and house-flies, which latter dishes are among the Lilliputians considered great delicacies, though the very sight of which, I must confess, was somewhat disturbing to my appetite. Along with these came generous quantities of vegetables, hors d'oeuvres, desserts, etc., much like our own foods which are for the most part exactly similar in kind, and differ only in size. Some had a flavor more delicate than our foods, and many tasted of appetizing spices which I could not identify.

From this point on the banquet was soon terminated. Everyone ate quite hurriedly. Whether this was the result of hunger generated during the previous five hours, or was merely custom, I am unable to state, though I surmised the former reason to be the cause. Soon we were all glutted, sodden, and sleepy. The Donkgop, as well as he was then able so to do, apologized for not having sleeping accommodations in the city for a person of such magnitude as I, but wished me, nevertheless, to consider myself the guest of his country, and to the end that I might better do so he had commissioned Nitpooperler Oxmut Hirear, Admiral Spraygrees, and Onk Watwil along with their wives to return to my boat with me to serve as hosts and hostesses.

Thanking him and bidding all farewell save those gentlemen and ladies mentioned, I took my departure, while the others were preparing to return to their homes in the city. After rowing a longer distance than seemed necessary (perhaps owing to my inebriation) we arrived alongside of the **Night-Hawk**, whereupon I clambered aboard by means of a rope ladder and let down a basket on the end of a rope to draw the others aboard.

A mishap occurred immediately after they had set foot on board. The wife of Admiral Spraygrees stumbled over the edge of a scupper and tumbled through it into the sea. By quick use of a search light and a boat-hook I came to her assistance and fished her out none the worse for her experience, excepting only the drenching and a slight scratch on her shoulder caused by the sharp point of the boat-hook. She was considerably frightened, but able to make light of the misfortune once she was on deck again.

Having been forewarned of their commission, all my "hosts and hostesses" came prepared with sleeping garments and articles for making personal toilet. Therefore nothing remained for me to do except conduct each couple to sleeping quarters in the cabin aft, where there were several separate berths each with clean linens, since they had never been used during the voyage. Then I retired myself — very, very weary. All went well with my friends, excepting (as I was informed by Hirear the following day) an accident to Onk Watwil growing primarily out of his intoxication. While weaving about on the edge of the toilet bowl in a very unsteady condition, he had lost his balance and toppled in. He was rescued at once by Admiral Spraygrees, but not before he had given vent to a rage which was for some unknown reason directed toward me.

Chapter VI

Wherein the author learns more concerning Lilliputian government and politics.

M<small>Y AWAKENING</small> the morning following the banquet was the first time I had experienced the dark brown feeling of a "morning after". My head was throbbing with a terrific pounding ache, and I had a sharp craving for water. After satisfying my thirst, and slouching half-clad into a chair, vague recollections of events of the previous day and evening slowly began to percolate through my poor aching head. I remembered having been struck by the Lilliputian "glass ball", — and then, after a long blank period, having been arrested, and finally, isolated events of the banquet. In that unhappy low ebb in spirits, for no particular reason, my sodden mind turned to thoughts of my late friend "Glyk" Spaddle, and a feeling of remorse crept over me. Poor "Glyk" Spaddle! He would not have been carousing with these pagan little people; he would have carried to them the great message of Christian truth for their salvation — a message of temperance, honesty, and piety. And I who had been able to complete a voyage to Lilliput by aid of funds raised for Christian missionary work — was I not betraying the trust of those who had contributed the funds, and betraying the trust of Spaddle himself in conducting myself as I had done on the night before? Yes, indeed, I was breaking that great trust, but I reflected that, although I had at times taken alcoholic stimulants, I had never before set my foot in the path of sots. I resolved to repent — to resist further temptation — to carry as well as I was able to carry the Christian gospel into the land of the heathen. Yes, I would repent — it was not yet too late.

This somber and sober meditation must have had a salutary effect upon my spirits, for after a time my head began to feel a little better, and the task of making my morning toilet did not seem quite so insurmountable as it had when I first arose. Until the moment when I began to shave I had forgotten my "hosts and hostesses" aboard. Upon remembering them I doubled my speed in order that I might quickly present myself to offer them the services and courtesy due them while they were aboard the vessel of which I was the master.

When stepping out upon the deck I found the three gentlemen, Admiral Spraygrees, Nitpooperler Hirear, and Onk Watwil, pacing about the deck, seemingly much engrossed in making an examination of their surroundings. A great coiled hawser lying near the windlass considerably excited the Admiral's fancy, as did a greased iron cable lying near it. Watwil was peering through a crack between a hatch, which remained partially open. Through the darkness of the hold he must have been able to see nothing whatever, though, as I approached, he persisted in his effort to do so. Nitpooperler Hirear was much taken with the height of the mainmast, which, though not as tall as some of the zingpups in the capital city of Lilliput, seemed to arouse his interest by its slenderness. At first he was unable to believe that it was made of wood — that, in fact, as I told him, it was the trunk of a single tree grown in my country. I resisted the impulse to tax his credulity further by telling him, as I might have done truthfully, the mast came from a tree not particularly large, as large trees are known in America.

During an exchange of inquiries as to how each of us had passed the night I learned that Mrs. Spraygrees caused the Admiral no little uneasiness, having in her sleep wriggled under a heavy pile of quilting lying at the foot of her bed so as to be completely hidden when the Admiral awoke. She was even beyond hearing his loud calling, so thick and heavy was the covering over her. Consequently it is hardly surprising that he became uneasy, especially in view of the fact that only the night before he had come near losing her when she had tumbled into the sea. At length, when his search had lasted nearly thirty minutes, and his shouting had awakened and pressed into service all the other Lilliputians on board, Mrs. Watwil noticed a slight movement beneath the quilting at the foot of the Admiral's bed, whereupon a hasty tunneling between the sheets revealed Mrs. Spraygrees peacefully slumbering away totally unaware of the Admiral's anxiety on her behalf. Having been thoroughly chilled by her wetting in the ocean and not having found the Admiral disposed to alleviate that condition by any contribution of his own bodily warmth, she had unconsciously crept further and further down beneath the bed clothing until she came to rest snug and happy beneath the quilting at the foot.

To serve breakfast to six diminutive people on a boat carrying no equipment suitable to their stature presented a problem which at first seemed too complex to admit of any solution, and, but for the assistance and ingenuity of my new little friends, I could not have accomplished that task. I invited the three gentlemen to the galley to keep me company while I set about the preparations, and the sight of the many large pots, pans, skillets, knives, dishes, chairs, table, etc. caused Watwil to make inquiry after a small stick of wood, it being his intention to carve eating implements for the company, since it must have occurred to him that I had not the proper facilities for accommodating them. Of course, I at first took his motive to be one proceeding from an innate desire to be courteous and helpful, therefore was somewhat disappointed to observe, soon after I obtained the wood for him, that such was not wholly the case. So skillful was he in the manipulation of his sabre, and so vain was he over that accomplishment that with an egotistical mien ludicrous to behold in so small a creature he set to work making the splinters fly, and in the space of a very short while had carved out six very good wooden trenchers the size of the plates commonly used in Lilliput. I almost burned the bacon and biscuits while my attention was absorbed in this wonderful exhibition. Not only did Watwil carve trenchers, but also carved forks of symmetrical shape and fine balance with an astounding rapidity. One could not help but admire this talent, yet the swelled ego of this little man over his accomplishments so warped his personality, at least while he was demonstrating them, that he seemed more despicable than praiseworthy. I suppose I have always lacked sympathy for those persons who, having caught the notice of the public by an achievement in itself laudable enough, are nevertheless so mentally unbalanced by a few rays of the limelight as to assume an overbearing and contemptuous attitude toward those who cannot excel them in their own particular *forte*. From that moment I never really liked Onk Watwil, though I could not escape recognizing his almost superhuman talent — in swinging a sabre.

We were able at last, by an arrangement of cracker, cigar, and hard tack boxes, to seat the small folk before a table improvised from the end of a provision crate, all of which were placed on the top of the long mess table. I had managed to make very small biscuits for my company while their bacon and potatoes were cut into tiny pieces, so that everyone had little or no trouble eating them. Hirear went to call the ladies who arrived just as the meal was ready to be served.

When I had lifted them all one at a time to the top of the mess table, where their breakfast awaited them, I seated myself and commenced to eat. For some reason incomprehensible to me, the others did not follow suit but sat ogling one another as though there was some deep current of distrust flowing among them. At length, Watwil broke the silence to ask the Admiral if the **Night-Hawk** lay outside the territorial jurisdiction of the Lilliputian nation, to which the Admiral replied in the negative, saying that it lay within that jurisdiction by several thousand scandunks.

"Then, perhaps, our guest would not mind moving his vessel beyond the twelve-*quink* limit," suggested the Admiral's wife.

Still not understanding what could be clouding the minds of my friends, I replied that I would be glad to move the ship, but for the fact that I had considerable difficulty in manning it alone, and that should I weigh anchor I ran considerable danger of not being able to anchor the **Night-Hawk** as advantageously as I then had her anchored, owing to the threefold difficulty of approaching the moving island, of catching anchor in undersea soil of that island, and of keeping the vessel from going aground.

"In that event," Watwil haughtily asserted, "we must either return to the capital without having breakfasted here, or we must prevail upon our guest, Man Mountain Gulliver, to provide us with drink to the end that we may obey the law in letter as well as in spirit."

I saw a gloomy shadow fall over the faces of all at this remark of Watwil as though a disagreeable truth had been uttered which would have left them happier had it not been said.

"Does your law require you to drink before breakfast?" I inquired.

"That it does," answered Hirear, "and on election days two ruquats before breakfast."

I could plainly see that Hirear and the Admiral were not elated over the prospect of having to drink so early in the morning, and I would have hazarded a guess that all of the others were of the same mind, but, being mutually distrustful, if not hypocritical, they were determined to make a brave outer show of observing the law, whether or no. Not wishing to have my friends leave, and wanting even less to violate again the Lilliputian law, I went at once to a cabinet where a bottle of *spiritus frumenti*[1] was kept for medicinal purposes. Bringing this out along with an eye dropper, four thimbles, a small salt shaker, and a miniature night chamber that one of the crew had

---

[1]Whiskey. During Prohibition whiskey was available from pharmacies by prescription under this name as a Medicinal Liquor.

been given as a souvenir in some dive along the river front in New Orleans, I proceeded to serve drinks in a manner which, while not strictly in accord with all the more fastidious points of Lilliputian fashion did, nevertheless, accomplish the same ends, — namely — satisfy the law, salve self-opinion of those who would appear noble and law-abiding in the eyes of their neighbors, and get everybody including myself busting tipsy again.

After I too had satisfied the law by the insistent entreaties of my "hosts and hostesses" I lost a large measure of my contempt for the law. After all, I reasoned there was something to be said in support of such laws.

It was only a few minutes until aching heads and the petty unimportant things in life were forgotten. As we breakfasted, the Admiral, who thus far I had considered a stiff, unbending sort of gentleman, gave me a surprise with his levity and jocularity in telling a number of anecdotes, some of which concerned prominent Lilliputians and all of which had a distinct frankness about them that either Boccaccio or Chaucer would have been glad to own.

I resolved to hold these men in conversation as long as I could that day in order that I might learn more of the Lilliputian manner of living, politics, and government. Of Nitpooperler Hirear I inquired how it was that the Donkgop and several other speakers at the banquet had been able to speak in such a loud deep voice.

"There is," said Hirear, "nothing odd in a politician's speaking loudly and clearly when he is endeavoring to corner votes. All of our most practiced and successful politicians soon acquire the gift of 'loud speaking' or big talk, as we Lilliputians call it. History records only two cases of men who, once they had acquired the knack, did not lose it when the purpose of their speaking was something other than seeking votes."

"But, sir," I protested, "you said there is nothing odd in that; it all seems very odd to me. How in the world does a person acquire a loud voice simply by making vote-seeking speeches?"

"Why, nothing could be simpler. Our **bakdsemis** (*professors of a science largely composed of psychology*) tell us that a man's life is shaped by his emotional impulses; that his bodily functions are molded and altered by those impulses; that all his acts spring from underlying emotional drives, and that even the form and size of his bodily organs may undergo changes so that he may the more readily meet life situations confronting him in the depths of the particular channel down which his particular emotions impel him. Thus, upon being insulted or threatened with physical violence a man tends to become angry, and the very physical process of becoming angry tends to make him stronger physically, hence better prepared for the fray. It so happens that in a politician there is but one overweening desire — one strong motivating urge — and that is to get votes. There is but one organ in the human body in any way adapted to aid in the fulfillment of this desire — namely, the larynx. When the politician is most fired with his great emotion — when he is making a speech soliciting votes — nature comes to his aid in the peculiar way you have noticed; his voice grows loud, clear, pleading, and very frequently even convincing."

Being more than pleased with his learning and keen ability as an expositor, I ventured to express to him my wish to make a thorough study of Lilliputian society and requested that he preserve the same patience in answering further questions for me that he had already manifest.

He graciously consented upon condition that I acquaint him with some of the customs of my country as we went along. To this I gladly consented. I also proposed to question Onk Watwil and Admiral Spraygrees concerning military and naval affairs, whereupon they politely promised to answer any and all questions, excepting only those which would betray state secrets, thereby rendering them liable for treason.

I had just explained to my companions that the paying of money to public officials to escape prosecution for a criminal offense, and the purchasing of votes, were in my country criminal acts of a very black stamp indeed, and asked for an outline of the philosophy which seemed to sustain an exactly contrary view of the matter in Lilliput, when another lamentable occurrence broke the pleasant trend of our conversation and set the party into an uproar. A half-starved kangaroo-rat emboldened by its hunger dashed across the table and snatched away a piece of bacon from one of the ladies. All of the company let out a shriek, and two of the ladies fainted. Onk Watwil drew forth his sabre and slashed wildly at the invader. In his nervous haste he missed his mark by a wide margin, and shaved all of the brass buttons from the front of the Admiral's coat. The rat, in its confusion occasioned by these mad gestures and the shrieking, scurried straight at the soldier, who became seized with a panic as the beast brushed his legs. Dropping his sabre, he leapt from the

mess table down to the floor, and only by a miracle escaped breaking some bones or meeting his death in so doing. After the rat had
vanished, and Nitpooperler Hirear had revived the ladies by the application of cold water to their faces, the Admiral finally succeeded
in finding Onk Watwil, who was beneath several layers of sail-cloth
lying on the deck. My reassurances that the rat would do them no
harm and that there could not be more than two or three left on
board, so diligent had I been in exterminating them, finally quieted
the party sufficiently for us to resume our breakfast, and to continue
the discussion that was becoming so interesting to me.

Nitpooperler Hirear was at first quite skeptical of the proposition
that there could be a country so foolish as to make the acts of paying
money to public officials for dismissals of criminal charges, or of
purchasing votes, criminal offenses. "Yours must be a nation where
corruption rules at high cost, and where both the people and the
officers of state have become masters of the art of dissimulation," he
hazarded.

These words, coming from one who knew nothing whatever of
my country, heated my blood considerably, but I repressed my feelings as best I could and urged the Nitpooperler to expound his meaning, realizing that he had probably meant no offense by what he had
asserted.

"Our country, too, would be ruled by corruption," he said, "if
a public official could only by criminal act buy a vote, or if a public
offender could only by another offense buy his liberty from an officer.
First, let us consider the purchase of votes. When the greater part
of the money finding its way into the pockets of the public official
must, of necessity, by the very compelling force of our system, find
its way back into the pockets of the citizen in payment for his vote,
even though the officials rob the treasury, lay burdensome taxes, or
resort to other nefarious means of gaining money, that money must
come to, and in the end, directly benefit each citizen in the nation.
If an officer will not spend more for votes that his opponents, he will
lose his office."

"But," I asked, "What guarantee has the citizen that an officer,
once he has lined his pockets, will not decline to run for re-election,
and thereby save his gleanings?"

"Our law provides that once a man has been elected to office, he
is automatically nominated to run for re-election, and he is bound,
on pain of life imprisonment, always to pay more per vote than he

did on the previous election. While this is not an air-tight method to insure against enrichment of public officials, it has always been a workable and sufficient insurance for a maximum of public benefit."

"Well and good," I ventured, "But your system, rather than avoiding corruption, seems to be squarely founded upon it"

"Not so, Man Mountain. Corruption is a creature of darkness which can breed and flourish only in obscurity. Light is fatal to it. Our whole system stands forth in the broad light of day. Everybody knows what becomes of an official's money, and everybody gets his money's worth. If votes could not be purchased openly, there would be throughout the land a dark undercurrent of bargaining, a fester of secret intrigue, and a blight of injustice. A few powerful persons or organizations could, in return for favors granted or promised, sway the minds of the voters by a bombardment of perfidious propaganda, threatened loss of livelihood, and broadcasted falsehood, rule the whole land. No voter would even know what to believe, and, not knowing his best interest, would nearly always vote against it, for he would be led to do so by the extravagant claims of the loudest liar. A few by the corruption would be enriched and the public at large made poor. Such a chaotic state of government in which neither the people nor the officials would govern, and where the real government would consist of a few wealthy, grasping, lying, stealing, ruthless individuals wielding the power of the nation, would be insufferable. Glory to our law, which does not lay our populace open to such exploitation. How thankful I am that every voter in Lilliput knows exactly how to vote to his best interest — for the candidate who will pay the highest price for his ballot. Little chance here of hoodwinking a voter into cheating himself."

The force of the Nitpooperler's words left me somewhat as a loss for words myself. I felt almost as though I had been called upon to defend my own country, yet a little reflection served to cool me off, since I knew that my friend, not having any knowledge whatever of my country, could not, as it seemed at first blush, have been directing his heated remarks toward it. I contented myself with asking him to explain what seemed to me even more corrupt than commercial traffic in votes — the buying and selling of dismissals of criminal charges.

"That practice," he replied, "rests upon the same strong foundation, the same broad principle of social justice, as the practice of vote buying. If a man be not allowed to purchase his freedom directly, he will do it indirectly and covertly, and if it should be done by the latter method, corruption and injustice would become a part of the warp and woof of our law. In return for covert favor in money or service, a judicial officer would warp the very structure of the law, and, by a process of judicial circumvention, obscurity, and hair-splitting, decide that an offender should go free even when the law clearly directs that he be punished. By openly setting a man free upon payment of a price, the travesty of a trial to which the conclusion has already been secretly determined is avoided, legal precedents are kept clear and uncorroded by the falsity of corrupt judicial opinion, and our judges remain free agents in the interpreting of the law unmoved by threat or the hope of gain —"

"Yes, but real offenders escape punishment," I interrupted.

"True – true, but it costs him money, and the net result upon society is ever so much more beneficial if he goes free openly than if he were to go free through a system of sneaking corruption which would ruin the splendid character of judicial officers and besmirch the case precedents of our law. Society suffers less in the long run, for if an officer could not accept payment to free an offender, there would be little stimulus to apprehend him. Our police are highly efficient, for every man is forever hopeful of capturing a criminal who can pay handsomely for his release."

"I begin to perceive, Sir, that at least a part of Lilliputian law is predicated upon the presumption that every person living is basely dishonest," I said.

Nitpooperler quickly replied: "That perception is not exactly accurate. Our system of government is built around the inescapable truth that 'man always does what pleases him best,' as said our ancient **disthedons**, in their philosophical discussions. The system also recognizes that the one thing that impels men to action is ambition — the hope of worldly gain. Our ideal is to let every man get what he can, openly and fairly, so long as he does not exploit his fellow man in so doing. When governmental functions are carried on openly, in a way intelligible to all, what room is there for dishonesty, Man Mountain Gulliver?"

To this I made no reply. But, seeing that everyone had finished breakfast and that the ladies were growing restless with our conversation, I proposed that we go on deck where there was a bright sun shining, and where the morning air was so fresh as to render the deck quite inviting. Again I served as a sort of human elevator by setting my friends upon the floor level of the deck one at a time.

Soon Admiral Spraygrees informed me that he had ordered a navy cutter to pick up the party to take them to vote. He knew that the Donkgop had requested me not to venture upon the island on the day of the election, for my presence, even if it did not directly lead to the injury of a native, might cause some to remain away from the polling places for fear of being trampled upon.

"That my 'hosts and hostesses' might be departing so soon had not entered my mind," I said "It is my hope that they will return to my vessel as soon as business no longer detains them on the island, for I would like to hold more enjoyable discussions in such an agreeable company."

"For my part," replied the Admiral, "having been commissioned by my superior, the Donkgop, to come here to be at your service, I shall feel obliged to return; but were I not under such compulsion, I wish to assure you that I should then be quite as happy to come providing I were certain the food and drink were of such excellent quality as that furnished for our entertainment this morning, and providing you could persuade my friend Onk Watwil, should he accompany me, not to slash off my buttons again. Watwil, not only have you put me in fear of losing my nose or some other protuberant portion of my anatomy, but you have deprived me of something I value highly. It has taken many moons to earn those buttons. Not only do they perform for me a distinctive service, but they also symbolize a lifetime of toil to rise to my present eminence in the Lilliputian Navy."

These sentences addressed to Watwil were even to me obvious banter, but Watwil, perhaps owing to a certain sheepishness growing out of his flight from the rat, was in no mood to notice banter, or return it as such. He countered in a surly tone, "Admiral Spraygrees, in the future I shall not draw my sabre for your protection from attacking beasts, but shall allow any creature so disposed to chew off you beard." At this juncture the cutter drew alongside the **Night-Hawk**, and I let the company down in the basket to the deck of the smaller ship as soon as I had been further reassured that I could expect them back before evening.

Chapter VII

Wherein the author attends the theatre in Mildendo.

AFTER I HAD BEEN sojourning in Lilliput for nearly three weeks Donkgop Medid Wherding, who had been re-elected to office by a large majority, gave me permission to wander where I would throughout the city of Mildendo, providing only that I would carry a bell to sound a warning of my approach, much after the manner of European lepers during the Middle Ages. The people were growing accustomed to me and none of them were any longer likely to be frightened. Children were at all times confined in school, on public playgrounds, or in their homes, consequently there was little danger of my trampling upon a child. I was repeatedly warned that I would be held amenable to the law governing injury by accident in traffic and it would be only wise caution on my part to avoid the places where traffic was heavy. The favor from the Donkgop was not purely a manifestation of courtesy on his part, but was partially the result of my own efforts. He was at first much disinclined to allow me to roam about at will throughout the capital, being mindful not only of the fact that injuries might be inflicted on someone, but also being apprehensive lest too much intercourse between the people and me might in some way not at all clear to me tend to indoctrinate some of them with theories subversive to good government. However, I was fully determined to carry out my designs. After the early frustrations and hardships I had endured in order to reach this fair little country, I would not be turned aside from my purpose to make a thorough study of everything concerning it. I discovered in one of my discussions with Hirear, who, all the while, had continued my chief companion and a "host" upon the **Night-Hawk**, that notwithstanding the mechanical ingenuity and advancement in Lilliput, they had no motion pictures. Since there was a projector on the ship with several reels of film which the crew had intended to use for amusement during leisure hours, I told him about it. He was immediately desirous to see it work and to become acquainted with its mechanical principles. For once in my life, at least, I was able to seize upon an opportunity before I had let it slip. Once Lilliputian curiosity was aroused by motion pictures, I could demand and receive favors in return for my revelation to them of the mechanical principles underlying the moving picture. If I had not carried out my bargaining well, I am confident that I would not even have gained complete freedom of the city of Mildendo. The Donkgop was quite as curious as Nitpooperler Hirear concerning motion pictures, and hence granted me every favor I had occasion to ask.

On one night in early summer a new play was opening in the *Looddlyn*, a large theatre in Mildendo. The Donkgop sent me word that if I wished to attend he would have the state engineers build me a seat outside the building where I might sit to view the performance through an opening in the roof. He had previously ordered constructed for me a periscopic device made of a steel tube of adjustable length and fitted with a series of magnifying mirrors. With the aid of this instrument I could easily look into buildings, through doors or windows, and see plainly a magnified reflection of everything within. It is needless to record that I accepted the invitation and was present at the theatre on the night appointed for the premiere.

The interior of a Lilliputian theatre in its general aspects resembles those of America and Europe, but differs in some important respects. Both the foyer and the stage lighting far surpasses anything of the kind I have seen elsewhere. Reflector-rays are employed for this as they are for all lighting in Mildendo, but in the theatre the light sources are completely hidden. There are no shining star effects such as I had seen out-of-doors at the banquet. Light just seems to be a constituent part of the atmosphere in a Lilliputian theatre. Balconies, galleries, and boxes are not present in the Looddlyn, nor, as I learned by inquiry, in any Mildendo theatre, but there is present in all an odd variation of them. Most of the audience is seated in rows on the main floor, just as in an ordinary theatre, but the highest priced seats are in a kind of enclosed booth suspended a short distance from the ceiling. Some of these booths hold one, some two, and some four persons. The front of each one is fitted with transparent steel over which the occupant may draw a curtain if he desires. To enter one of these seats, it is necessary that the whole booth be lowered to the floor and the door opened, which service is rendered by employees of the theatre. To avoid lowering a booth upon the heads of people in the orchestra seats directly below, all seats work in a mechanical conjunction with any booth vertically above. As a booth is lowered on its cable three or four rows of seats may be seen to slide in locked grooves to one side or the other, thus making way for the descending booth. Upon first seeing these "box seats" I could not understand why anyone would want to view a performance from one rather than from an orchestra seat which appeared to me infinitely better. But there is in Lilliput a certain premium set upon "privacy in public", or a sort of ostentatious exclusiveness.

The penchant to pursue the fashionable mode leads many wealthy Lilliputians to commit acts which never could in my eyes appear to be other than absurd follies. For instance, one old lady, the wife of a rich merchant of Mildendo, engaged the most skillful silversmith in the nation to design and make for her a silver gown. She, herself, directed that it be fabricated with holes to reveal certain portions and extremities of her person which a little good sense and a modicum of modesty would have impelled her to cover even had she then retained those charms that in a young girl might excusably have given rise to feminine pride. She paid the artisan a huge fortune to refrain from making any other silver dresses, once he had completed hers, which being the only one of its kind in the whole country attracted nation-wide attention. The uncomfortable weight of the dress should have been enough to deter most women from wearing it, but not the merchant's wife. She never gave up wearing it because it had galled her shoulders, neck, and waist, even though it caused several running sores to appear on her body; she only ceased to wear it because, having ventured forth clad in it one day, the summer sun so heated it as to severely blister large patches of her body. So badly was she burned that when I left Lilliput she was still confined to the hospital. I would not have digressed to describe the folly of the merchant's wife had it not been, as I conceive it, that something of the same vanity, something of the same mad craving for the gaze of others, however it be attracted, is partly responsible for the popularity of "box seats" in Mildendo theatres. That there may be other reasons making them popular I am prepared neither to affirm nor deny. One may surmise what one wishes.

The cheapest seats in a Lilliputian theatre are nothing more than a space in an aisle where many people sit on a cushion brought with them. Unlike America, Lilliput has no fire laws to prevent such practices, for the excellent reason that loss by fire has been nearly outgrown in the latter country. There "fireproof" is not one of the catchwords of smart advertising but really means fireproof, and most of the buildings there have been fireproofed. Tile, stone, brick, and concrete are in use, but metal is the common building material, exceeding in a ratio of about ten to one. I have seen few pieces of wooden furniture there; nearly all of it is made of steel. Even the upholstery is made of splendid fabrics woven from wire, or from the very fine fibres of asbestos found in abundance all over the rocky parts of the island.

Through my periscopic instrument I obtained an excellent view of the whole interior of the Looddlyn. The stage, although like those familiar to Americans in respect to contour and general arrangement, was different from them in that it appeared to have no curtain. While the large crowd was filling the place, which held about two thousand to three thousand seats, the stage appeared as a great vacant space, bare except for a few live shrubs growing from earthen pots.

The colorful and fantastic costumes of the people defy description, since each and every one of them, in the strictest accord with the fashion of the times, differed from every other one. It would require a lengthy catalogue merely to list them, but a brief notice of a few may serve to present a general notion of the bizarre scene I gazed upon. I hesitate to assert that in choosing a costume a Lilliputian endeavors to symbolize his or her own peculiar personality, although I have been told such is the case. At any rate one young dandy, the son of a steel manufacturer, came dressed in a suit that was amusing even to the others composing the audience. To begin with his footwear, he wore a pair of shoes, one white and the other black, which curved outward in a wide semi-circle in such a way that the toes resembled the horns of a mountain goat. These were continually getting under other peoples' feet or hooking around their legs and tripping them. His breeches consisted of one short red pant leg reaching not more than half way from hip to knee leaving the remainder of his leg bare, while the other pant leg was of black material as wide as a hoop skirt, and flopped down around his foot. He wore a transparent shirt made of a shining material resembling cellophane, and a jacket of loosely woven straw bearing inscriptions such as *yoopee*, *hawtcha*, *honey*, etc. There were accompanied with drawings of feminine faces and forms. Notwithstanding the humidity and heat of a summer evening, he entered the theatre wearing a long coat made of fur closely resembling dog fur, though it may have been Blefuscudian raccoon. For a head gear, if such it may be called, he wore a thin, flat, multicolored piece just large enough to cover a small spot on the top of his head. The thing was so small and I was so far from him when I first noticed it that I may be wrong in stating that it was a head gear at all. Quite possibly it was a small drop of something spattered on his head.

Just as I was wondering what would happen if two or more individuals should appear in the same group dressed alike I beheld the answer in the crowd. Two young ladies had unfortunately conceived the same idea at the same time. Each came to the theatre wearing nothing but a cool thin strip of potato peeling. When their sight fell upon each other, mortification deep and blushing set in at once, though strangely not through any shame arising from their scant attire, but through the shame of being out of style. So aroused were they over what was, after all, only a mishap, that both left the theatre immediately and did not return for the play.

One eccentric old lady came decked out in a sprig of geranium blossoms, and another in gossamer tights of frogskin richly ornamented with shining fish scales.

Just before the performance was scheduled to begin, an orchestra, concealed in some spot I never did locate, began to play. Lilliputian music, while undeniably very rhythmic, was almost unbearable to my foreign ears. It is nothing but a confused scramble of wailing, shrieking, squeaking, moaning, tapping, clanging, clattering, pounding, grating, crashing, squawking, rumbling, and raucous noises such as would draw the very nerves out of one's body and slit them into fine shreds.

When at last the preliminary concert was over, much to the relief of my offended ears, the stage became invisible, not, as I have said, by means of a curtain, but by means of a thin black ray directed across it from one side to the other.

Then a man appeared when the black ray was turned off. Quite briefly he introduced another who was to act as master of ceremonies; then appeared the individual introduced – a small man even for a Lilliputian, dressed in an odd costume consisting of tattered breeches, high boots, a calf skin vest, and a tall hat. For several moments he stumbled over his own feet while he toyed with something which may have been a yo-yo; I could not discern exactly what it was. After some clownish pantomime he began to speak in the embarrassed manner of a small boy, saying that all he knew was what he read in the funny papers, and added that he was no longer a subscriber. He made two or three remarks about friends of his. One friend, it seems, was going to be late to the show because his only collar button had dropped into his beard and he was still at home looking for it; another in his overweening desire to get to the Looddlyn on time, had forgotten that it was his night to stay home and feed the baby, consequently he had just been sent home by his wife. The humor in all of his remarks was completely lost on me, yet the audience hung onto every word and punctuated every remark with riotous laughter and applause.

The new play was entitled **What Happened in the Bedroom**. The first scene opened revealing a young man and woman engaged in a heated discussion over what seemed to be something very psychological, although very obscure to me. The next scene was the interior of a living room, and the characters were the same as in the first. The heated discussion continued along with some action consisting mainly of amorous advances by the young man, and the repulsing of them by the young lady. In the third and last act the scene was laid in a bedroom, and, since I entertain some hope of publishing this account of my adventures, I dare not narrate what took place in that act. Besides, it would not be worth the trouble, for the play was utterly rotten even to the Lilliputians. Toward the end of the play several persons in the audience began to protest vociferously. Many had left before the opening of the last act. The shouted protests increased and the play was almost stopped by the confusion that ensued. However, it was completed; the ending I thought rather touching.

Nitpooperler Hirear emerged from the theatre muttering something under his breath concerning what a terrible play it was. Everybody seemed in quite a huff about it. I agreed. A viler production I had never before witnessed. The whole piece was immoral from beginning to end. Its crudeness and depravity were beyond any possibility of excusing or condoning. I wondered whether or not Lilliput maintained any censorship over her theatres and ventured to put that question to Nitpooperler Hirear as we were on our way to the beach, he sitting upon my shoulder as usual.

"Yes – yes. We have a board of highly paid censors, but the *dink swak slaginzebobs* (*Lilliputian profanity*) must have been cold sober and loafing every day of their lives to allow such a *dink swak* show to pass. What did you think of it, Man Mountain?"

I replied that I too shared his opinion – that it was inexcusably lewd, lascivious, and sexy.

"Sexy – sexy – ho, ho – sexy?" he roared, almost bursting with laughter.

"Yes," I replied, "sexy – it was too sexy – nothing but sex."

At this answer the Nitpooperler laughed so uproariously that he nearly fell off my shoulder.

"What kind of plays must you have in your country? Sexy – ho – ho – Don't you know why the people were displeased? They were displeased because that lukewarm nursery tale had no sex theme in it – no stimulating suggestive action – no warm blooded sex relationships in it. Ho – ho – ho!"

"Do you mean the people's protests were not because the play was so immoral?"

"No – they were protesting because it lacked excitement – because there was nothing stimulating in it – because the board of censors had let through a tepid and feeble piece of poppycock. It is their business to see that they are lively – hot."

Something in this enlightenment saddened me. Again I felt the need for a "Glyk" Spaddle to cope with something I now perceived to lie beyond my power.

Chapter VIII

Wherein the author is suspected of being a disease carrier and makes the acquaintance of certain members of the Lilliputian medical profession.

O NE SUNNY HOLIDAY MORNING while Nitpooperlers Hirear and To-matocumber, Onk Watwil, Buzknut, and I were basking on the sands of the beach, and I was entertaining them with tales of America, our pleasant occupation was interrupted by the arrival of a company of mounted police. With some difficulty, owing to the fact that the horses took fright at the sight of my huge bulk, the company rode up within a foot of where I sat, and took a semi-circular formation confronting me. Of course, I could not be other than apprehensive lest I had again unwittingly violated some law of the land. Approaching me as near as he could, *Chief Squeesegraft*, the chief of the company stood up in his stirrups and handed me a written document. By aid of a magnifying glass, which I always carried to enable me to read the small signs posted throughout Mildendo, I was able to read the contents of the missive. In translation it read:

From the Board of Sickness and Wellness of the City of Mildendo, on the Island of Lilliput, in Mid-Ocean, to the Man Mountain, Arthur C. Gulliver: Greetings, Salutations, Greetings:

Comes now the Head Officer of the Board of Sickness and Wellness, Division of Sickness, Subdivision of Epidemics and states:

I. That there is now prevalent in Mildendo an epidemic of a disease hitherto and heretofore unknown on the island;

II. That said epidemic began nine days after the said Gulliver's first visit to the said city of Mildendo, on the Island of Lilliput, in Mid-Ocean;

III. That said epidemic has been spreading and increasing ever since.

Upon information and belief, the said Head Officer of the Board of Sickness and Wellness, Division of Sickness, Subdivision of Epidemics further states:

IV. That said Man Mountain, Arthur C. Gulliver, is the carrier of the germ causing the said epidemic, in the City of Mildendo, on the Island of Lilliput, in Mid-Ocean;

Wherefore, it has been ordered and adjudged that within one day after the service of this instrument upon the said Man Mountain, Arthur C. Gulliver, he, the said Man Mountain, Arthur C. Gulliver, must, and is hereby commanded so to do, submit to a medical examination, and should the medical examination prove that he is a disease carrier, the said Man Mountain, Arthur C. Gulliver, must, and is hereby commanded so to do, submit himself to the direction and care of a board of Medicos appointed for the purpose, at such place as the board shall stipulate.

Done in the City of Mildendo, on the Island of Lilliput, in Mid-Ocean, this 193rd day after the last day of the last week of the festival of Scoratias, in the year of rank cheeses, under the hand and seal of the Head Officer aforesaid.

Signed and Sealed,

Scabpincer Blodglut

Head Officer of the Board of Sickness and Wellness,
Division of Sickness,
Subdivision of Epidemics.

After reading the document there seemed nothing left to do but hand it to the Buzknut. He scanned it a moment, then addressing the Chief said, "The law requires that such an order as this direct the examinee to appear in the Mildendo Hospital. This order does not so direct, therefore it is squashy. I advise the Man Mountain that it is null and squashed."

"Sir," replied the Chief, "I am not a lawyer, and it is not my duty to argue with lawyers. My orders are to see that the directions of this document are carried out, and that I shall do. However, with reference to your statement, I might say that I overheard the Departmental Attorney and *Scabpincer Blodglut* discussing the point you have raised, and they decided that Lilliputian law does not require the impossible. Man Mountain cannot possibly appear in the Mildendo Hospital."

"Then," the Buzknut reasserted, "he need appear nowhere."

My mind even in this situation was working to gain further means for learning more about Lilliputian society.

"Friend Buzknut," I asked, "is the medical fraternity of Lilliput split into various factions, according to how their basic theories differ, or do all doctors belong to the same school?"

"Friend Gulliver, the healers of this country are many and various, though I am unable to see how that matter bears upon your situation."

"Well and good," I said, "Whether or not it bears upon anything is of no import. Although, as you say, I am not legally bound to obey this summons, I will gladly obey it voluntarily, provided certain conditions which I shall enumerate are met by the Board of Sickness and Wellness."

"Man Mountain Gulliver, you will be arrested upon the order of the Board and no conditions will attach," the Chief replied in a most officious manner and tone of voice.

"So?" My temper rose a little. "So? You would arrest me contrary to the legality of the thing, thereby injuring me in law and rendering me liable to criminal prosecution for having allowed myself to be accidentally wronged? No, that shall not be. Did you know, Chief, that I am a necromancer, a magician, a fortune teller? Did you know that I can predict the future?"

The chief stared bravely up into my face as I lowered it near to him in asking these questions.

"No, I did not know you were a magician," he answered. Then after a thoughtful pause – "What do you predict?"

"That when you come to arrest me you will be seriously hurt in a very bad accident." (I dared not threaten him with willful injury for not only the act, but even a threat of violence, is criminal in Lilliput.)

Again there was a long thoughtful pause, during which the Chief stared unflinchingly at me. Finally:

"What are your conditions?"

"That at least one member from each of the different schools of the healing profession be sent to examine me and that no one of them will consult with another," I replied quickly, realizing that I was succeeding in the project I had formulated in my mind.

"Are those the only conditions?"

"Yes, that is all. I will be waiting on the **Night-Hawk** for the delegation of healers."

"I shall deliver your message to Scabpincer Blodglut," the Chief said; then he shouted a command to his men, whereupon they swung into a double file formation and rode swiftly out of sight over a low sand dune.

"I see," observed the Buzknut, "that you are learning our ways and customs, and that you have absorbed some of the rudiments of Lilliputian law. For a time I feared you were going to threaten Chief Squeesegraft. What, please tell, impels you to want to be examined by many healers? I should think an examination by one would be ordeal enough."

"Friend Buzknut," I said, "I wish to learn all I may about the society of your state, and I seized upon an opportunity to learn much on a subject of which I now know nothing. Perhaps, to prepare me better for the 'ordeal', as you call it, you would be so kind as to tell me something concerning the various schools of Lilliputian healers."

"That I will, and gladly, as best I can. So numerous are they, doubtless, I am not cognizant of some. First, the largest and most conventional group is the 'cutters', whose remedy is the knife; secondly, the 'dosers', whose remedies are very numerous, but all alike in one simple respect – in that they consist of directing into the body by one means or another some foreign substance calculated to affect the organs in some unnatural way, and thereby affect a cure; thirdly, are the 'rubbers', whose remedy consists solely in rubbing the patient; then there are the 'wetters', who claim to effect cures by the application of water both internally and externally. There are 'lighters', whose remedy is the application of light rays to the body; there are 'stretchers', whose remedy is stretching and bending the body; there are the 'starvers', whose theory is that eating causes all human ills, and that consequently the only proper remedy is to quit eating. Very numerous of late are the healers known as the 'non-volitionists', whose theory is that illness or pain is only a figment of the imagination or thought, and therefore that any illness may be cured by the simple expedient of ceasing to think at all. There are the 'bone twisters', whose cure of all diseases is accomplished by the snapping and cracking of bones, especially the bones of the feet; also 'breathers', whose cures consist of inhalations and exhalations according to a scheme for every known disease. It is very interesting to visit a sanitarium where patients are taking a cure under a 'breather'. Each one sits, stands, reclines, or assumes some combination of these positions while before his eyes is placed a sheaf of inscriptions somewhat like the music sheets placed before musicians. Every patient breathes in, out, or ceases to breathe according to the rhythm and time as directed by the chart before him.

"Of course, each of these branches of the healing art have developed specialists, and some of the specialties have almost developed into separate schools themselves. For instance, among the 'cutters' there are specialists whose cutting is done only in the human throat. So popular have they become that now they profess to cure many obscure ailments in other parts of the body."

Before the Buzknut had finished speaking I was pondering seriously how I had, indeed, let myself in for an 'ordeal' as he characterized it. Should all of the healers mentioned each try his specialty upon me I should be a dead man ere half had tried – especially since their methods would of necessity be crude and cumbersome on one so large as me. The gloomy prospect before me considerably abated my thirst for knowledge.

Finally, as my companions and I were leaving the beach to take the row-boat out to the anchored *Night-Hawk*, I determined to go through with the business of the examination by the healers and use force if need be to prevent any nonsense which might possibly injure my health or body.

Toward evening a messenger in a scazpop fitted with paddles came skimming across the water to the *Night-Hawk*, where he delivered to me a message from Scabpincer Blodglut which stated that a delegation of forty-two healers, selected in keeping with my conditions, would attend me on the morrow immediately after the breakfast hour.

All of the healers commissioned to examine me were private practitioners save two from the Department of Sickness and Wellness, so I was not surprised that when they arrived next morning there were but thirty-four, the other eight being detained with dying or near-dying patients. In spite of the wide diversity of professional opinion among them, the group of Lilliputian gentlemen I hoisted aboard that morning were surprisingly alike in appearance. The long hair on their faces and the dearth of adornment on their heads would have rendered them conspicuous anywhere.

The whole process of my examination occupied about four hours, during which time I was subjected to many prickings, slappings, thumpings, tappings, poundings, etc. I was examined by each healer separately as I had requested. In all fairness to these Lilliputian healers I must state that none of the thirty-four were of the opinion that I was the carrier of the germ causing the epidemic then prevalent in Mildendo, and that all but five noted in their examination an incipient carbuncular condition on my right posterior. The dentist, having noticed this condition recommended that I have seven teeth extracted to clear it up; the throat specialist recommended the removal of my tonsils to clear up the carbuncular condition; the cutter, after a very lengthy and unpleasant probing and pricking with a pitchfork in many parts of my body, advised a carving off of the right posterior and a cropping of my ears to effect a complete and permanent cure.

These words of advice I listened to with patience, and thanked each, but firmly refused the proffered services each seemed only too ready to give.

The "rubbers" offered to bring a hundred strong men to rub me; the "wetters" suggested the employment of the fire department, both men and water pumps, for administering colonic irrigations and salt water baths; the "doser" left for my use several phials of drugs, some ointments, and mineral waters. The "lighter" suggested the application of red fluid rays, and offered an ingenious plan for my obtaining the treatments. If, said he, I would go to the Mildendo Hospital the following day he would have his ray machine placed in a second story outside room so that he would be able to apply the light to my posterior through an open window before which I should drop my breeches and assume a position convenient to the operation. To him also I gave my thanks, stating that owing to lack of time and pressure of other matters requiring my attention, I would not in the immediate future be able to accept his services.

While the "non-volitionist" was pacing up and down the side of my bed delivering me a lecture, the gist of which was that I had no sore, no pain, or ailment of any kind whatever, but only thought I had, he got his feet tangled in the folds of a sheet and fell. His head struck my toe nail and he received an ugly gash over his right eye. The remarks he made upon this occasion were about the most profane I had ever heard uttered by a Lilliputian. He left my presence still swearing and holding a wet handkerchief over the cut on his forehead.

When at last I had been examined by all of the healers, I, myself, with the aid of a needle gave the pimple on my posterior the attention it needed, put on my clothing, and went on deck to find Nitpooperler Hirear. I found him engaged in earnest conversation with *Healer Slisepaarts*, the "cutter", who had examined me.

"It was against my better judgment," he was saying, "that I came upon this mission. Against all the ethics of my profession I have been required to associate with the chief quacks of Lilliput, and to enter upon a case in which their disreputable services were demanded."

"Yes, but you must admit that the case was quite unusual. The size of the patient alone should be sufficient to excuse you for breaking ethical rules on this one exceptional occasion."

"Healer Slisepaarts," I asked, "would you be so kind as to answer for me a few questions? Being foreign, I am naturally unacquainted with your ways, and being curious, I wish to ask questions."

"Gladly, Man Mountain, will I answer if I am able. What are your questions?"

"Well, first, would you mind expounding for me the theory underlying your advice that my ears should be cropped?"

"That question I should not answer had I not already given you my word. That theory can be understood only by a trained cutter; it lies beyond the grasp of lay intelligence. Furthermore, I ordinarily would not attempt an explanation of it for the simple reason that medical terms tend to frighten a patient. Explanations are futile. It is the business of the patient to trust his cutter without bothering his head about the method by which his cutter has arrived at his professional opinion. The fact is your ears should be cropped because the peculiar excrescence of the super medulla ganglia of epidermal vortex in the tintafibula membranes surrounding the false tibia has given rise to a fistulous neurosis in the hemimorphus portion of the bicameral metacarpal."

"Thank you, sir," I said. "Would you now, please, tell me whether or not you would send to a 'rubber' or a 'stretcher' a patient who came to you with an ailment which you knew rubbing or stretching would cure more readily than cutting?"

"Your question is unanswerable, because you predicate it on false assumptions. There is no disease or ailment which is not curable by cutting; rubbing and stretching are pure quackery."

"Do you ever receive patients to whom you were recommended by a 'rubber' or a 'stretcher'?"

"No, rubbers and stretchers, being interested only in relieving their victims of their money, promise to cure anything by their methods, so never recommend anybody but themselves. However, a doser occasionally sends me a patient, and I sometimes supplement my cutting with certain dosing. These two healing practices are both scientific, but the latter is a very limited one. Cutting is a well developed, accurate, and effective science."

Our conversation was interrupted at this point by the nonvolitionist who, still bleeding profusely, came to ask for the ministrations of Cutter Slisepaarts. In a few moments the latter had by a few deft slashes with his scalpel removed the original wound by cutting around it. Then he sewed the edges of the opening together and soon had the bleeding stopped. As I watched the operation, an errant thought entered my mind: "Was this a demonstration of homeopathy surgically applied?"

After the healers had departed, Nitpooperler Hirear and I held a long debate concerning the healing profession. He warmly defended the dosers and cutters, whom he considers very highly advanced scientifically, and I, while not condemning any, nevertheless contended that a little common sense would be useful to all. Why, I argued, should each school consider that its system of treatment was the best treatment for all afflictions? Why not a little co-operation and the recognizing of what seems to be plain to the layman – the fact that one kind of treatment is effective for the cure of certain ailments and another effective for the cure of others.

"That," asserted the Nitpooperler, "would lead to an undesirable end. If a person went to a 'cutter', for instance, and the cutter advised him to go to a 'rubber', the patient would lose faith in the 'cutter'; and so it would be if a 'rubber' advised his patient to go to a 'cutter'. Soon no one would have faith in any kind of a healer"

"You are probably right," I asserted. "There is likely more efficacy in the patient's faith than in the healer's remedies."

Next day I learned through Tomatocumber, who paid me a morning visit, that the non-volitionist who had received the cut the day before had been lodged in prison for having received an accidental injury. Feeling that I had been at least indirectly to blame for his misfortune, the plight of the non-volitionist aroused in me no little concern. Immediately I sent word to the Buzknut to do whatever he could to obtain the release of the man, and if such could be done at a reasonable cost, I would bear the expense. I was happy to learn a few hours afterward that he had been released. This act of mine, which he always viewed as a great kindness, made for me a warm friend who later stood me in good stead. Indeed, but for the friendship of this little man, the reader might never have perused these lines, for I would not have lived to write them.

Chapter IX

Wherein the author views a Lilliputian execution and visits the government workhouses and prisons.

HAVING ENTERTAINED THE IDEA, growing out of some of my experiences during the first two months of my stay in Lilliput, that the civilization of the country was completely emerged from all but a very slight taint of congenital barbarism, I was somewhat shocked when one morning Nitpooperler Bittzzora, the young Barrister who was the chief executive in the Department of Prisons, Crime, Injustice, and Liquor Consumption, came to invite me to go to the great Mildendo Prison to witness an execution. I had a strong distaste for any such business, yet I neither wished to offend this brilliant young official nor to pass up an opportunity to learn more concerning Lilliputian society. So, taking the periscopic instrument that had stood me in such good stead on the occasion of my visit to the theatre, I set out with Bittzzora to attend the execution.

After arriving on the beach, I walked, as it was always necessary for me to do in Lilliput. We arrived at the prison some two hours ahead of the time scheduled for the execution, Bittzzora having ridden in my coat pocket somewhat, as he said, against his better judgment and to the detriment of his dignity. He, noticing my interest in the prison, which housed some fifty odd thousand inmates, kindly consented to conduct me about.

The great State Prison on the northern outskirts of the city of Mildendo occupies approximately two acres of ground, much of which is given over to agriculture, raising food products for the inmates. It is surrounded by a wall about eight feet high and a foot thick, composed of some metal alloy almost as heavy as lead, but decidedly harder than that metal. Large gates, operated mechanically at the touch of a hidden button by one of the guards, swing open upon the approach of persons definitely known to have business at the institution. The buildings within the walls, unlike most of the buildings in Mildendo, are low two-story affairs, and, strangely enough, as it seemed to me, only one small wing contained the barred windows to be expected on prison buildings. I soon learned, by putting my periscope to a few windows, that only the one wing mentioned contained actual cell blocks. All the other buildings were nothing but well lighted and well ventilated factories humming with scores of busy machines operated by hundreds of busy hands. All of the prisoners, or State Workmen as they were called, excepting about two-hundred who were locked in the cell blocks and those who worked in the fields, worked in the factories, which turned out a great variety of finished products. In one plant there was being manufactured a wide woven metal ribbon which Barrister Bittzzora informed me was used in the construction of paved scazpop highways since the rough hard surfaces of the material afforded excellent traction. It was also widely used as a flooring material, especially in zingpups. In another plant sacks were manufactured, and in still others, workingmen's uniforms.

The well-fed healthy appearance of the inmates was strikingly noticeable, and was, according to Bittzzora, attributable to the first-class fare and medical attention furnished by the state to every inmate. A thing that particularly attracted my attention was the sign worn on the back of each prisoner. With some difficulty I was able to read a few of those nearest the window through which I obtained my view of the interior. One read:

> I, **Madluuk Whingdid**, have become a State Workman for having injured myself in a fall down an elevator shaft.

One elderly fellow, whose wearied downcast look contrasted with the appearance and demeanor of the others, wore a sign which read:

> I, **Zat Blabblathre**, have, for the period during which the State shall sustain my life, become a State Workman. I once talked against the government.

Another inmate wore a sign reading:

> I, **Sat Waaxwroth**, am for a time a State Workman. I murdered an old lady for her money.

The inmates in the cell block as well as those active in the factories wore signs upon their backs. One of these signs reads:

> I, **Woostow Saavecassh**, having evaded taxes, and having mismanaged the State property formerly mine, and having diversely talked against the government, contrary to the law and the terms of my

sentence, have been condemned to death by evaporation upon my refusal to take oath to enter upon the performance of my duties under the said law and sentence aforesaid. May my substance freshen the crops in rain.

"Friend Bittzzora," I asked, "is it customary to sentence tax evaders to death in Lilliput."

"Tax evasion," he answered, "is the most serious crime known to the law. It carries the harshest penalties, which are always imposed upon criminals with stern swift certainty. It does not, however, carry the death penalty. Tax evaders are sentenced to have all of their property confiscated, and they are taken bodily to manage for the benefit of the State during the remainder of their life any business they may have owned. When there would occur a serious loss to the State in the event of a convicted tax evader's death, medical aids are sometimes employed to prolong his life and its consequent benefits to the State. Strictly speaking, Man Mountain Gulliver, the death penalty is now unknown to the country for any but a few crimes. The incurring of an injury so serious as to render the criminal unfit for any service to the State coupled with an inability to pay for ordinary sustenance gives rise to a situation in which the death of the criminal provides the only sensible solution. Being injured, he can be of no use to himself alive, and would be a distinct burden to the State or to his friends. You see, Lilliput imposes penalties designed to return the greatest benefit to the State and individual concerned. Treason is also punished by death, since one guilty of treason is always apt to be a menace to the government."

I took advantage of an opportunity to tell Bittzzora that in my country the law did not punish injured people, but instead punished those whose carelessness caused the injury of another. I also told him that murder was punishable with death.

"What an unsound, malicious, and despicable doctrine that is," said he. "Why has your law such an insane doctrine that it must punish murder by murder?" he exploded. "The State must be so foolish as to kill an actual servant because he has caused the death of a potential one. Lilliputian law permits the murderer to live, produce, and make up some of the loss his willful killing has occasioned. The Lilliputian government punishes a person injured accidentally for it has ever held health and soundness of body paramount among virtues. An injured person is not an asset, actual or potential, civil or military, to the State. On the contrary, he tends to become a distinct burden upon it. Common sense — ordinary rat reason — demands that each individual be held strictly responsible for his own safe-keeping. Punishment of the agent through which an injury is incurred is to inflict injury upon the only sound person in an already bad and undesirable situation. To punish the injured party is to foster and build strong individuals, able to take care of themselves — strong in character and in pride. People in your country must always be getting injured."

"Yes," I replied, "injuries are frequent in my country — people are sometimes careless of their own welfare; but, Sir, does not Lilliputian law encourage carelessness toward others?"

"I don't believe it does particularly. In the first place, gross carelessness is apt to appear as willful misconduct, which is criminal; furthermore, care for one's own safety, involves as a necessary concomitant, care for the safety of others."

This latter statement might have been more convincing if I had not had the memory of the knot on my head which was occasioned by have been struck by the scazpop. The drunken driver of that wild, leaping, bounding "steel ball" had not appeared greatly concerned with the welfare of others.

During a discussion with Nitpooperler Hirear several days later I happened to mention the same matter — that I thought the scazpop driver who nearly broke my head seem to care little enough for anyone's safety. His reply to me was that the driver only seemed careless to me because, having been so careless myself, I sought, perhaps unconsciously, to project my fault onto another. Had I not been at fault, said he, I would have had little reason to think the scazpop driver careless.

At the wing of the prison wherein the steel cell blocks housed recalcitrant, unproductive, or politically dangerous prisoners, there occurred an accident which, but for the intervention of lucky chance, would have proved most unfortunate for my companion, even without raising up a great scandal, which, in fact, was the surprising result later.

While I was straining my eyes trying to read some of the signs worn by the prisoners in the steel cells, some of which I could not discern owing both to the smallness of them and to the unsatisfactory quality of the light, Bittzzora, recognizing by the frowning expression on my face that I was trying to read, made a move to aid me in this respect. Without having warned me of his intentions, he was just in the act of climbing from my pocket onto the wide sill of one of the barred windows when I shifted my position in an attempt to improve my view of the interior of the cell-house. Bittzzora leapt madly toward the window and succeeded in grasping one of the bars. A fall from that height to the hard pavement below might easily have resulted in grave injury, or even death. As it was he did have a fall, but not to the pavement. He fell into the prison!

The bar which he clutched was rusty, and, having become loosened on the inside, bent inward when his weight fell against it. Down he tumbled into the midst of these violators of the laws. Whether the fall, or the sight of these men, who were behind bars as a result of his efforts as the prosecuting officer, caused Bittzzora's face to blanch somewhat, I could not determine. However, as he picked himself up and made a valiant effort to recover his dignity and composure, he was obviously a little pale. The strained expression of the three in the cell remained fixed during a long interval of silence; then came the dawn of recognition.

"Ah — Bittzzora — the Honorable Bittzzora is with us," gloated one as he made a step toward the newcomer and made a gesture as though he were going to throttle him.

Bittzzora made no audible reply, but merely pointed a finger to the window where I knelt to peer through the bars, having temporarily abandoned my periscope. Thrusting my arm into the cell, I beckoned to Bittzzora to come within my reach so that I might affect a rescue. One of the prisoners attempted to block his way to the window, but Bittzzora executed a sudden lunge which sent him spinning into the corner, grasped my hand, and I soon had him safely outside.

He denied having received any hurt in answer to my inquiry, although I would have been blind not to have seen the look of pain which crossed his countenance when I set him on his feet. Without comment I offered him my hand again, and he, understanding that I had detected his distress, clung to my fingers while I lifted him into my coat pocket. "Hadn't we better call a guard to inform him about the broken bar?" I asked.

Barrister Bittzzora's answer was hesitant, but negative. "I would prefer that a guard not see it yet," he said finally in such a manner as to make an explanation unnecessary. Bittzzora had an injured foot, either sprained or fractured, and any act on our part which might lead to a discovery of that fact would lead to trouble for him. A scandal would result, and his fine reputation would explode like a bubble.

At my unfortunate friend's request I made my way toward a far corner of the prison grounds where the execution was scheduled to take place in a very few moments. We found a large crowd already gathered in a space surrounding what appeared to be nothing more than a pan of about six inches in diameter sunken into the metal pavement of the area. I was able to approach no nearer than thirty feet from the pan without running grave risk of treading upon some of the spectators. This, of course, would afford me an excellent view. But Bittzzora, whose eyes, being like the eyes of all Lilliputians, were not capable of seeing a long distance, said that we must go nearer, since he was legally bound to witness the execution.

The people were so very numerous that I was quite reluctant to move nearer, but did so finally at Bittzzora's insistence. After much pushing and scrambling, a pathway about a foot wide was opened through the crowd, and we moved slowly to a point within a yard of the death-dealing instrument, which I prefer to call a pan for lack of a better name. Following the clanging of a bell somewhere in the distant part of the prison grounds, four guards appeared marching a thin, wry-faced, little man who was the victim. He was dressed in a shining, unornamented, silvery-hued suit which, I soon learned from the whispering around me, was made of magnesium foil. This suit of foil, so it seems, played some chemical part in the execution.

The victim's face, wry and drawn though it was, was less suggestive of dread of impending doom than of past sufferings and tribulations. He marched slowly, though unhesitatingly, before the guards up to the brink of the pan where he came to a halt. His back being turned toward me, I was just barely able to read the sign in broad black letters hanging across his shoulders. It read:

> I, **Stickeo Banzatti**, having been thrice convicted of accidental injuries; having been convicted of tax evasion; having deliberately mismanaged my confiscated property to the detriment of the Lilliputian State; having by word of mouth attempted to incite overthrow of the government by violence; having refused to work in the workhouse; having willfully destroyed some of the workhouse schipidtpots by throwing sand in the gears; and having incurred a disease putting me past the possibility of being useful to the State, go now to my death. May my substance freshen our crops in rain.

A man whom I took for the warden stepped forth from the crowd, directed the victim to step into the pan, and in a monotonous voice, as though he were chanting a piece of long familiar ritual, asked the doomed man if he had any last words to utter. The prisoner meditated a moment as though he had not heard, while the throng stood in silent anticipation as though not a soul among them were breathing.

"Yes," he said in a clear unwavering voice, "I have something to say. The last line of the inscription on my back expresses no wish of mine. Freshen our crops in rain — Bah! I would that I were going to p--- on them!"

"Is that all?" the warden asked.

The doomed man nodded, and a brilliant burst of a white light flashed where he stood. A whiff of white smoke and steam drifted slowly upward over the pan into the blue sky. The pan was left utterly empty. I had witnessed a Lilliputian execution.

Much to my displeasure the thrills for the day had not ended. Just as the crowd was breaking up, and the spectators starting to leave the prison grounds, a sharp ray of light streaked across the space between a wall and the cell house. Two men fell to the ground in an effort to dodge the glimmering streamer directed at them, but were caught and encompassed by it, and lay motionless in its dazzling glare where they had fallen; a third escaped the ray and made a wild dash toward the wide gate which had just opened to allow the audience of the recent execution to leave the enclosure. The man failed to heed the command to halt shouted by an armed guard stationed on the top of the wall. Lifting his gun to his shoulder the guard again shouted a command that went unheeded, then fired two shots which felled the would-be prison breaker almost within reach of the open gate.

I was unspeakably shocked to discover when the fallen man was lifted into a stretcher that the guard, instead of wounding him in the lower portion of his body, had fired both bullets through the poor creature's head. I recognized him immediately as one of the two in the cell into which Bittzzora had tumbled. The two others detained by the paralytic ray shining from the lamp atop the prison wall were undoubtedly confreres of the dead man.

Bittzzora was fully as astonished as I had been by what had transpired, and must have been anxious to leave the prison, for as soon as the two men in the grip of the powerful ray were in the safe custody of guards and that frightful needle of light switched off he requested me in a nervous whisper to hasten away to my row-boat on the beach, avoiding as much as possible the thickest traffic arteries of the city.

Taking a devious course in a semi-circular line along a highway skirting the city through a few outlying suburbs, we soon arrived at my boat and shoved off at once toward the anchored *Night-Hawk*. When we arrived aboard, Bittzzora's ankle was so badly swollen that he was unable to bear his weight upon it. He displayed considerable uneasiness in refusing my offer to go for medical aid, and implored me to minister to his injured member as best I might.

"Please do what you can for it," he begged, "and whatever happens, pray do not mention my misfortune to anyone. I'm a ruined man, if anybody but you learns of my fall into the prison cell."

"But won't the convicts at the prison inform against you?" I asked.

"I'm afraid so, but in that event I count upon you to see me through. Your word and mine should carry over that of convicts. Your must stand by me."

"But *perjury* — is there not such crime in Lilliput?" I used the English word "perjury" for I did not know the Lilliputian equivalent.

"Yes, indeed," he replied. "Either true or false testimony aimed at achieving an illegal end is a criminal act, but surely you would not hesitate to —"

"Commit perjury," I interrupted. "Well perhaps not, but let us now see to the ankle. Maybe when you have rested and had time to think you will be able to formulate a plan of action which will not involve the both of us in the commission of another crime."

I examined the injured ankle as did Bittzzora himself, and we were both of the opinion that there were no fractured bones, but a bad sprain. When he had immersed his foot in hot water for a time I applied arnica and several turns of stout bandage. I took him down in the hold to rest in one of the seamen's bunks out of sight, should a visitor come aboard to call upon me, as happened nearly every day.

Chapter X

Wherein the author goes to court as a witness and has an opportunity to see Lilliputian courts of justice in operation.

L ATE ON THE EVENING of the day of my excursion to the Mildendo Prison with Barrister Bittzzora, Nitpooperlers Garnite, Flebrow, and Hirear came aboard the **Night-Hawk** while Bittzzora and I were lingering over a last after-dinner cup of coffee. Their arrival caused the lawyer to grow quite nervous, but he gained control of himself and, heeding my advice, remained where he was seated on top of the mess table. He had put his sock over the bandaged ankle and was wearing his shoe. As long as he did not attempt to walk he would not betray himself to his friends by a tell-tale limp. Anyway, walking was out of the question.

The new arrivals were excited over the news in the day after the morrow's newspaper, a copy of which the Nitpooperler Hirear brought along to show me. Upon seeing Bittzzora with me, the three Nitpooperlers in vociferous unison became insistent that the Barrister elaborate for them the news story they had read. Neither Bittzzora nor I had seen the paper; consequently we were at a loss to know what had leaked into the news until we had perused the copy brought us by Hirear.

A Lilliputian newspaper, if there is such a thing, is the fruit of human perversity at its acme. Every newspaper in the city of Mildendo has an assortment of twisted, uneven, distorted, crooked type galleys and frames into which every news story and editorial published must fit. The result is a newspaper with nothing in it straight. Headlines flare across the top in wavy lines suggesting a snake. Columns are twisted, deflected, and wrenched into fantastic angles, spirals, trapezoids, French curves, and other shapes not even bearing a name. The type which fits well into the printers' frames of the newspaper prints a fairly plain reading matter. But much of it does not fit well. The inability of the printer to cram the type for some news stories into his particular crooked frame results in spots in the paper which are blurred, blotted, or entirely blank. At other times, when a story will not completely fill the printer's particular frame, much tin, brass, and lead from the publisher's private store is used to pad the matter out in some fashion to make it as nearly presentable as possible. In short, a Lilliputian newspaper, especially the larger ones in the city of Mildendo, are nothing short of exasperating. It is seldom, if ever, possible to get to the bottom of any matter published in them, so badly do they present it.

In the paper brought by Nitpooperler Hirear was an article which, as best I could make out, described the attempted prison break of the afternoon, and contained an alleged story of one of the convicts charging Barrister Bittzzora with having plotted and engineered the prison break. This was what had aroused the curiosity of Nitpooperlers Hirear, Flebrow, and Garnite.

Bittzzora gave them a rather full account of our day's adventures, omitting only the incident of his tumble into the prison, for which omission, I believe, he might at that time have been justly pardoned. His friends seemed quite satisfied, but naturally were somewhat puzzled over the queer story of the convict.

The following day the newspapers carried more stories based on statements of the convicts who had attempted escape. Accusations against Bittzzora broadened. It was stated by one convict that he had, with the help of the Man Mountain, broken the bars from a cell window, and that he had entered the prison through the window to propose escape to the three prisoners. In short, a scandal was breaking, and I was being drawn into the maelstrom along with Bittzzora. The speaker in the national *tricamerate* (*Lilliputian legislature*) came forth and promised a full investigation which should disclose the facts. A committee of nine *tricamerators* (*legislators*) was appointed to launch the investigation.

Since my presence before the investigating committee was desired, the committee elected to hold hearings on board the **Night-Hawk**, where my bulk was better accommodated than it would have been in any of the governmental buildings. At the very outset, I resolved to answer all questions truthfully, as Bittzzora advised that I might, since, said he, neither of us had anything to fear from the committee. There would be, he said, a great smoke raised, much tumult, books of publicity, talk galore, and a lot of time wasted, but nothing would ever come of it, because there were few tricamerators who dared reveal any really scandalous matter concerning another official, since they too (the tricamerators) were always skating on thin ice.

Bittzzora's words were prophetic. The committee spent nineteen days carrying on the investigation, and, without arriving at any conclusion, finally, out of pure inertia, let the matter drop. However, the incident was not closed by any means. Somebody had, in a manner unknown to us, gained some knowledge of Bittzzora's ankle. Bittzzora was arrested and I was subpoenaed as a witness. I was somewhat surprised that Bittzzora chose to stand trial rather than pay his way off, but he explained that the extent of his fortune was too well known in Lilliput for him to adopt any other way of getting through the difficulty. It would have cost his entire fortune. Besides, to have paid out would have left him bereft of his reputation, since the very act would have involved an admission of the truth of the charges against him, whereas a trial afforded at least a bare chance of eventual vindication.

I was given notice to appear at the trial on a certain Monday, and on Thursday of the same week the case had not yet been called. During this time I was obliged to remain in the courtyard waiting all day every day. This would, indeed, have been very wearisome, had I not been able to observe and listen to the court proceedings for several cases. I assumed a comfortable attitude atop a wall about three feet high, and, by the aid of my periscope, was in an excellent position to follow proceeding in several courtrooms which had windows opening upon the part of the yard where I remained.

Lilliputian judges wear white robes as a symbol of purity, and conduct their courts with stern, severe dignity. One old, gray-bearded guardian of the law, who had spent the greater portion of his life upon the bench, is deserving of our special notice. I became quite absorbed in his deft manner of administering justice among those who came before him. He presided over the divorce division, and, though there was a steady stream of applicants coming in before him, there were few who succeeded in obtaining a divorce, the Lilliputian law in this regard being very rigid. It seems that there is only one certain ground upon which divorce may be had in that country — namely, mutual consent of the parties. Questioning is done by the court and is very close. The least hint that one party is not in absolute accord with the other — that there is not an exact mutual consent — results in the divorce being denied.

Adultery, desertion, failure to provide, cruelty, etc., are not recognized grounds for divorce in Lilliput, for there it is reasoned that these acts partake of a criminal nature, and that no punishment could be devised that would be more effective and suitable than requiring the guilty party to remain wedded to the wronged spouse, thereby having to submit daily to nagging reminders of his crimes and shortcomings.

One poor little woman appeared in the divorce court and asked that she be given a divorce because of the continual beatings her husband gave her.

"Madam," the judge exploded, "you don't want a divorce — you want a club. Apply to the bailiff for a strong wooden club, and in the future see that you deliver as well as receive whenever any beating is done. Next case!"

One divorce proceeding which lasted somewhat longer than the others gave some promise of success to the applicant wife, or so I thought until the prayer for alimony was injected into the case. The wife's attorney, having read from numerous documents statements which seemed to clearly indicate a mutual consent, turned his attention to the demand for alimony, whereupon the husband's attorney raised voluble objections on the ground that the amount demanded was excessive. The plaintiff, not being disposed to lower the figure, lost the case entirely, for the husband, upon being so directed by his lawyer, took oath before the court denying that he consented to the divorce, which, I have no doubt, was the true state of his mind after hearing what it might cost him to be free.

At length I turned my periscope away from the window of the divorce division and trained it through the window of the petty crime division. Many things coming to my knowledge in this way proved highly shocking to me, and a narration of a few events that I witnessed in the court may serve to convey to the reader the reason for the astonishment I experienced.

The courtroom itself was far from pleasant, being small, dingy, and ill-smelling. It was so crowded with humanity of such character and quality that it reminded me of a rabbit-hutch I had once seen as a boy — a short low box containing far too many unclean mangy rabbits. But for the indelicate connotations of the word "scum", I would use it to describe the people crowded into that dark gloomy temple of justice. Even with the indelicacy which I would rather shun, "scum" better describes those people than does the word "rabble", for some of them were well-dressed, and there is something incongruous in the phrase "well-dressed rabble". The judge of this court too wore a white gown, or rather a gown which would have been white if it had not been besmirched with irregular spots and grime which, no doubt, had come upon it when he wiped his hands. But for the robe and the slight eminence he enjoyed from the vantage point of his elevation of the bench, the judge would have been indistinguishable from the persons around him, for in point of facial feature there was little that distinguished him from the criminals upon whom he pronounced judgment. There was about him something even suggestive of the criminal type, though this, if not completely attributable to my imagination, may have been the result of his environment and long contact with the criminally inclined.

The first case I attended in this court was the trial of a sad-faced, middle-aged man who was accused of having stolen a quarter of beef from a meat packer. When asked by the court if he admitted having stolen the meat, he replied in the negative and asserted that it was not he, but another man, who had committed the offense. His defense, although quite ingenious, was too weak to win his acquittal, primarily because, except for one healer, he was the only witness in behalf of the defense. In answer to the questioning of the defense attorney, the healer stated that it was a scientific fact that the bodily substance of a man completely changed and renewed itself once in seven years, and, since it had been nine years since the offense in question had been committed, the man on trial could not possibly be the one who committed it. The force of this evidence was considerably lessened by the defendant's own testimony when he told his story. This was to the effect that nine years previously he had been employed in a meat packing plant and had slaughtered twenty-two thousand nine-hundred eighty-nine head of cattle every day, but that the wages he received for this work were not enough to keep himself and his family in food and shelter. One day in a moment of weakness, when he had not eaten meat for a year and a half, he did take by stealth a quarter of beef. He took it home, and he and his family feasted on beef tea for one month. All gained so much weight that the authorities became suspicious that they were getting enough to eat, whereupon a search was instituted and the theft discovered.

Needless to say the man was found guilty and sentenced to prison. The scientific contention of the prisoner was swept aside by the judge who ruled that, in law, a man once born remained the same man until he died, regardless of how much or how little he might, in point of fact, change physically, mentally, spiritually, morally, or otherwise during his lifetime.

It was my privilege next to hear a case most of which exceeded my comprehension, owing to the numerous fine points of Lilliputian legal procedure which occasioned much heated argument among the lawyers. A flashily dressed young man was accused of cheating or fraud of some kind, which was in some manner accomplished by numerous writings produced in court. The prosecution sought to introduce the writings in evidence against the accused, but each time met with an objection by the defense. First, there was an objection that the writing sought to be introduced was on pink paper; then that the ink used was a lighter blue than allowed by law; then that the paper was not quite square, and too nearly round. These objections failing, others followed: that the paper had a hole in it; that it was one-ten-millionth of a Lilliputian toad's eyeball-breadth too thick; that it looked funny, smelt bad, and tasted worse; that the clerk who had been its custodian had lifted it by the wrong corner; that the prosecuting attorney had not placed his left foot forward properly when he made the original proffer; that contrary to his oath and in contempt of the "august tribunal" the prosecutor had wiggled his ears and drooled in his own beard.

At last, after many more objections and haranguings, and after the judges and lawyers had examined, scrutinized, handled, and re-handled the document until all of the writing on it had become soiled and completely illegible, it was admitted into evidence and the clerk called upon to read it. Being unable to do so, owing to the illegibility mentioned, he was given a stinging lecture by the judge, after which a repetition of the whole scene was commenced over another doc-ument. In the end the defendant was found guilty, although none of the documents around which the wrangling centered were ever read by the court. As near as I could discern the judge decided that a person who wrote so many letters (or whatever they were) as this defendant had written must be guilty of the fraudulent business with which this man stood charged.

During one of the long recesses, (which, by the way, are both more numerous and lengthy than the court sessions) I, using the En-glish word *jury* for lack of a Lilliputian equivalent, asked Bittzzora if any such institution was known to the Lilliputian law. I have sel-dom found him unfamiliar with an English word, but *jury* held for him no concept whatever. Whereupon I described for him as well as I was able that institution as I know it. It was beyond his belief, he said, that any nation pretending to enlightenment and civilization would require the unanimous agreement of twelve laymen to convict a criminal, for, said he, disagreement among men was a mark of their intelligence, therefore twelve intelligent men would rarely if ever agree. Conversely, agreement among the twelve strongly indicated a lack of intelligence, and, because of that very lack, any conclusion agreed upon by all twelve would in all probability be wrong. It must be, he said, that your penal system aims more at making an example of someone, no matter whom, rather than at the punishment of real culprits.

"That," I answered with some warmth, "is not true. Our law is very jealous of the life and liberty of a man, and provides every safeguard against the possibility of punishing the innocent —"

"And," Bittzzora added, "against the possibility of punishing the guilty as well, if — what do you call it? — the *jury* is widely used."

I desisted from further discussion along this line, not trusting my temper, for I deeply resented this scoffing at an institution dating as far back into the past as the Magna Charta, and revered universally throughout the English-speaking world. Bittzzora, like a few other Lilliputians in high authority, was a bit too self-complacently critical of things he knew little about, and even though I overcame the irritation such criticisms engendered, I had nothing to gain in raising a controversy.

Next I turned my periscope upon the proceedings of the highest court in the state of Lilliput. Seven judges sat in that court, and it was my great good fortune to hear arguments by eight of the most prominent lawyers in the land. The particular case to which I listened grew out of a controversy between a contractor and the party for whom he had constructed a building. Over twenty-two years had elapsed since the building had been completed and the contractor had commenced the original suit in the lower courts to compel payment of his claim under the contract. While the terms used by the lawyers were much too technical for my comprehension, I did gather from one very learned legal argument that the statute upon which the case turned had been amended by the tricamerate nine-hundred two times since the suit itself was first filed. The main body of the argument centered around the exact interpretation of the statute and which particular one of its nine-hundred two different contexts was the proper one to be applied. One lawyer argued that the statute as last amended was the one to be invoked, since, if anyone were to gain money, or anyone fail to gain money then and there, it should be done or not done in accordance with the existing law. Another controverted this contention saying that if any of the nine-hundred two contexts of the statute were applicable (and he doubted that any were) it should be the one in force at the date the building was completed, for if any money were owing or not owing it was owing or not owing as of that date. Several lawyers opposed this theory, and one especially astute in his reasoning steadily maintained that the statute, as it stood at the date of completion of the building, was manifestly not the one to apply for two reasons: (i.) That any money owing or not owing was owing or not owing, not because of the operation of the statute at any given time, nor because of the contract, nor because of the conjoint force of the contract and the statute; (ii.) But any money owing or not owing was owing or not owing by reason of the final judgment of the court, and, since no final judgment had yet been rendered by the court, no money was yet owing or not owing, and would not be owing or not owing until such judgment was rendered, Therefore if the statute in any of its nine-hundred two forms should be applied at all, it should be the last form, for that would be the one in force when the obligation did or did not arise by virtue of a final judgment.

In opposition to this theory of the case there arose an old, bald-headed gentleman of the Honorable Profession, whose suavity bespoke long practice in an atmosphere of high dignity and decorum. "If it please the court," he began, "may I call attention to page ten-thousand, three-hundred two of the plaintiff's brief wherein it is pointed out that the statute as last amended cannot be the one applicable, if for no other reason, for the very practical one that no one knows — yea — not even the members of this court know — what the last amended form of that statute is. Every member of our great profession knows that before he has time and opportunity to read or study any statute, the tricamerate has long since tinkered with it and amended it in one or more respects. Furthermore, may I call attention to the eight-hundred eighty-ninth form of the statute and all subsequent forms of it available. So worn is the state printer's type from hard usage that, beginning with the form mentioned, the printing is so illegible that it baffles the wit to discern any letter in it."

For three days I listened to these and similar arguments in the great case, after which time the court took it "under advisement" which meant, according to Bittzzora, that sometime within the next two or three years a final decision would be pronounced and the case ended.

Altogether I spent nineteen days awaiting Bittzzora's case to be called for trial. On the twentieth day the case was called and the indictment read. In a low hum-drum voice, so monotonous as to be nearly inaudible, the judge of the Criminal Officials' Court read the sheaf of papers, some two-hundred forty pages in length, at least ninety of which were covered by *zishawshawws* (*the Lilliputian equivalents of the words 'whereas', 'wherefore', and 'said'*). The gist of the charges was that he had plotted and conspired a jailbreak, had made me either an unknowing or an unwilling tool in the conspiracy, and had accidentally injured himself. Other fine-spun technical crimes were also charged, but they all grew out of facts already known to the reader. Somebody had seen Bittzzora limping on the deck of the *Night-Hawk* — no doubt somebody in high office who visited me there and posed as a friend of both Bittzzora and myself, but who was not disclosed. The informant who swore to the charge of limping was only a common beach comber. He said he had seen Bittzzora through a telescope from where he used to sit every day on the beach. Added to this was the testimony of convicts who positively stated that Bittzzora had broken his leg in jumping through the window into the prison. Ridiculous though this statement is to anyone acquainted with the truth, it was a sharp thorn in the side of the defense during the trial. Bittzzora dared not demonstrate his lack of a broken leg for he yet had an ankle too sore to permit any cutting of capers, and, of course, it was fully as important to conceal the real truth as it was to disprove the convicts' absurd allegation.

Toward the close of the prosecution's case Bittzzora began to realize only too well that the prosecutor had skillfully spun a fine strong web from the evidence — that he had built a rib-rocked case out of a mass of circumstance — and that he, Bittzzora, would need every iota of his cunning and cleverness to extricate himself from the net. Obviously the special prosecutor, *Flink Swaff*, would ask in his argument: What was Bittzzora's purpose in calling on me and inviting me to the execution? Was it not strange that he had never called before? Was it not strange that he should ask me to go to the Mildendo prison on an execution day instead of some other day? Why did he induce me to go? Did he have need of me? What need? Breaking barred windows? If he had not plotted and conspired to incite the prison break, were not most of these things strange? Why did Bittzzora remain on the *Night-Hawk* a fortnight after the Mildendo prison break? For a man who had shown nothing more than a mild distant interest in the Man Mountain before, was not this sudden and extended display of friendship a little odd, especially, involving as it did, the utter abandonment of attention to pressing official duties which really demanded attention? Had Bittzzora broken his leg? No? Well — maybe just sprained it accidentally?

Flink Swaff asked all of these questions with an innuendo of tone and insinuation of gesture that no written word can convey. It was all very convincing, and from my observation of the slight play of feeling and thought across the face of the judge, it was plain that he too thought the case rather strong and convincing. Unfortunately he remained of that mind.

Bittzzora had engaged one *Scance Wardorg*, a lawyer famed throughout the land as a clever successful defender of those accused of a crime. But the good fortune and success that had attended his efforts in so many other trials struck snags at the very outset in his defense in this one. He had gone over my proposed testimony with me many times previous to the trial, and at all times seemed confident, not only that my testimony would be of a nature designed to gain freedom for Bittzzora, but also that it would draw me from beneath the shadow then hanging over me. It was planned that I should tread on the verge of falsehood at but one point in my story — in reference to Bittzzora's ankle. Wardorg insisted that I could truthfully testify that I did not know whether the ankle was really injured or not. In fact, at the time, he really had me convinced that I did not know, for, as he said, it was true that I could not feel the pain in Bittzzora's ankle, and there were no broken bones to be felt. At first he had asked me to admit that I had intentionally tossed Bittzzora into the gaol as a joke. But I knew only too well that in so doing I would have incriminated myself. Therefore, I flatly refused.

When Wardorg called me to the court window to testify, troubles began. The prosecutor objected that since I could not properly take the oath, I could not qualify as a witness. First, said he, I could not understand what the court swearer said when he administered the oath. Unfortunately this was true and readily demonstrated when the prosecutor asked me its meaning. To be sure, I was by this time becoming well versed in the Lilliputian tongue, but for the life of me I could understand no word spoken by the court swearer. Secondly, insisted the prosecutor, being a creature of so great a size, I could not possibly crawl through the hole in a panel leading to the witness chair, and this, it seemed, was an ancient iron-clad requirement of the law. He went on to make much of the point. Not only could I not crawl through the hole in the panel, but I could not even enter the courtroom, and "in all the vast sea of legal literature, from times immemorial to the present moment, there is not one precedent — not a shade of an iota of a precedent — permitting a court session to be held elsewhere than in a courtroom!"

The upshot of the objections were that I was not allowed to testify at all. Poor Bittzzora was adjudged guilty of all charges, and forthwith sentenced to prison. As I left Mildendo to row out to the *Night-Hawk* the evening of that unhappy day, my mind wandered through a melancholy haze. So narrow, I pondered, was the thread by which a man's fortune, fate, and very life hung suspended that he never knew when he would fall into the chasm of disgrace or death would overtake him.

Chapter XI

Wherein the author amuses himself with a perusal of modern Lilliputian literature and art during a period of watchful waiting following the Bittzzora trial.

FOR THE FIRST TIME since my arrival amongst the Lilliputians, I was permitted to spend several days alone on the **Night-Hawk** following the Bittzzora trial. At all times before, there had been at least one and often many "hosts", either appointed or self-appointed, aboard the vessel with me both day and night, but no one accompanied me when I rowed out to my lonely ship on the evening the trial ended, nor did anyone appear the next day, nor the next. I had resolved to remain aboard, owing to certain apprehensions I entertained concerning a possible hostility of the populace toward me, which I had some reason to fear, mainly because of my association with the unfortunate Bittzzora. As has already been noted, my learning in the Lilliputian language had steadily been advancing, so that reading and speaking the language was beginning to come easy for me, though I must confess, however, that writing in that language always remained both laborious and painful for me because of difficulty in learning to form the characters (which are in nowise similar to the Latin), the difficulty in making them on the Lilliputian scale, and an equal difficulty in enlarging them to a size commensurate with my own when copying from small samples.

During many of my excursions around the city of Mildendo I had purchased Lilliputian books, both ancient and modern, intending to make some study of the literature of that country when opportunity would permit. One single American dime would purchase as many of these tiny volumes as I could at one time conveniently stuff into my pockets, so in a very short time I had a collection comprising several hundred volumes. Being alone and not wishing to venture into the city for a time, I began to amuse myself by reading. Of course, a strong magnifying glass was necessary, and, to read conveniently and with any comfort, I had to devise a mechanical means to hold the book, for Lilliputian books are only slightly larger in height and breadth than an ordinary postage stamp. Consequently, a reader so large as I could not hold one without getting his thumbs directly over a part of the print. Also, turning pages is more than difficult — it is nearly impossible without mechanical aids. I hit upon the scheme of holding a book with one pair of tweezers, which I found among the surgical instruments on board, while I used another pair for turning the pages. In this way, after mounting the magnifying glass on a fixed stand made of a stiff wire and a piece of wood, I was able to read my diminutive tomes with some facility.

Picking at random among the pile of books I had placed on a shelf in one corner of the cabin aft, I chanced upon an anthology of modern Lilliputian poetry, and having once had a fancy for English and American verse, I plunged into this Lilliputian collection. For a considerable time when I first began reading it I doubted whether I had really come to any mastery of the language, for I could make no sense out of what I was reading. It seemed utterly meaningless, so for my own edification and better progress I attempted certain translations into the English language. Some of it, as I remember my translations, I will here set down for the reader, should he care to peruse it, keeping in mind that translated poetry always is far different from its original owing to the necessity of sacrificing sounds to retain meaning, thus necessarily losing even a part of the meaning itself. For my versification I offer an apology; but I offer none for my translation since I took pains to make it accurate. I soon found that it was not my weakness in the Lilliputian language which rendered it nearly unintelligible to me, but rather it was the inherent obscurity of the poetry itself which made it difficult to understand.

Here is a short poem, **Skonkup Schklel** (*Sea Suds*), by a modern poet named **Stonk Ammzstyo**.

When sea suds of the rat's ears purl in view
And stands the pickle bloated in the height of time,
I knock the pate upon the shell of peach stones and adore
To set my thoughts in metre and rhyme.

Now, you may see the yellow moulding streaks
On past day's rotting apple core
While I can see nought but the crags and peaks,
And rust upon the dirty parlor floor —

Yea — even though the sad days of my life are yet to come,
I little love him with no marrow in a bone;
For rather would I see a buzzard spewing rum
Than calculate the cubic volume of a cone

And would I rather see a peanut than a pill?
You don't know that passion strikes me dumb —
My soul still lacks a beauty large to fill
The hollow ache now gnawing in my thumb.

Oh, whither go my funny wandering feet?
Among the sands upon the dappled hill?
No — no! 'Tis merely that they're made of meat
And find it hard to travel standing still.

But yet, why waste the sunlight on an idle muse?
Cannot my poor thin breeches bear the heat?
Why not a cruise around for subtler news,
And save what yet remains of cover on my seat?

If perchance the foregoing stanzas are difficult to comprehend, imagine my struggle in first reading the following verses by one **Spogden Pash**, another modern Lilliputian versifier. Not only does he cast his verse from the very substance of vague (and to me maniacal) dreams, but even coins words symbolical of something only to himself. This creative genius for word-coining and misspelling seems to proceed from a two-fold desire — first, to put a rhyme where he could not possibly put one if he were to observe any of the conventionalities in language, and, secondly, to be hilariously funny, which latter objective he never attains, at least in my humble estimation. He lacks humor for two reasons. His words created for rhyming purposes are not understandable, and furthermore would not be funny even if they were.

Perhaps, I would have done better to postpone any expression of my own opinions until I had presented some of the verses lest I infect the reader with my own prejudices; yet my remarks may be disregarded easily and an independent judgment arrived at from the following lines, which, I believe, are fair samples.

The man who first said — "Sober as a judge"
Must really not have known so very mudge.

———————

Whene'er I hear the big brass tuba
Playing with the boys,
At once I stare to see the booba
Making all the noise.

———————

Candy's not splendid
And liquor is blended —
But I'm not offended
Whichever I'm hended.

A round unseasoned red tomato
Is just a plain old ripe tomato —
But when it's sliced, or even grato,
Or mixed in with a cold potato,
Then it becomes a salad straighto,
And I say I haste to stato —
That if it's oiled I surely hato.

Although I did read more in the works of the great Pash, out of a deference to what little sense of the aesthetic I have, I attempted no more translations of that author. After all, time does have a certain value even to one alone on a large boat anchored off the shores of Lilliput. In tweezering my way further into the same anthology I came upon a type of writing which, if it was verse or poetry, was of a variety unknown anywhere but Lilliput, and if it was prose, was of a kind flowering nowhere else in the world. At first, I was reminded of Paul Verlaine and one or two American poets who, affecting his style, for a time produced a type of sawed-off, half-cracked prose; but that kind of literary product in Europe and America had some justification in being rather frankly experimental, whereas, judging by the volume of the Lilliputian variety to which I allude, it must in the minds of the natives find some other *raison d'etre*, which was not revealed to me by several hours of earnest reading.

One author who styled himself **Snarle Kandrug** had the following to say about something or other:

Cornhuski

Cornhuski is a fat patute; he saves nothing to take him somewhere; a patute without any suitcase and lots of time; Ah, yes, he is a patute — a funny bird with a humped skull all knotted with knowledge of femininity — old, young, dead, gone, and how they all got their shapes.

Let us not talk too loud today about Cornhuski because he is slow getting goin', but he is ready to go somewhere on nothing if only he knew where and could get started; Oh, Cornhuski, why do you keep sweeping the driftwood out of your front yard; why not let it dry in the sun so you could cook it in your vegetable soup — or set it under the skull of your dead hen along with the boiled eggs you save in ice-cream cones; why not hammer it round, and chisel it square — make an egg of it to hatch into new eggs — one, last, hard, earthy, hard-boiled ice-cream cone?

Cornhuski, don't advertise the person of the Prime Cause — you won't even carry in his new-laundered shirts off the clothes line; you will go fumbling and stumbling like a drunk mouse at a *Scanezi* wedding when a Blefuscudian plays ribald tunes on a snare drum — The Prime Cause has a hole in his attic for you, Cornhuski.

Before making any further remarks concerning my readings, both an explanation and an apology for the sketchy character of my reproductions is needed. Had I a better memory, the reader would have a better idea of Lilliputian literature; or had not misfortunes which later befell me divested me of my every worldly possession including my whole Lilliputian library, notes, translations and all, I could have gone ahead with the project of publishing an anthology of Lilliputian works in translation. But misfortunes did befall me, and fate spared me nothing but my life and an incomplete memory of my readings.

When I had done with puzzling over much modern verse, I turned to the various writers of prose. The novel has gone through several remarkable phases in its long development in Lilliput, and, of course, having but comparatively little time to devote to the study of it, my knowledge of that particular form of literary expression never became anything but highly superficial. Yet from the more modern works I did gain certain impressions which I think were fair and accurate. In the first place, the later Lilliputian novel bears, in my estimation, a certain likeness to the English novel of the Eighteenth Century. For instance, they are long, and, in this respect alone reminiscent of Richardson and Fielding, while in the tendency to numerous frank references to matters sexual and scatological they outstrip the English Eighteenth Century in lasciviousness and even the crudest of Rabelaisian literature in ordure. Although Boccaccio, Chaucer, Rabelais and later writers who affected their vein may have waxed both sexy and dirty in some of their writings, they usually are saved from being pure unadulterated filth by an honest humor that wafts away the bad smell; but sex and dirt are ends in themselves for the Lilliputian novelist, while the realistic representation of perversity in sex has well nigh attained the distinction of being the highest form of literary art. Lest I unfairly create a prejudice in the minds of some who may later enjoy the privilege of an acquaintance with Lilliput and her arts (and many will some day), let me hasten to add that not all Lilliputian novels are pornographic in nature. This type of novel, for the time being so popular in that country, is written primarily for, and read primarily by, those members of society who are pleased to regard themselves as the intelligentsia — the college professors, the literati themselves, the literary dilettante, grass widows, and young girls intelligent enough to have outgrown youth's innate fear of big naughty words.

For an esoteric few of this group there has blossomed and flourished of late a type of literature, in both novel and essay, which depends more upon the intellect than upon passion for its sustenance. It is concerned emphatically with pointing out individual, class, and social diseases and deformities, while the authors skillfully treat of such matters in a way to insinuate that, excepting themselves, only idiots, imbeciles, morons, moral lepers, weaklings, bombastic nincompoops, grafters, etc. live on the island of Lilliput, or have anything to do with the conduct of the country's commerce or other affairs. Such literature further cleverly conveys the idea that, if the authors would but deign to step down from the pinnacle of their high attainments and self esteem, and risk soiling their hands in systematically annihilating those they stoop only to ridicule, the world might then be made a fit place for them, the authors, to inhabit. This school of the super-intelligentsia have even begun the publication of a magazine which, as I have it on the good authority of Nitpooperler Wickdomp Ooick, is bound in a green cover, not only to attract the public by its brilliant coloring, but also to deceive donkeys by leading them to believe it to be a fine morsel of fresh hay.

Below the timber-line there flourishes the great forest of Lilliputian writing which has little in common with the crags above. Here is to be found the literature of the reading hordes. Stories and novels in both book form and in the cheaper magazines bring simple tales of love, adventure, and crime to the Lilliputian equivalent of the fireside. Happy endings, the reward of good and punishment of evil, and the glamorous romance of Lilliputian city and desert constantly provide the stimuli that impels youths to become successful baggage clerks, factory hands, or beauty parlor operators. Life in the streets of Mildendo glitters when spread upon the pages of these magazines for the people; wealth and happiness lie just around the corner, and any boy may become the Donkgop.

One kind of writing that particularly caught my fancy was to be found in all of the daily papers. Each newspaper, it seems, has on its payroll one or more writers whose chief excellence is a well exercised ability to write a great deal about a very little. Most of them are very proficient in creating the illusion that they know very intimately everybody of any distinction, though several of my Lilliputian friends told me that one, **Zerro Zero Cracklfire**, who cuts quite a figure with his daily gossip in several Mildendo papers, really knows fewer than half of the people with whom he claims to have taken breakfast; they also told me his reputed penchant for fine clothes, if true, would account for the quality of his journalistic productions, since he would of necessity have to spend about four-fifths of his time at the tailor's or haberdasher's getting measured and fitted. While my translated reproductions of some of his work may not be strictly accurate owing to the fact that again I must rely on my memory, I trust that I will do the illustrious Zerro Zero Cracklfire no injustice. The parentheses, of course, are wholly mine since the personages are unknown to the reader, to me, and probably to Cracklfire.

Mildendo —

Diary. Somewhat distressed over a bit of dandruff on my coat collar today — likewise a slight sniffle, but more distress over a delivery delay in **Mrs. Zang Dit**'s *(a famous actor's wife)* bid to sup, thus missing **Siz** and **Lit Fandan** *(some other well-known females)*. So whirring in my scazpop with wife to **Cay** and **Syla Zocks**' *(a married couple in Mildendo's four-hundred)* and the Prince and Princess Bagtouun there. Then in a lackadaisical meander through the **Custonk** district where we came upon a fabricator of spittoons, the almost forgotten **donjon**, and the dog-eared offices of old Zoapsudder.

Coran Bazelle Fitchbock and **Pristine Dennpahn** to dinner, then a fourth time to the new play — **Hodspordth** liking it better than any this week. Between scenes talked to **Zat Whingoe** and **Hilly Zuncle** *(theatrical producers)*. Later with **Susy Csort** to **Artillerist Boyn**'s midnight banquet for **Zarkk Pabl**, where talked to **Zang Monkay** *(financiers, army officers, actors, actresses, etc., etc.)*.

Cred Bould *(theatrical comedian or something)* moved from **Tree Mound** hut to live in a dome atop **R.B.C. Ouest Zingpup**. Their old hut burglarized eight times in two days. Cred threatens to crash in also to see what he can find since it is becoming the fashion.

Twill Prahot is **Lawain Mish**'s usual stage lover. In only a few is he out of the amatory zest. This I am told is mere stage setting, there being really only an old convivial bond between them centering mainly around the playing of **scatchmanmond** *(an ancient Lilliputian indoor game invented by a lunatic to while away his time while convalescing from a severe sunstroke)*.

The rumor will not down that *Z. P. Ecks*, the *Eorlish (foreign country)* actor wears a wig. Even his professional associates say so. Quite a lengthy piece of gossip about it. You may remember he was born in Corkpire, Eorlent, made his first hit in Mildendo in the great year of Catfits, and again returned to play in **Craker Crawfish** in the Hot Year for Rabbits.

Personal designee for the member of the younger set who uses the most pleasing perfume — *Calama Saytor* — daughter of *Zina*.

Everybody loves the three little swine of story fame. Lallia and Dallia are two swan-like ballroom dancers of Port's. Just here from somewhere in **Sude Lillenia** *(an island country south of Lilliput)*. On their second appearance in this strange country the Donkgop's wife and the Donkgop's mother saw them dance at a university club private dinner. Afterward they were presented, and, in a sudden explosion, requested autographs. Mrs. M. Wherding wrote: "Much obliged for your wonderful dancing." Mrs. S. Wherding wrote: "Your dancing is very pleasing." But most important of all the High Lady before leaving said: "I hope to have you appear at the **Skeetut** *(official dwelling of the Donkgop)* some day." Are those dancers gliding on rainbows!

Small tripe: Young **Kladanks** *(a noted Lilliputian actor)* touches the tips of fingers to his lips and then to **Zalia Trink**'s before dining at the public trough. Very foreignly sophisticate ... **Sarlez Kaugh** *(another actor of considerable fame)*, long a well known juvenile, is going to conduct a brass band ... **Twan Gohing**, the new High Lilliputian attorney, is coming after crooked lawyers ... And it's none to soon ... **Skad Skuztop** *(the richest scazpop manufacturer in Lilliput)* personally selects and approves all material disseminated to the public over the **pale blue ray phone** *(a device in use only in Lilliput with which a speaker may be heard in all parts of the country by everyone simultaneously)* ... **Learnandoc** *(Professor)* **Skintine** *(the most famous scientific professor in Lilliput)* will attempt to explain his theory of thirteen dimensional infinite space to anyone who will inquire about it ... **Skordlon L. Bungnot** owns four scazpops but only one pair of socks ... **Tendric Kandlavum** *(a prominent author)* carries an artist's palette, paints, brushes, and canvas for painting in his watch pocket ... So does **Squapl Pepperbot** ... Prices in all Mildendo flower shops have doubled.

I like fuzzy, chirrupy, old men whose sputter is worse than their spark. After a heap of pigskin luggage had been symmetrically stacked under the canopy at the **Staidorf** *(a Mildendo hostelry known throughout the length and breadth of Lilliput)* a big carrier queried: "Is that all your bags?" Almost choking on a snort he had half-way down the guest squawked, "All? How much to you want me to tote from the farm into this bleeding village?"

Among the books I had purchased was an illustrated guide to the Mildendo Art Gallery, which contained small colored prints of most of the paintings in that wonderful collection. That is, I suppose it is wonderful, for every Lilliputian who professes to know anything about art says it is wonderful. My intentions when I bought the book were to study it, then make a visit to the gallery itself, but one survey of the exterior of the building convinced me that I would never be able to see any of the pictures while they remained there, for the windows in the gallery walls are smaller than common in most Lilliputian buildings, and horizontally the building is more spacious than the governmental buildings, therefore, even with the aid of my periscope, I could not get a good view of any of the paintings. As may well be imagined, the largest of them are scarcely larger than a post-card, so the difficulty I would have in viewing any detail at a distance of ten or twelve feet even with a magnifying periscope is easy enough to understand. But I did have the guide book, and was able to acquire some knowledge of the pictures in the gallery vicariously, as it were.

For my own part, I am neither an artist nor a student of art. Frankly, I know nothing whatever of the subject, so I hope that those of my readers more fortunate than I in this respect will pardon my ignorance and take what I have to say at its face value only, remembering that ignorant as I am of the principles of art, had it not been for me they, the readers, however much they may know of European, Oriental or American art, would still be completely ignorant of Lilliputian art.

Some of the first pictures in the book had large insects for subjects. One I remember in particular was of a large grasshopper (not a Lilliputian one). It was of the winged variety, and, according to the appended history, had fallen from the sky upon one of the principal streets of Mildendo during a high wind. Many artists had painted this awe inspiring creature and, even in the samples contained in the guide book, the photographic detail was remarkable. This attention to minute detail was in fact the most notable thing about most of the earlier Lilliputian paintings. Pictures of quail, ducks, fish (mostly dead ones hanging upside down), bouquets of pansies, ripe strawberries, tomatoes, oranges, bananas, pears, grapes, red apples, colored vases, and cows in a meadow were plentiful in the first part of the guide book. These were representative of a past era. In the latter part of the book which covered the modern works of art, excepting in a very few, detail seemed to have been discarded completely by the artists. Perhaps the invention of photography impelled them to desert the field it came to occupy, for in Lilliput that science is in itself an art as well with which few paint and brush artists could successfully compete. All Lilliputian photographs are in the original colors; and this without any process of retinting whatsoever. Also, all of their photography is stereoptical in effect. Flat gray or brown photographs were never made there. A few artists still paint subjects recognizable by the authenticity of outline and color, but most merely attempt the expression of abstract ideas or feelings without producing recognizable form. One highly praised modern painting was called *Green Horses,* and by the same artist was one called *Pink Horses.* I own to a lack of appreciation on my part, so without intending any criticism of the pictures, I must say that the only horses I could see in either picture were the ones printed in the title. To be sure, there were some sorts of odd creatures outlined in colors, but to me they simply were not horses.

Another of these moderns was called — *Nude Sliding Down Banister,* but it was also beyond my depth. I perceived in it nothing but a maze of vague lines and planes. There was for me neither banister nor nude — and that, by the way, reminds me: Photographic detail, I said, is no longer an element of Lilliputian art. But, save only in the case of the last mentioned picture, there is one great class of modern paintings in which faithful reproduction of detail stands uppermost. In modern Lilliputian paintings of nude women clarity and completeness of detail leaves utterly nothing to be desired, except, perhaps — well — the model.

Chapter XII

Wherein the author receives assurances that the people of Lilliput are still interested in his welfare and hold him in nowise implicated in Bittzzora's crime; wherein he makes the better acquaintance of Mezarra Watwil; and wherein he becomes acquainted with the educational system of the country.

O N THE SEVENTH DAY after I had begun amusing myself alone, mainly by reading, I was in mid-afternoon interrupted in such occupation by the arrival of a delegation of women who drew alongside of the **Night-Hawk** in several water-going scazpops. There were about twenty in the group, and the leader was the wife of Onk Watwil. At her request I hoisted them aboard, scazpops and all, this being the most convenient method to avoid the possibility of a wetting, since transferring from a scazpop to a basket is a ticklish undertaking, owing to the tendency of a scazpop to spin in the water.

When finally all had been lifted aboard and the ladies stood before me on the deck, **Mezarra Watwil** addressed me in a tone and manner so affected and diffident as to betray the fact that her words had been carefully chosen and memorized beforehand. Although I had seen this lady on numerous previous occasions, especially with her husband in the company of others when they had visited the **Night-Hawk**, my attention had never, until that moment, been particularly arrested by her. In this moment of her leadership, a slight flush of excitement bloomed in her face, which, I noticed for the first time, was really beautiful — not the doll-like beauty of most Lilliputian women, not the stiff kind of beauty which comes from a smooth fineness of feature and coloring alone, but the kind of beauty that comes from a fineness of feature and coloring *plus* the glow of a radiant personality behind it. In the eyes of any Lilliputian male, she must have been almost irresistibly captivating.

"We, of the Federated Amalgamation of Unions of the Federated Amalgamation of Women's Federations," she began with spirit, though a little brokenly, "have been conducting a public campaign in your behalf, Honorable Man Mountain Gulliver, and have chosen this happy occasion to inform you of our happy victory, and incidentally of yours. Since the Bittzzora affair, there has been current in Mildendo, a current of unthinking gossip and rumor, which I knew, and our organizations knew, were unfair and slanderous to your character. Whatever the crimes of the former attorney have been — whatever may have led you unwittingly into association with him, I knew, the women of our clubs knew, as every fair-thinking person must have known, that you had no part in those crimes. Your own fine character, your sensibility, fairness, and gentleness, which I and many others have observed in you while in your company aboard this very ship and elsewhere, bespoke plainly, finely, and flatly of your innocence. If that were not enough, the very fact that you are the descendant of that great personage known to every Lilliputian school child, Man Mountain Lemuel Gulliver, the Saviour of Lilliput, should have been enough to free you from any suspicion in the eyes of any Lilliputian worthy of the name. It is our mission to inform you that all rumor and gossip in any way disrespectful to you has been silenced, and it is our pleasure to invite you in the name of the Donkgop Medid Wherding to a banquet to be held before the gates of Mildendo this evening in celebration of the recent Wherding victory at the polls. Here, I deliver you the written invitation from the Donkgop himself."

As I knelt down to receive the missive from Mezarra Watwil, I was embarrassed from a confusion of causes. The very situation itself was enough to produce this result — so ponderous a man as I being defended by a handful of Lilliputian females — but moreover I could not escape noting, in the warm brown eyes of the spokeswoman who addressed me, something disconcerting — even distressing. I dared not believe — really could not believe what I fancied I saw in the faint blush and vibrant smile of the beautiful little upturned face, yet quite soon I had ample reason to believe it.

In a stammering voice that I fear every one of the ladies in the delegation must have detected, I expressed to them my thanks and appreciation for the interest and faith they had shown in me. "And may it be my good fortune," I added, "to return, at least in part, the great favor you have done me."

The interview being at an end, the ladies clambered into their respective scazpops which I lowered to the surface of the water one at a time on a boat-hook. Mezarra Watwil lingered behind, hesitant, beside the door of her shiny scazpop. Evidently she had something further to say to me.

"I hope," she began, this time groping for words, since they were not from any memorized speech, "that you — that you do not think ill of me for what I have done — I mean for what we women of the clubs have done in interceding with the Donkgop for you."

"Why, of course not. Why should I?" I replied, and then remembering that I had an urn of tea brewing in the galley — "Would you have a cup of tea with me? I was just preparing some when you arrived."

Through the railing she cast a quick glance over the water toward the retreating scazpops glistening in the bright afternoon sun as they spun toward the shore, appeared to ponder for ever so brief an interval, then answered, "That would be ducky." (I forget if she said "ducky" or "goosey"; at any rate it signified consent and approval.)

The novelty of being alone aboard the *Night-Hawk* with a Lilliputian lady gave me a queer feeling and a childish diffidence which was not easy to master. I showed Mezarra Watwil to the cabin where I had lately been reading, and excused myself to fetch the tea. When I returned I found her perched on the arm of the chair, fingering through one of the books I had left there. Upon noting the particular book it happened to be, I felt even less inclined to be at ease, though I made a valiant effort, chiefly by pretending that I had not noticed what I had. But the matter was not so easily evaded.

"Do you find this book interesting?" she inquired.

"Yes — rather," I faltered as I clumsily placed a thimbleful of tea beside her on the arm of the chair.

"What do you suppose it is in the heredity or environment of such a woman as the heroine, Meldara, to make her a *shari*?" she queried with a sort of nonchalance perhaps born of preoccupation. (*Shari is the Lilliputian equivalent of Lesbian*).

After I had stood a moment collecting myself from the shock, I mumbled some incoherent answer intended to convey the idea that I had given no thought to the matter at all.

There followed a long interval of silence during which I seated myself in another chair opposite her and mechanically began to sip my tea. After having intently fingered through more pages of the book, she again spoke as though she were merely thinking aloud to herself — "And Meldara's husband was such a splendid man, too. How strange it is. Is it fiction or could it be real?"

Having had in the protracted period of silence an opportunity to regain my tongue, I was able to answer, "Oh, yes — yes, indeed, it could be real enough, I suppose."

She lifted the thimble of tea to her lips and her eyes stared in my direction as though it were somewhat of a strain upon them to catch a clear view of me across the cabin. Lilliputians can see plainly only a very short distance, yet, as she looked at me, I thought I could detect something of feminine guile in her conduct. For just a brief moment she gazed, then tottered on her precarious perch as though she had either scalded her mouth with hot tea or felt suddenly faint. The thimble dropped to the floor, and I sprang to her rescue.

"I suddenly became dizzy from the height," she explained as I held her about the waist. "I'm sorry about the tea."

"Oh, that's all right. Let me get you another thimble — or maybe you would rather have some wine."

"No — no — not now, thank you," she said in slow musical tones, and I, being in a quandary as to what had best be done, chose the easiest course, which was to seat myself in the chair upon the arm of which she was sitting. "Do you wish to get down?" I asked.

She made no reply, but her eyes brightened with a soulful look as startling as it appeared sincere. In a moment she was so near that I could feel her warm cheek pressing against my neck. How it came there I never knew, but then I did know and understand why it was that this lovely little creature had taken such a lively interest in me — why she rallied the women of Mildendo to my support, and had not stopped till she had successfully pressed the Donkgop to intercede in my behalf by ordering any contemplated legal proceedings against me squashed.

Out of a respect for my benefactress, I must here take leave of this trend in my narrative, for, although in continuing it I might bring satisfaction to certain idle curiosity, I would only be relating to the reader things his fancy and reason can better arrive at un-aided. Suffice it to say that, while it is true that Mezarra Watwil came frequently to visit me on the **Night-Hawk**, she did so openly and honestly — blindly, I might say, never once suspecting what a stir a few wagging tongues in empty heads can create. Married though she was, she was young, and her lovely brown eyes had seen lit-tle of evil in the world. Life was still a game to her, to be played not according to musty rules rooted in superstition, ignorance, or reasonless tradition, but according to simple, plain rules one knew instinctively. I never encouraged these visits; I never invited her to return when one ended, yet she, no less and no more than any Lilliputian, was always welcome to come upon the **Night-Hawk** at any time. Mezarra Watwil simply chose to come often, and but for certain unhappy events to be later related, I would have been glad that she did. I have spent no pleasanter afternoons in my life than those spent with her — drinking tea, and discussing some Lilliputian book.

★   ★   ★

At the banquet celebrating Donkgop Medid Wherding's reelection, I happened to address to Wickdomp Ooick, the Nitpooperler of Education, Labor, and Cockroach Extermination, a few remarks concerning what Lemuel Gulliver had written about education in early Eighteenth Century Lilliput. On that occasion I was told that education had greatly changed on the island, and the Nitpooperler promised to conduct me to some of the schools, if such were my wishes. I gladly accepted his kind offer, and his promise was soon kept, for in about three days thereafter I received word from him that he was free upon an appointed day and would show me around if I would meet him at a certain hour just inside Mildendo.

My excursions to the university of Mildendo and several vocational, secondary, and primary schools occupied most of four different days. Nitpooperler Ooick accompanied me on each day, and it was through his kind guidance and patience in answering my questions, as well as through my own observations, that I came into possession of the information I am about to relate.

It may be recalled that even in the days of the Lilliputian Empire, when Lemuel Gulliver paid his visit to the island, education was a state institution — so much so, in fact, that parents, save only the lowly cottagers and rural inhabitants, were completely deprived of their own children. All children were placed in state nurseries, where parents were not even allowed to see them but one hour twice a year. A tuition payment was required of every parent for each of his children in the public nurseries. This old system is no longer in vogue in Lilliput, education there having undergone many rapid and radical changes. Education is still one of the large functions of the state, but the old public nurseries idea has long since been discarded, primarily because the principles of morality upon which it was based worked as well to destroy it as to support it. The principle serving as a foundation for the early system of public nurseries was as follows. I quote from (Lemuel) **Gulliver's Travels**:

"Their notions relating to the duties of parents differ extremely from ours. For, since the conjunction of male and female is founded upon the great law of Nature, in order to propagate and continue the species, the Lilliputians will needs have it, that men and women are joined together like other animals, by the motives of concupiscence; and that their tenderness toward the young proceeds from the like natural principle; for which reason they will never allow, that a child is under any obligation to his father for begetting him, or to his mother for bringing him into the world; which, considering the miseries of human life, was neither a benefit in itself, nor intended so by his parents, whose thoughts in their love-encounters were otherwise employed. Upon these, and the like reasonings, their opinion is, that parents are the last of all others to be trusted with the education of their own children; and therefore they have in every town public nurseries, where all parents except cottagers and laborers, are obliged to send their infants of both sexes to be reared and educated when they come to the age of twenty Moons, at which time they are supposed to have some rudiments of docility. ..."

Even before the end of the Empire, the difficulty in collecting tuition gradually began to disclose that the principle referred to was a two-edged sword. If perchance a parent evaded payment, or was unable to pay, the State could not say: "Here is your infant — take him back, if you don't pay" — for the State had taken the infant, and to return him to his parents would defeat the very ends the State sought to accomplish — the parents would have the child. The State could not even say to the parent: "From now on you are a cottager, and you may have your child as do the other cottagers" — for it was only too obvious that a nobleman, a doctor, a lawyer, or a politician, however impecunious he might be, was not in any sense of the word a cottager, and could not easily be thrust into that class.

Tuition evasion and a curse of hard times brought the public nurseries to the point of collapse; there were not enough available funds to carry on, while day after day the numbers of infants in the public nurseries grew as parents, finding it possible to escape the responsibility of paying tuition, accepted the irresponsibility of parenthood foisted upon them by state theory, and set about the jolly business of doing their bit to add to the burden of the already overburdened nurseries. Finally matters came to such a pass that general taxation was resorted to for the support of nurseries. Necessity must have been the force behind this move, since the government of a civilized country presumably would not allow its children to starve; yet, it operated also to free the already irresponsible parents of the nation from their only remaining obligation — to pay tuition. Tax, no more than tuition, could not be collected from the penniless or cleverly dishonest parents, though it did fall upon bachelors, who theretofore had borne none of the country's expense to educate the young. Support of education by taxation merely palliated the fever the public nurseries experienced. More and more children came steadily into them, since under the new system married people seemed more than ever obligated to demonstrate their fecundity, and especially since no longer would they alone be called upon to pay the fiddler. Soon even taxation, unless it were made unbearable, would not furnish adequate funds for the conduct of nurseries, so what was inevitable happened. While the Lilliputian government retained complete direction and supervision of education, and continued supporting it with taxation, it abolished public nurseries and put the children again in the homes of their parents. Thus a long-tried experiment in completely state-controlled education, noble in purpose as it was, came eventually to an abrupt ending, not so much because it had failed as a proper method of rearing and educating the youth of the land, as it was because it found that the removal of the children from the nation's homes destroyed the mature mental balance and the better moral sensibilities and ideals of the parents. In time the truth dawned that it was of more benefit to the State to balance the lives of its adults with the weight of their own children than it was to rear and educate the children perfectly, if such perfection necessitated the distortion of the adult population's moral horizon.

While children now remain with their parents, all of them of both sexes are required to attend school until they are sixteen years of age, therefore very few of them are free to leave school before they have gone at least half-way through the **bibancrib**, which roughly corresponds to the American high school. Beyond the bibancrib is the **Mildendo Goosaree** (*Mildendo University*), which is a national institution of higher learning serving the whole island and the outlying Province of Blefuscu. Tuition there is moderate enough, but few students can receive their education in this institution without being put to heavy expense in the observance of the ancient and honorable traditions of the Goosaree, nearly all of which cost money. For instance, any new student dreads not being fed soup by some group of older students who happen to dwell together under the same roof. Soon after the newcomer's arrival, if he has not been winked at, and if he does not have the spilled soup on his necktie to prove it, his social standing in the sphere in which he moves becomes comparable to that of an untouchable in Brahmin India; therefore, nearly every student by the simulation of some eccentricity such as wearing dirty clothes, rolling a peanut uphill with his nose or buttocks, going swimming fully dressed, habitually being clean and nattily clothed, or by some other affectation equally as original, manages to get the wink and the opportunity to spill his soup. If the new student be a female, the refusal to allow any member of the opposite sex the pleasure of her company, or the ability to dance like a dandelion whisker in a March wind without perspiring may win for her the coveted soup-stains. For either male or female student so fortunate, the winning of the soup-stains, obligates him or her, by ancient precedent and inviolable tradition, to make regular, irregular, and special payments at frequent intervals for life to the end that broken soup bowls may be replaced, and the unbroken ones refilled.

Of late (I was informed by Nitpooperler Ooick), the custom of commercial houses in Lilliput to request Mildendo Goosaree coupons from their prospective janitors, scrub women, farm laborers, scazpop repairmen and shiners, painters, hod carriers, butchers, stenographers, fuel salesmen, metal workers, gardeners, bartenders, plumbers, factory hands, etc., had resulted in an invasion of the institution by hordes of students seeking the green slip that would attest the fact they had sat so many hours on a certain seat. I, myself, observed that the Goosaree was literally swarming with thousands of students.

An enumeration of the studies pursued at the Mildendo Goosaree could serve no useful purpose, so nearly did the subjects correspond to those in our own universities — the sciences, arts, philosophy, etc. — including many courses scarcely capable of classification under any of these heads, such as *Advanced Matrimony, Love Among the Peafowls, Technique of Fingernail Chewing,* and *Advanced Methods in Canine Ablutions.*

The quality of instruction offered, as nearly as I could discern from having watched several classes through my periscope and having listened to several lectures, was good. Most of the professors exhibited much learning in their respective fields; that is, they gave evidence of having knowledge when circumstances permitted, which they seldom did owing to the peculiar classroom and lecture hall formalities which occupied most of the time. Each student wore, hanging on a cord around his neck, a multiplated slate upon which the professor was obliged to make a series of marks with a pencil at some time during each class meeting. As for the students, this formality deprived them of many hours of instruction; but it seemed to make very little difference, since during the rare moments when the professors found time to do a little lecturing scarcely a student paid any attention, but improved the time by rearranging some article of clothing, dozing, gazing out the window, or intently contemplating the physical contours of one of the opposite sex.

The figures on the slates worn by a student, as may be guessed, were records of his progress at the Goosaree, but, oddly enough, those records had little to do with his studies. A Goosaree record relates in statistical form such accomplishments as kicking a pig-bladder eighty feet across a green turf, heaving a rhinoceros egg four feet, dancing for two weeks, skill at Lilliputian ping pong, telling dirty jokes in a suave manner from a semi-public stage, jumping five inches high, excelling in quantity consumption of beer, rowing a boat five-hundred yards swiftly enough to reach the limit of human endurance without bursting the heart, etc. *ad infinitum*. The green coupons eventually awarded students when they have sat long enough depends largely upon their Goosaree records, while their financial success, at least in early life after they have left the Goosaree depends almost entirely upon that record. A student may graduate into the profession of law or medicine, or into a business occupation, but the foundation of his fortune will lie in a Goosaree record attesting high ability to smack a dried raisin skin over a fish net with a paddle fabricated of twisted wiener casings.

In these pages, much more could be set down regarding higher education in Lilliput, but it was the primary and secondary schools which I found most interesting. Subject matter as known in American and European schools is totally unknown in either of these classes of schools in Lilliput. In the *child-focused* schools in which learning is accomplished by the so-called ***scramblivity*** methods of teaching, I saw some things which utterly dumbfounded me. The first school I visited was a primary school employing scramblivity methods. I beheld a teacher, an unattractive, middle aged, squeaky-voiced, hungry looking female, standing near the center of a spacious room. She had removed one shoe and was holding it in her left hand while a small boy diligently filled it with sand from a sandbox; all the while she was thumbing her nose with her right hand, and actually wiggling her ears. Nitpooperler Ooick, who entered the room to pay a visit, explained these antics to me later. Under the new Lilliputian theory of education children are seldom opposed in their desires, for, so the theory runs, to do so would be to block some channel of learning. Little **Honksnort**, the youngster who was filling the teacher's shoe with sand, had the teacher refused to allow him to engage in this activity, might never have learned that once a physical container is filled with a physical substance it spills over and no more can be put into it; little *Jizpip*, the tiny girl who asked the teacher to wiggle her ears, learned the great moral truth that perseverance leads to success in even the most difficult of things, for teacher could not wiggle her ears the first time Jizpip requested that she do so; and little **Skreekwow** learned how really bad a person could look when fingering their nose. While, of course, the children in the room were all very small, the din which arose from their talking, yelling, scuffling, and other activity was almost deafening. That such things could be carried on in the name of education was totally beyond my comprehension. After briefly describing for Nitpooperler Ooick a typical American school as I knew it, he remarked: "Your schools are years and years behind the times. We once had such old-fashioned methods here. We taught reading, writing, arithmetic, geography, history and so forth, each in a separate class as a separate subject; but we have learned the error of our ways — we now teach not arithmetic, or reading, or history, but we do teach *children*. We will not allow a subject-minded teacher in our schools; we want them and get them child-minded."

"Yes, I dare say," I commented, "but how in the world does a child ever learn to write if he is not taught writing, or how does he learn history if he is not taught history?"

"Great Man Mountain Gulliver, you do not in the least comprehend the social philosophy underlying our educational system which is designed to produce totally *scrambled* individuals; we aim at integrating into a scrambled composite all of the knowledge and skills needed by an individual in actual life. Under the old system a student might reach maturity with a fair knowledge of, say, English, history, physics, psychology, and chemistry, but there was no interrelation between these bits of learning — the subjects were not integrated, they were *unscrambled*, consequently such learning produced *unscrambled* people. To answer your question, first of all let me say that a child may not need to learn to write — it may not be what *he* wants to do; he may not need any knowledge of history, for it may not fit in with what he wants to do. But we find that many do learn to write, or do learn some history incidentally, as a means of accomplishing what they want to do. Ah, but these are happy *scrambled* children, who are now growing and developing, by doing whatever their little hearts dictate!" And the Nitpooperler's voice waned into an effeminate falsetto expressive of the beautiful sentiment behind his words.

As we were leaving the primary school the Nitpooperler stopped to speak to a little girl who was seated disconsolately alone on a bench in one corner of the wide playground.

"What's the trouble this fine day, little girl?" he asked.

"Boo — hoo," she sobbed. "Teacher told me I must do what I wanna', an' I don't wanna' do what I wanna' today — Boo-hoo!"

'Well, indeed! I'll look into this. Teachers mustn't tell little girls they *must* do things.'

The secondary schools we visited were similar to the primary, only the din was much louder. Nothing there was taught as a subject. Everybody did just about what he wanted to do, and kept the teachers busy helping him do it. On the afternoon of the last day as we were leaving the last school I visited, my companion, the Nitpooperler, remarked sadly, "We sometimes find it difficult to procure well balanced *scrambled* teachers; so many of them were educated under the *unscrambled* system and know too much about too little for the best interests of education. Then too, many persons who would otherwise make excellent teachers have such inordinate appetites that they wish to eat every day, and for that reason either refrain from entering the profession or soon leave it. I really have a hard job — and cockroaches are so thick this year, too."

Experience I had already had in Lilliput should have taught me to avoid a critical attitude, but I could not resist saying in jest: "My dear man, I believe I have a simple suggestion which, if put into effect, would lighten some of your heavier duties. It has occurred to me that there are persons in Lilliput who are perfectly *scrambled* individuals, and therefore would make very superior teachers for your schools. A young baby before he has come to that sordid stage in life when he can discriminate between his toes, fingers, or the nipple on this bottle is a perfect *scrambled* individual; history, geography, mathematics, home economics — in fact, all branches of learning are one and the same to him. Why not put babies in charge of your schools just to see how it would work?"

The Nitpooperler twisted around in my coat pocket, and, looking upward, eyed me somewhat contemptuously, for (as I thought) having punctuated his serious remarks with such nonsense. At last, still quite serious, he answered:

"Friend Man Mountain, we have had for many moons in the city of Mildendo just such an experimental school as you suggest, and its results are truly marvelous. Only one thing stands in the way of its adoption as a pedagogical method throughout the nation; that is the reluctance of parents to have their babies absent from home all day, and their insistence upon government buying the milk for baby teachers while in service. We simply haven't the funds to purchase the milk the universal adoption of the system would entail."

Chapter XIII

Wherein the author is permitted to go upon a rural excursion; and wherein he learns much regarding farm life, farm methods, and farm economics on the island.

Q UITE EARLY one hazy morning, a messenger appeared on the *Night-Hawk* to deliver a message from the Donkgop. Upon opening it, I was pleased to learn that a request that I had previously made had been granted upon certain conditions. The message read as follows:

At the Skeetut
Diddle Moon Day, Hot Time, 988

To the Great Man Mountain, Guest of the Land,
Greeting — and Greeting:

We, Medid Wherding, Donkgop of Lilliput, and the Nitpoopo assembled — Nitpooperler Flebrow, High Civil Officer of Elections and Politics; Nitpooperler Garnite, Head of the Bureau of Garbage Disposal, Onion Culture, and Sandburr Conservation; Nitpooperler Gravinap, High Officer of Health, Disease, and Mortality; General Ossdoc, High Commander of the Army; Admiral Spraygrees, High Admiral of the Lilliputian Navy; and **Barrister Scantak**, Head of the Department of Prisons, Crime, Injustice, and Liquor Consumption; and the Judges of the Top Court — do advise, all having duly considered your request to be granted leave to go upon an excursion into rural Lilliput, have given our consent to, and have granted that request aforesaid upon the following conditions, to wit, to witter, and to wit:

I. The Man Mountain Gulliver shall at all times proceed cautiously, using care and diligence not to frighten any livestock away, trample upon livestock, crops, or children;

II. The said Man Mountain Gulliver shall use the highest degree of care and diligence not to trample upon sandburrs;

III. Should the said Man Mountain Gulliver injure or damage any crop, chattel, land, hereditament, fixture, or easement appurtenant thereunto, he shall reimburse the owner thereof in silver, and in addition shall fertilize the said owner's property as Nature demands and as the nature of the situation shall best dictate;

IV. The setting out by the Man Mountain Gulliver upon the said rural excursion shall constitute an acceptance of the binding force of this commission.

Done at the Skeetut in the City of Mildendo, on the Island of Lilliput, in Mid-Ocean, the said Diddle Moon Day, Hot Time, 988.

Signed:

Medid Wherding

Donkgop of Lilliput

P. S. Have you any more chewing gum? I find it great sport to feed it to the cat. She chews it in a manner most ludicrous, getting it tangled in her whiskers, and after she swallows it, she has the cutest comical convulsions. You should see it.

I lost little time in fitting out a knapsack with a few articles of clothing and blankets that one would be apt to need upon such a walking expedition, a canteen of water, hard-tack, and dried meat enough to last me three days. Although I could easily have returned to the **Night-Hawk** each night, since I was never over six and one-half miles away from it, to have done so might have resulted in my missing some very interesting phase of rural life. I would have had to leave off my visit in the country in mid-afternoon in order to escape walking upon the highways at night, which not only would have been a difficult feat, but might have resulted in grave injury to some of the inhabitants, their dwellings, livestock, or crops. When one realizes that a Lilliputian sheep, for instance, is no larger than an ordinary mouse in other parts of the world, it is not difficult to imagine the havoc I could wreak should I stumble inadvertently into a sleeping flock.

Skirting around Mildendo on the circular highway following the outer wall, I struck out in a westerly direction from the city and had gone less than a half-mile when numerous farms began to dot the expanse on either side of the road. I left without having learned whether the country folk had been forewarned of my coming, but judging from the lack of consternation exhibited by the first two men I met, I judged that news of my projected visit had preceded me.

On either side of the road there stretched away in the distance, almost as far as I could see, small squares, triangles, and other many angled geometrical shapes in every color and shade imaginable, made by fields of growing things, most of which I could not identify as anything I had ever seen before. The whole countryside was one wild, blazing crazy-quilt, glittering with dew in the early morning sunlight. While I had stopped to ponder over what strange crops could be growing in some of the fields of pastel green, pale lavender, pink, old rose, light yellow, soft orange, and a peculiar glossy black, two characters — typical rustics of rural Lilliput — slowly approached down the dusty road in a chugging scazpop that obviously had seen better days. Although it was made of the usual transparent steel, the whole surface of it was so worn and scratched that its general aspect was that of being frosted rather than transparent. Soon it drew up before me and came to a halt, whereupon its two occupants alighted and addressed me. While fashion abhors any uniformity of dress in the cities of Lilliput, outlying districts remote from the centers of population have for the most part defied the dictates of modistes and men's tailors. This is mainly for reasons economic, but also by reason of the fact that the average Lilliputian farmer holds his city brothers and sisters in mild contempt and will not allow his own pure and simple ways of life to be contaminated with too many metropolitan fads and fancies.

Of course, I did not know all of these things when I first met the two characters alluded to, but the description of them at this point will serve at least partially to account for the odd similarity in the costume of these two and many other rustics I subsequently met. Both of the farmers were dressed in coarse linen suits exactly alike. The flaming crimson color of their pantaloons and jackets contrasted sharply with the brilliant green of their woven grass hats.

It was a long time before I could understand what they were trying to say to me, for they spoke a Lilliputian dialect filled with local idiom and distorted with a twanging accent that made it a language quite different from that I had become accustomed to hearing in Mildendo. Gradually my ear grew attuned to it so that I was able to understand what was said to me, with the exception of colloquialisms I had never heard before. I was made to understand that they wished to administer the customary Lilliputian greeting, and was requested to assume a position convenient for its accomplishment, which I did, silently hoping as I did so that every farmer and hired hand in this portion of Lilliput would not insist upon the same performance. Having returned the salutation to each of my new friends with a flick of my little finger to the portion of the anatomy appointed by custom to receive it, I started down the road, the two country gentlemen going slowly before me in the dilapidated scazpop. At noon we stopped beside a tiny brook to eat our lunch and rest beneath the shade of some exceedingly tall trees, perhaps seven and one-half feet in height. We had passed numerous farms where hay, oats, barley, rye, corn, millet, and other crops familiar to the reader (though not familiar on the Lilliputian scale) were beginning to ripen in the warm sun, but we had come to a stop at a point where again the crazy quilt of many hues splashed the landscape on both sides of the highway. I ventured to ask one of my companions what crops grew in these fields.

"Sandburrs," he answered, "chromatic sandburrs."

At first I was skeptical, but upon reaching over a fence in several places and pulling up a number of plants of different colors, I readily verified the truth of his statement. They were sandburrs indeed, exactly like those which grow in other parts of the world, in all except color.

"What are these colored sandburrs used for?"

"Paper's scarce 'n' mighty dear in Lilliput," was the enigmatic answer of the elder of these two farmers.

"But, I don't see — " I said, "Do you make paper from them?"

"Naw," replied the younger of the two with a trace of scorn at my evident ignorance. "They uses 'em in houses like that 'un younder."

He pointed a grimy finger at a small unpainted weather beaten structure of rough wood which stood somewhat apart from a cluster of farm buildings across the road. The only point noteworthy about this building, so crude in all other respects, were tiny openings artistically carved in the shape of a crescent and stars both in the door and in the upper portion of each side. No doubt, these served not only as an adornment, but the useful purpose of admitting light and air as well.

The elder farmer, perhaps detecting a sign of my bewilderment in my face, volunteered some more information.

"They likes them colored ones down to Mildendo 'cause they matches the colors o' their fancy bathrooms, an' now ez colored paper caint be bought at no price anywhere, we sells a lot of burrs down there. There ain't no crop makes money for us nowadays but burrs."

As I fingered over the plants I had pulled and felt sharp needles of the burrs spear into my skin, I could not help reflecting upon the hardihood and adaptability of the Lilliputian race, which, faced with a crisis — a serious shortage in one of life's necessities — turned to a lowly weed, the sandburr, and applying their native ingenuity, not only made of it a substitute for paper in one of its widest uses, but by a genius in botany produced new varieties in a thousand colors to satisfy their aesthetic yearnings.

When we had finished lunch and had resumed our journey, I began to observe that many of the farms we passed had buildings upon them quite ugly in appearance owing to an advanced state of unrepair. The outbuildings in general did not present a very pleasing appearance, and, in particular, the type of diminutive structure previously referred to — those perforated here and there with crescents and stars — on many of the farms looked as though they were about ready to collapse or tumble. During the course of a discussion with the elder farmer, who by that time had been persuaded to travel in the coat of my jacket that we might the better converse, I learned the cause of these phenomena.

"Most farmers out this way ain't made no money 'ceptin' a little on burrs for a long time. They cain't afford to fix up their farms an' **crinkplunks**. An' it's a bad all-fired shame, too — take fer instance, **Sticck Naills** that used to live over at **Kerwilly** (*a cross-roads country village*), he made a livin' in this country buildin' crinkplunks mosta his life up until goin' on thirty moons ago. An' he made dern good ones too — but no more. He don't even git nuthin' to eat unless we neighbors gives him some garden truck once in a while. Folks cain't afford to hire him to do jobs they kin git along without havin' did, an' besides one of them big steel factories up to Mildendo is makin' crinkplunks outa' this here shiny new fangled steel now, an' everybody's hopin' if ever they gits a holt o' any money again, to buy one o' them. **Corziltah**, my wife, fer instance, thinks a nice lapis-lazuli colored one ud be nice. **Skordut Hordapyl**, a rich farmer down in **Skaldit kire** (*a political subdivision somewhat like a county*) has a bright red one made o' steel, but he found he had to fit it up with a little asbestos here an' there 'cause it do get all-fired hot there in the summer, an' it's more than jest a little cold in the winter."

Although there was field after field of ripened grain along the way ready and past ready for harvesting, there were no harvesting operations going on in any of them, except here and there where we could see a few men with cutting machines drawn by horses leisurely cutting a few square inches, and even ceasing to this when I approached, owing to the drivers' curiosity about me and their fear lest their horses run away.

"Naw, we don't gather much grain this year," said the man in my pocket, answering my question as to why the farmers were allowing so much grain to stand in their fields. "We ain't got no money to do it, an' wouldn't have that much if we did. They's enough grain in this country to make bread and breakfast silage fer everybody for five years now. The distillers and brewers down at Mildendo an' up to **Wauskivilli** (*the Lilliputian city second in size*) will buy some grain this year an' we got to sell it at a loss 'cause that's the law. But the rest we gotta let rot 'ceptin' what we feeds, eats, or burns. That ain't so bad though, 'cause Donkgop Wherding's government pays us well nigh enough to cover the cost o' plantin' whenever we rots a crop."

"You are indeed fortunate to live in a country so well supplied with foodstuffs that no one ever need go hungry," I ventured.

"Yer _____ _____ right!" he ejaculated. "But I'd give my right upper molar fer a banana or a juicy pineapple right now. I ain't had enough money to buy one since that young man in that there scazpop was high enough to reach my boot-top, an' by gar the _____ things won't grow in any o' this land hereabouts."

Finally I took leave of my two red-clothed friends, but not until I had promised them I would see them again on the morrow at the fair then to be held at Kerwilly in my especial honor. When they had disappeared in the scazpop over the crest of a hill, I sat down in a wide spot in the road and watched the strange activities of three laborers in an adjacent field of growing flax. All three of them were dressed the same as the other two already described. One was walking behind a plow hitched to an animal which, as nearly as I was able to discern, was like a rat — not a rat of the Lilliputian variety, but a large rat such as is common in countries inhabited by peoples of my stature. He was plowing half-grown flax plants into the ground as though intent upon destroying them, as indeed, I learned, he was. Two others in the same field were working together doing something incomprehensible to me; one would lie prone and grasp the stalk of the plant firmly near the root, while the other would stoop over and take the same plant higher up on the stalk and pull upward as though he wished to stretch it. Having pulled upward rather vigorously two or three times, the man with his co-worker would move on to another plant and repeat the operation. While I was still wondering what could be the meaning of such antics, an old gray-bearded fellow in a faded hat of yellow meadow grass and a ragged red linen suit approached and, without a word, greeted me in the usual manner where I lay staring at the workers in the field. After returning the salutation with a flick of the finger and spending a few moments passing the time of day, I asked the gray-beard to explain for me the labor being carried on in the field before us.

"Wal," he drawled, "thet feller plowin' is turnin' in the flax plants. Fer every row he buries the government is gonna pay him such-an'-such a much. Them other fellers is stretchin' them flax plants that ain't gonna be turned under so ez when it's ready to pick they'll be as much flax in that plot o' ground ez they would ha' been if none had never been turned under. Altogedder thet farm'll jest about break even on the crop this season — mebbe make a little."

The afternoon was well advanced when, at length, I left the old man sitting by the roadside whittling willow whistles and still willing to continue relating experiences from his younger days. I had heard much concerning the great Wauskivilli fire in the year of Twin Heifers, the Beer War in the same city during which hundreds of people who opposed the repeal of taxes on beer were drowned in beer kegs, and the early rat races in Kerwilly where my narrator "used to be a jockey ridin' the best darn rats in Lilliput." Some of his yarns might have been interesting, but I had reason to suppose that most of them were exaggerated. At any rate, they taxed my credulity a little more than it would comfortably bear. As I took leave of him, he stroked his beard and hesitantly asked me if I could "spare a coin fer an old man ez has to buy a crust o' bread for his orphants." He really presented such a picture of dejection at that moment that I gladly would have given him a dime, which, no doubt would have set him into a frenzy of joyous wailing, so valuable is an American dime in comparison to the almost microscopic silver pieces of Lilliput. But that would have set a precedent that would have dogged me out of the country when the news spread around. I set out for the banks of a wide river which, as nearly as I could determine from the old man's directions, lay not over a half-mile down the road.

It was, to be sure, a broad stream as streams go in that country, about forty feet across and well over my head in some of its deeper pools. At this point in the road there were no longer any fences and a rolling expanse of prairie and sparsely wooded land bordered the river. Numerous cattle, sheep, goats, and swine were to be seen in herds here and there, so I was obliged to move with caution to avoid frightening or treading upon any of them as I walked slowly a short distance downstream in search of a suitable place to spread my blankets in preparation for spending the night. I found a spot beneath some live oaks which, after I had removed some of their lower branches so that I might the more easily crawl in beneath the overhanging boughs, gave promise of being comfortable enough, and fairly well sheltered. When I had finished the task of removing limbs and spreading my blankets, the sun had just set beyond the western horizon, and the air was becoming quite noticeably more chilly. The bawling of small calves somewhere in the near vicinity, and the answering lowing of cows at not a great distance from my bower, attracted my attention to a farm house about forty yards distant from where I then was. The sound of the cattle lowing increased, and soon I saw a herd of some fifteen cows driven by a small boy approaching the barnyard adjoining the farm house. At that instant lights appeared in the barnyard. Suddenly I was seized with the desire to view the milking operations as carried on in Lilliput, but I dared not go nearer the barnyard for fear lest my approach stampede the herd. Then, too, I knew there were sheep and other animals all about me which, since it was beginning to grow dark, I might trample underfoot. Luckily I had brought with me a pair of binoculars which, although they did not focus very well on small objects at such a short distance, served well enough to enable me to perceive what took place in the milking shed.

It was here that I became acutely aware that science and mechanization were setting grips as firmly upon rural life as upon city life. There was no hand milking done on that Lilliputian farm. The boy and the older man simply gave each cow a dose of something from a bottle. Then, one at a time, each cow had a hose-like contrivance attached over her nose and mouth, and a queer looking machine at the other end of the hose was set in operation. The result was startling beyond belief — the cow was quickly inflated to about twice her normal size, and the milk that spurted from her udder, apparently as a result of the inflating process, was caught in a trough that led into a contraption at one end of the shed. When all of the cows had been thus milked, the boy drove them back to the pasture, while the man busied himself removing from the machine into which the milk has been conveyed certain parcels which I took to be packaged cheese, boxes of powdered milk, and cans of condensed milk. Later I verified this matter. The packages actually contained fresh cheeses, powdered milk, and condensed milk, and they had been made by the machine from the milk run into it less than three minutes before. I well realize that this tale has something of a Baron Munchausen flavor about it, but it is true none the less. Cows throughout most of rural Lilliput, on all but the most poverty-stricken farms, are milked, and have been milked for many years, in just the manner I have described.

It is a matter of record in the office of Nitpooperler Flebrow, the High Civil Officer of Elections, under whose department is the Bureau of Dairy Products, that experiments at the Wauskivilli Agricultural College, which is a branch of the Mildendo Goosaree, have resulted in producing several cows that give a very fine quality of condensed milk without any processing at all, though this milk was never put on the market before I left Lilliput. Experiments designed to produce cows capable of giving cream cheese directly, as well as powdered milk, were then being carried on, and the first results were successful enough to make the experimenters hopeful, but neither of these commodities has as yet actually been so produced.

⋆   ⋆   ⋆

My night under the live oaks would have been delightful but for dreams, which like the dream of the man from Peru in the famous limerick, were perfectly true. I dreamed of being nearly devoured by a swarm of ugly, voracious bugs of a species unknown to me. When at last the dream became so realistic that I awakened with considerable fright, I was almost frozen stiff with the realization that there was something — several somethings — under my shirt and undergarments, biting hungrily into my ribs. After I had sat for several minutes, paralyzed with such horrible visions as poisonous snakes, lizards, spiders, Gila monsters, tarantulas, and nameless other deadly creatures, I either mustered some courage, or became terrified enough to tear off my shirt and undervest as though they had been on fire. A sow and a brood of about nine suckling pigs tumbled onto my blanket, emitted a few startled grunts and squeals, then scampered away into the underbrush. Evidently they had rooted their way into my bed, having been attracted there by the warmth of my body.

⋆   ⋆   ⋆

The following day, as I was wending my way along the road toward Kerwilly to attend the fair, I passed numerous country people all going in the same direction. Here and there, as I approached nearer the village, I encountered more people — men, women, and children — decked out in clothing more in accordance with the eccentric fashions of Mildendo than any I had previously seen in this part of the country. Some of them had preserved "best dresses" from former days of greater affluence, while those dwelling near the village were more moved by the demands of sartorial elegance than were their brothers and sisters from the hinterland. At any rate, the crowds in their holiday attire, when all gathered in Kerwilly, made quite a colorful splotch against the green countryside, albeit a splotch well encrimsoned throughout with large numbers of farmers who either possessed no holiday clothes, or preferred their everyday "beet clothes", as they called their red linen suits.

Just before noon, a brassy blast from some kind of trumpet sounded on the edge of the village to call the crowds to the opening of the fair proper. The mayor, or *sprugswel* as the Lilliputians called him, mounted a high platform draped with tinsel rain and dried moss, and launched into a long speech pertaining mainly to the mighty and marvelous physical proportions of my person, which, it seems, was, for the sprugswel, the principal attraction of the fair. As I had feared, the usual thing which spoiled nearly every public Lilliputian function of this kind for me occurred at this one, and the "marvelous proportions" about which the sprugswel had said so much became the more marvelous in one of its larger portions by reason of its newly reddened and inflamed condition.

Following these formal rites, I was called upon to speak to the assembly, and I responded to the best of my ability by saying something, most of which I do not remember, though I do recall some of it had to do with sandburrs and sandburr culture. One poor fellow, evidently a hired hand who had partaken too liberally of stimulants in some of the grog shops which lined the main thoroughfare of the village, became so terrified at the sound of my voice that he fell dead on the spot; another, a middle-aged farmer, broke into a frenzy from fright, and later I learned, much to my chagrin, he never did regain his right mind.

There followed diversions such as might be expected at a country fair: horse races, foot races, wrestling, squash hurling, acrobatic exhibitions, etc., all of which differed very little from similar performances at country fairs in other parts of the world. I was obliged to retreat some distance from the scene of these activities to lessen the danger to the crowds should I unwittingly frighten some of the horses taking part in the races or being put on show. Taking up a position at the summit of a gently rising knoll about twenty-five yards west of the race track and grandstand, I lay down to be the less visible to the livestock, and, making use of the same binoculars that had served me the evening before, I was able to survey the whole field and enjoy the program of events there taking place. After the races and games already alluded to, a queer game between two teams — one consisting of eight yellow-hatted men, and the other eight green-hatted men — was commenced. Each player had strapped across his back what appeared to be an inflated rubber cushion. The two teams lined up in parallel rows some thirty-five paces apart, one line standing with backs to the other. Each player on the team, looking to the backs of the opposing team, had some kind of a hard ball which simultaneously with his team-mates he flung violently against the cushion on his opponent's back. The balls rebounded in every which direction, while those who had thrown them scrambled to get them as the players who had been struck raced to knock over any opponent not in repossession of a ball. The resultant melee looked very rough, as indeed it must have been, for several players were knocked unconscious and had to be carried from the field, their places being taken by fresh players. The object of the game and its methods of scoring and determining which team was the winner, I never learned, although I asked seven or eight persons whom I had heard doing much yelling and shouting at various exciting moments during the progress of the game. An opportunity did not present itself to question any of the players upon these points, for following the game they were all either injured or so exhausted that they went immediately into an inn for recuperation.

As a climax to the games of the day, a beer drinking contest open to all comers was held. To begin with, there were no less than fifteen-hundred entrants of both sexes who took their places at the long drinking board hastily set up in the middle of the field. Scazpop after scazpop laden with barrels spun up near the board and discharged their burdens. About three-hundred attendants assumed their places beside the barrels and performed the labor of keeping the contestants always supplied with beer, while another three-hundred with pencils and slates kept score on the contestants' consumption.

I was not present at the end of the contest, since it was not finished until late the following day, but I heard that the winner was a corpulent middle-aged woman who attributed her success to the fact that as a little girl she "allus et her spinach every day".

Chapter XIV

Wherein the author visits several factories and centers of the industrial arts, and learns more concerning Lilliputian economics.

NOT MANY DAYS after my return from Kerwilly to Mildendo, Mezarra Watwil with **Whillila Fluzez**, an unmarried female, and her escort, one **Scar Tilutug**, a student from the Mildendo Goosaree, came aboard the **Night-Hawk** especially to enjoy with me a dinner, which Mezarra had previously planned, and which had that afternoon been prepared by a Mildendo caterer and fifty assistants.

That evening, after having dined leisurely and well, I essayed to entertain my company in the cabin by running off a few reels of motion pictures. The picture machine was of the old silent variety and the films old ones which had so long outrun their day in the United States that they actually had been, by reason of their novelty, quite amusing in the eyes of some of my unfortunate crew. Motion pictures of any kind were new to any Lilliputian, so this method of entertaining my friends served its purpose excellently, the uniqueness of the experience making up for the lack of quality in the film.

At the close of the entertainment, when I switched on the light in the cabin, it fell in a white flood through the open door where, to my surprise, stood Onk Watwil, silent, pale, sullen, and weaving somewhat from the effect of too much drink. For a moment the brilliant light pouring over him blinded him, then, his eyes having become accustomed to the glare, he saw Mezarra. His face twitched with convulsive movements of primitive anger, and the words he attempted to shout were fairly choked off with the wrathful tension in the muscles of his throat.

"You — you — " he gurgled, looking insanely at his wife — "You slut! You — you — !"

With an intent obviously murderous, he drew a revolver from his pocket. Mezarra screamed a blood-chilling screech and fell from the arm of the chair where she was perched, just as I, having regained some presence of mind momentarily effaced by the suddenness of Watwil's appearance, switched off the light and plunged the cabin into darkness. The enraged man, having sensed my design turned his fury and his weapon upon me. Eight popping noises in rapid succession accompanied by eight spurts of flame blasted and cleaved through the darkness. I felt a sharp stinging pain like a hot needle suddenly jabbing through the calf of my right leg; then my own anger got the better of my judgment. I turned on the light, seized the mad little drunken wretch who had fired the shots, quickly disarmed him, carried him by the nape of the neck to the port rail, and threw him overboard. Immediately I fished him out again with a boat-hook, but the poor deluded fellow, still being infuriated, bit my hand savagely, whereupon I promptly thrust the curved point of the boat-hook through the back of his military coat and ducked him repeatedly beneath the surface of the sea. At last I drew him up half drowned, sputtering, and coughing, but sobered and cooled to a state of mind in which he could be much less impervious to reason and rationalization.

Throwing the boat-hook down upon the deck with the dripping Watwil still caught on it, I returned to the cabin, where, seeing the unfortunate Mezarra Watwil reviving from her faint under the competent ministrations of Whillila Fluzez and Scar Tilutug, I looked to my own wounds. Two of the bullets from Watwil's gun had passed through the calf of my leg just under the surface of the skin. From the neat little holes left by their passage blood was trickling, but I was pleased to learn they were little more than mere scratches. An application of iodine and a few turns of bandage were all the attention they required. When I had accomplished this, I returned to the deck, freed the would-be murderer, and pushed him, ashamed and shivering, into the cabin. Mezarra, somewhat hysterical until then, rushed to her downcast, dripping husband, and clasping his cold wet form to her breast, kissed his tight blue lips as though she were ready to devour him. His hearty and repentant reciprocation was pleasing to behold, and I rejoiced in this happy turn of events from the near-tragedy of a few minutes before. Handing Onk Watwil a thimble of brandy which he accepted abjectly, though he gulped it down avidly, I suggested their retirement to the cabin aft and took a flashlight from my desk drawer to show them the way. Tacitly they accepted the invitation, and I am sure that soon they were in sweet forgiving bliss which makes of lovers' quarrels something more than an unmitigated evil. Poor Mezarra had not expected her husband to return for several days from the sham battle maneuvers on the distant coast. And poor Watwil — was it possible that he was such a jealous, unreasonable fool as to suspect his young wife of indiscretions with me? What an idiot! The very absurdity of such a thought caused me to laugh aloud — I guess the whole affair had unstrung me a little too.

Whillila and Scar at once took leave of me to go ashore upon my return to the cabin where Watwil had done the shooting. We first agreed among us that nothing should be said regarding the unfortunate occurrences of the evening, since it was more than probable a complete reconciliation between the young married couple would be effected, while bits of scandalous gossip floating about could only complicate matters, and might prove embarrassing to everyone concerned.

★   ★   ★

An excursion to the industrial district, which I had long wanted to make, I postponed several times because of other matters pressing upon my attention, but finally I resolved to go especially since one *Jaaypie Ganhorg*, a wealthy banker and the manufacturer of Lilliputian *Brillitite Mustache Twisters*, *Whisker Burnishers*, and *Milady's Graduated Tin Hip Squeezer*, had paid me a visit upon the **Night-Hawk** and delivered me a very insistent invitation to inspect his industrial plants. On the occasion of his call I became very interested in some of his gadgets which he brought along to show me; likewise was I interested in his hectic career. For sheer business acumen, sagacity, and an uncanny power to make a fortune where others failed, I have never seen his equal.

Jaaypie Ganhorg started out as a poor boy with big ideas. While he was still on the farm, he heard of the fashion then current in Mildendo which required a certain definite plumpness in feminine figures, and having noticed how the country lassies seemed to grow naturally into the then fashionable proportions, he reasoned that it must be the diet of bacon, roast pork, ham, cornbread, and fritters that produced such results, and that if such foods would produce such results in country girls, they would do the same for city girls. But how was he to get city girls to eat such foods in quantities that would accomplish the ends sought — i.e. – rounded, plump ends?

That might have been hard for some people, so he said, but not for Jaaypie Ganhorg. He simply bottled up a mixture of bacon fat and corn oil in concentrated form, sweetened it with wild honey, and advertised it as *Honey-Plump-Glorified-Form-Former* on little hand-bills printed by himself, and in three hours had sold out his entire stock on the streets of Mildendo. He began to buy pigs and corn from neighbor farmers. These he converted into more bacon fat and corn oil, and upon mixing it with honey soon had a larger stock of *Honey-Plump-Glorified-Form-Former* than before. This time he advertised not by medium of hand-bills, but by a small advertisement in one of the large daily newspapers in Mildendo.

Be Fashionable

Have Those Thick Healthy Hips —
Those Plump Popular
Curves
Every Red-Blooded Woman
Wants
&
Every Man Admires
Buy Today! Buy Today! Buy Today!
A
Bottle
of
HONEY-PLUMP-GLORIFIED-FORM-FORMER
On Sale at the Buzzard Drug
Store

The resultant demand for Ganhorg's product was overwhelming. In three weeks, so he says, he had five-hundred men employed making *Honey-Plump-Glorified-Form-Former*, and in thirty moons had a factory employing five-thousand men. He showed me statistics to prove that within the space of eighty moons *Honey-Plump-Glorified-Form-Former* had raised the feminine tonnage in Mildendo from 733,489 to 1,008,302. In one-hundred and sixty moons this marvelous product had raised the whole nation's gross feminine avoirdupois. Every woman in the land, except a few hopeless invalids, and a few old spinsters who never seemed to be in style, had blossomed out as dimpled darlings, and Jaaypie Ganhorg was well on his way to becoming the richest man in Lilliput. But he was too shrewd a man to rest on his laurels, or to allow his money to remain idle. When he found he had surplus profits, over and above the necessary capital to carry on his *Honey-Plump-Glorified-Form-Former* business, he started a bank. Very soon Mildendo people were depositing their money in his bank, and he was lending money to a razor factory to enable it to make razors to meet the growing demands of men for clean shaves. Ostensibly, he said, he lent the money for that purpose, but really to serve his own better interests. He still had ideas, and one of them was to ruin the market for razors, then foreclose his mortgage on the razor factory site, since it was a splendid piece of industrial property. Covertly and by cleverly executed plans, his propagandists — a barber here, a tailor there, a haberdasher here and there — all at strategic points, began to complain about the annoyance of shaving, calling attention to the ugliness of the masculine bare face, and to extol the virtues of a manly beard. Almost overnight the feat was accomplished. The style had changed; men began to grow beards, the demand for razors fell off to nothing, the razor factory defaulted on payments for its loan from the Ganhorg bank, and Ganhorg became the owner of the razor factory. The market for razors having gone entirely flat, he immediately had the factory equipment remodeled and rebuilt to accommodate the manufacture of the *Ganhorg Whisker Burnisher*, production of which, beginning as it did with the whisker craze, soon trebled the fortune of our industrious "get-goer", Mr. Jaaypie Ganhorg, for it soon came to pass that no self-respecting man who even pretended to be presentably groomed would think of going out unless his whiskers were polished, and the *Ganhorg Whisker Burnisher* was the only whisker shiner ever put on the Lilliputian market which would really impart a brilliant brass finish to the whiskers. Other manufacturers quickly set about imitating the Ganhorg gadget, which was a kind of a small revolving brush electrically propelled, but none succeeded well. In the first place, the whisker paste essential in the process of burnishing or silver-plating beards had a secret formula which nobody could imitate. In the very first sales campaign Jaaypie Ganhorg struck upon the wise expedient of selling *Ganhorg Whisker Shine Paste* only with the *Ganhorg Whisker Burnisher*. The natural tendency of this policy was to increase the sales of the Burnisher, for even if a man already owned the machine of some competitor, he could not get a satisfactory whisker polish without purchasing Ganhorg's, and to do so he had to buy the Burnisher. Having once bought it, every man began to use it, because it was very definitely the best machine of its kind then being manufactured.

I was at some loss to understand why a people whose sartorial fashions dictated diversity and eccentricity should struggle to be as nearly alike as possible in the matters of figure and of face. Jaaypie Ganhorg had a plausible explanation. He said that it was the more natural for people to want to be alike than it was for them to want to be different; this desire to be different was something recent in Lilliput, was very superficial, and really did not touch the hearts of the people. A clever dry goods merchant who had bought a hundred-thousand bolts of goods which had become stained and damaged in all manner of form and color when an explosion had occurred in a dye factory, by subtle advertising and propaganda created the desire for diversified clothing, and incidentally turned all of the cloth at a handsome profit.

The ease with which he had ruined the razor market made Ganhorg realize that a fortune based on one whim of fickle fashion was not on a solid foundation, so he has always followed the principle of doing an about-face before the turn of the tide. The razor business was ruined because whiskers became popular. "Well," said he, "the opposite of whiskers is no whiskers, and no whiskers means razors — we reequipped our factory to manufacture the best razors and shaving accessories in Lilliput long before whiskers again went out of style, and again the demand for them arose."

"Likewise," said he, "I knew that pleasing plumpness in women would not always be so pleasing, and that the market for *Honey-Plump-Glorified-Form-Former* was limited by the element of time; therefore, I says to myself, 'What is the opposite of plumpness?' and the answer seemed to be no plumpness — slimness. How to attain a slim-figure? Easy — *Milady's Graduated Tin Hip Squeezer*."

This latter implement was being sold in great numbers at the time of my visit in Lilliput, and in none of his many manufactured products had Ganhorg exercised so much ingenuity. As nearly as I am able to describe the thing, it was a cross between a coat of linked mail and a diving suit, although it was designed for everyday wear beneath a lady's outer garments. The principle upon which it worked was simple, and its use was quite effective in chafing off the outlines so sturdily built up by *Honey-Plump-Glorified-Form-Former*. Being a garment easily adjustable in three dimensions, it could be fitted most tightly over those areas requiring the most constant chafing to wear them down to the desired contours without danger of scouring into a perilous fragility those points already sufficiently slender.

And the *Brillitite Mustache Twisters*, another brain child of

Jaaypie Ganhorg, is at least worthy of a brief notice. While beards, once the high tide in tonsorial modes, had nearly disappeared, the mustache lingered to adorn the otherwise cleanly shaven faces of our Mildendo gentlemen. Ganhorg marked well the great amount of energy expended by the masculine element of the population in twisting the waxed points of mustaches to that peculiar curled tip so admired by the Lilliputian women. As a labor saving device, the *Brillitite Mustache Twisters* has few equals. All that the fortunate owner of one needs to do after his morning shave, if he wishes his mustache to remain undroopingly in perfect unimpeachable form throughout the day, is to apply this little power driven mechanical contrivance to the hirsute appendage on his upper lip and presto — it is waxed, curled, and twisted for the whole day. He need give it no further thought. All day long he may feel the calm self-assurance that comes from the firm knowledge that whenever he smiles, the fine adornment on his lip will add a pleasing something to the force and effectiveness of his smile.

When I visited the Ganhorg razor factory, I was somewhat disconcerted by the appearance of the thousands of men working there. Excepting only a few, all wore beards. My wonder was natural enough. It was odd that contrary to the prevailing mode, men working in a razor factory should go unshaven. I became so bold as to stop a group of workmen when they were leaving the factory and press them for an explanation of this oddity. "That's easy," one red-whiskered fellow replied gruffly. "We make razors — not money." And with that the group hastened to get a place aboard an endless belt conveyor much used as a means of getting from place to place in Mildendo by those members of society who cannot afford the initial price or the subsequent upkeep expenditure of a scazpop.

In the factory producing *Milady's Graduated Tin Hip Squeezer*, I was pleased to note that all feminine workers were stylishly slender, therefore assumed that they were able to purchase the product into the making of which they had expended their own labor. But no. When I, impelled by a curiosity that blinded me to the indelicacy of such a question, asked a comely young lady if she wore a *Milady's Graduated Tin Hip Squeezer*, she blurted somewhat indignantly, "Why — why — certainly not! I ain't never et enough to get fat — an' you'd be politer not to ask such questions!"

From the hip squeezer plant I proceeded to a great scazpop plant. Ganhorg does not manufacture scazpops, but through his influence I was permitted to visit the largest scazpop factory in Mildendo. This one factory alone employs thirty-thousand skilled workmen and turns out thousands upon thousands of scazpops. In one great room, which seemed to be a storage hall, I saw several thousand finished machines of almost every imaginable style and color — mottled, speckled, shiny, dull, green, striped, red, pink, plain, and fancy. These, I learned, were outmoded products the manufacturer was saving for such a time as the public would have forgotten that it had ever seen such models, and there would be, by reason of that fact, a market for them again. Competition is so keen among the scazpop makers that each factory designs and produces a new model every six days or oftener. Buyers demand new and showy scazpops, and the new models are created to satisfy this demand.

One feature of scazpop manufacturing I never would have believed to exist, had my own eyes not convinced me otherwise. This great mechanical industry has reached such a state of perfection that the most ordinary of scazpops could last for a lifetime. Were they not specially processed to prevent such longevity, it would be a catastrophe great enough to throw the whole industry into absolute ruin. In the particular factory I visited there were three-thousand men employed to do nothing but apply their skill to putting latent defects in the mechanisms of otherwise perfect scazpops. A poorly tempered valve, a hidden flaw in the transparent steel body, a soft solder-filled crack in a pressure line, a coat of some substance to produce excessive heat, and a hundred and one other subtle tricks to insure future quick wearing out are used for the more prompt creation of new sales openings in a market that otherwise in only a few moons would become completely glutted.

★   ★   ★

Near the very center of the trade and industrial district in Mildendo, I witnessed one of the queerest activities I have ever seen carried on by human beings. At this spot there stands a great circular wall, perhaps three feet high and enclosing an area of about fifty feet in diameter. Inside the wall and affixed to it are numerous booths, each shut off from the others and the central area by partitions. Entrance to these booths is by means of a door opening inward with reference to the great circle. Over every one is the name of an individual or an organization operating a business of some kind therein. The middle of the enclosure was a bedlam of shouting, scurrying, pushing, pulling, yelling, running, tearing of hair, slapping of backs, squalling, bellowing, shrieking, and running helter-skelter by thousands of men, many of whom were almost hidden under a load of rubber *suckorities*, the one great commodity dealt in there.

At first I thought I was looking upon some kind of a holiday game being played in the arena, but, upon noting the great earnestness written into the lined faces of the participants, I was obliged to recognize an error in my first surmise. Suckorities came in many shapes and sizes, some like hot-water bottles, some large, some small, some red, some green, some thick, some as thin as toy balloons, some worn, and some shining and new; but all were made of rubber or some substitute thereof, and were designed in such a way as to be capable of bearing considerable inflation. On the floor of the arena men were buying and selling suckorities, and, after gazing upon the confusion and listening to the ear splitting hubbub for an hour I began to perceive some meaning in the mad activity before me, the object of which seemed to be to purchase at a price as low as possible the suckorities containing the most rubber, run to one of the booths by the wall, quickly carve some of the rubber from each suckority purchased, patch it up, inflate it to such a size as to be in dire and imminent peril of bursting like a bubble, run from the booth onto the floor again, sell it at the highest price possible, then with the proceeds of the sales buy more suckorities, and repeat the whole process.

The serious demeanor of the men engaged in this mad scramble led me to believe, just as anyone else would have been led to believe, that rubber must have some great intrinsic value. But in that supposition I was wrong. I learned from a bystander atop the wall, who was surveying the orgy below, that rubber is a common commodity in Lilliput and very cheap, owing to the vast quantities produced on the island of Blefuscu. In earlier days, it seems, suckorities were symbolical of some very definite interest or participating share in some well known business or industry, but in modern times these same suckorities, while still theoretically symbolical of like interests, have been so cut, diluted, vulcanized, remodeled, and altered in complexity of form that no one who purchases one knows precisely of what it is symbolical — nor does he even care. The game of suckority purchasing, carving, vulcanizing, inflating, and selling, like some rites in time-honored religious ceremony, has taken on such an interest in and of itself that its original significance may be entirely lost, yet the custom may go on for centuries.

During the course of my sojourn in Lilliput, more than one sad sight caused my sympathy to go out to some sorrowing soul. The hardened criminal executed at the Mildendo prison, Bittzzora in his hour of defeat and disgrace, and poor sodden Watwil boiling over with jealous wrath, served in their time to arouse my compassion. But of all Lilliputians weighted down by the burdens fate heaped upon them, the one I most pitied was an old man in the wild melee of the suckority arena at Mildendo. Blithely and in exuberant spirits, he purchased two dozen or so fine looking suckorities, but failed to see the fine strings attached to them running to the evil hand of some professional manipulator hidden in the milling crowd on the trading floor. With hopes akin to rainbows, the old fellow inflated his balloons to a great size only to have them explode and burst into a million bits just before he made a sale. The manipulator had pulled the strings, and the old man who had lost a fortune slumped abjectly into the corner of a booth and wept brokenheartedly as a little girl weeps when her only doll is shattered beyond any hope of resurrection. How pitiful indeed is the lot of an honest gambler in a den of thieves.

Chapter XV

Wherein the author learns of certain defamatory remarks made against him by Watwil; discussion with Admiral Spraygrees and General Ossdoc concerning naval affairs and national defense; an unfortunate occurrence.

ONE MORNING when I lay abed late suffering from an aching head and trying quite unsuccessfully to recall more clearly certain events of the previous night, which then were, and still are, mere unrelated incidents in my memory, I came finally to the realization that the tapping noise I first took to be gnawing by another of those infernal kangaroo rats was really someone knocking on my door. When I had bid the callers to enter and opened the door for them, in strode General Ossdoc and Admiral Spraygrees, both very erect, business-like, and solemnly dignified. They indicated a wish to greet me formally, perhaps to preserve the iciness of the encounter. I then vaguely remembered having seen them the night before at another of those irksome Lilliputian banquets I had been obliged to attend. Both of these gentlemen knew that I rather disliked Lilliputian greetings, and for a long time had submitted to none on board the *Night-Hawk*, having made my friends, including the two before me, understand that I looked upon their calls as informal, and therefore did not feel obliged to adhere to formal conventions. The suave dignity of my distinguished visitors remained until first the Admiral and then the General attempted to speak concerning the central purpose of their call. A slight hesitancy, born of what I took to be embarrassment, cracked away some of their starchy stiffness.

Finally the General got under way with his speech, arriving in due course of time at the core of the matter. "Last night you were at the banquet — er — ger — umph — er — were you not?"

"Yes," I replied, putting my hand to my throbbing temple. "I was one of the biggest patriots there, was I not?"

"Indeed — indeed! But another honorable gentleman — a good, law-abiding gentleman, who now lies in the Mildendo Hospital has made — well — er — has made some very scandalous remarks about your conduct — er — with his wife. Now, we come as friends — that is, friends of both of you — but you must understand that if what he says is true, you have grossly offended a very fine patriot, who even now is suffering from a nervous affliction brought on by his assiduous attention to patriotic duty —"

"And," I broke in, "is that nervous affliction of which you speak characterized by hallucinations involving — say — snakes, green monkeys, nine-legged elephants, or like fauna peculiar to a deranged cerebrum?"

"Well, to be sure, he did say something about his bed being infested with red billy goats, but you must understand that he had mostly to say defamatory things about you —"

"In short," the Admiral blurted, coming to the aid of the faltering General, "you have been accused, within the hearing of several persons, of having seduced a man's wife."

"But, gentlemen," I protest vigorously, "can't you see the utter absurdity of it — the utter impossibility — that such a charge is simply froth in the rum-soaked grey matter of Onk Watwil — a confirmed dipsomaniac?"

"Yes, but you will admit that Mezarra Watwil was concealed under one of your trouser legs when you left the banquet last night — I saw it myself."

"What!" I shouted, completely dumbfounded.

"Half the people at the banquet saw it," the General chimed in.

"How can you insinuate such a thing? What if she did cling to my leg? What are you driving at?"

"Mezarra Watwil wandered home just a short while ago."

Almost at my wits' end, but with a splitting head and this nonsense, I asked curtly, "What of it all? What are you going to do about it? What do you want me to do about it?"

The Admiral paused a long time before answering, looked about him as though he wished to assure himself there was no one else present, then, stepping somewhat nearer with a bright humorous twinkle in his eyes, said in a voice just above a whisper, "You might tell *us* how you manage to fare so well with the ladies."

★   ★   ★

Later as the Admiral, General, and I lingered over our coffee cups, I had the long awaited opportunity to learn exactly what reason such a nation as Lilliput could have for maintaining an army and a navy.

The Admiral informed me that Lilliput held several great island possessions lying at a great distance to the southwest of Blefuscu, and that those possessions as well as Blefuscu were openly coveted by a powerful little island people in a kingdom northwest of Lilliput. "Yes," said he, "there is every reason for having a strong navy. We are even in danger of an invasion of our mainland. The *Scanezi* are planning a conquest of Lilliput. Our Intelligence Division definitely knows this to be true. Even without the facts of which this division has definite knowledge, the brazen military effrontery of the Scanezi kingdom should be enough to convince any observer that Lilliput has every reason to expect trouble from that quarter."

"And what makes it worse," remarked the General as he deftly brushed a fly from his glazed mustache, "is that the tricamerate continually hamstrings national defense by not pushing the buttons to release more cash. *Zachpedst!* (*A rather vulgar profane word for a General merely conversing.*) The people of Lilliput must think we are just entering upon the millennium instead of verging upon a war! Time and again we sound the tocsin in the halls of the tricamerate and in the public press, but the jangle awakens nobody. The nation lies sleeping — waiting for the blood sucking Scanezi to drain her dry."

"Man Mountain Gulliver," put in the Admiral, "would you believe that in such a crisis the tricamerate would deny us enough money to build a modern fleet?"

"Well, if things are as you say —"

"As I say? Of course, they are as I say! Come to the navy yards with me and see for yourself."

"I meant if there is a cri —"

"Come, come — See how our navy is being built."

Both because it seemed useless to try to question these two gentlemen concerning the crisis, as they called it, and because I had a sincere desire to see the navy yards, I forewent any attempt to carry the conversation further, but accompanied them ashore.

Under the direction of the Admiral, who was in my left coat pocket, I soon carried them to the place designated. All the way the General, who was in my right pocket, enlarged upon his argument anent the niggardliness and stupidity of the Lilliputian people and their government, soon veering away from a strict adherence to the original motif of national defense and entering into a monologue on politics, economics, and labor.

"You wouldn't believe it," said he, "but the government, instead of putting two million unemployed men under arms in the army where men are needed, has them busy digging up old sewers, and policing traffic corners where there are already men on the job for that purpose —"

I suppose this babble flowed on and on, but my interest became absorbed in what I looked upon in the shipyards. There were perhaps eighty-five or a hundred ships under construction. The din from riveting machines, hammers, saws, and wrenches in the hands of many busy little workmen would have been enough to drown out the words of the Admiral and the General as we drew nearer, even if I had not become more interested in looking than listening. Previous to this occasion, I had seen ships under construction in America, but then I had been able to perceive some progress being made by the workmen. Not so here. The air rang with industrious activity; busy hands were everywhere pounding rivets, chiseling rivets, tightening nuts, loosening nuts, hoisting steel, lowering steel, delivering materials, taking away material. For a long time I could discern only isolated details — unrelated to each other. One crew of workmen would come along and skillfully rivet on a series of side plates to a skeleton hull, and it would not be ten minutes until along would come another crew that set to work, either with hammers and chisels or with electric torches, to tear away from the hull the very plates just affixed by the preceding crew. A crane would hoist a girder into place where some workmen would bolt it down, and in twenty minutes that very girder would have been removed again, loaded onto a quadruple-scazpop conveyor, and moved out of the shipyards. It was all positively amusing. When at last I began to get the grass out of my eyes so as to gain a perspective of the meadow, I realized that every vessel under construction was being torn down just as rapidly as it was being built; that as far as progress might be reckoned in completed fighting ships, the hundreds of workmen energetically engaged before me might just as well have been sweating out their lives on a gigantic treadmill.

Some of the navy ships I had seen maneuvering off the portside of the **Night-Hawk** were in dry dock in these yards. A few of them were having guns exchanged and re-exchanged; a few were being scraped and repainted — then scraped and repainted again.

Upon leaving the shipyards I was only too willing to have the Admiral Spraygrees attempt to rationalize for me the seemingly insane activity I had just witnessed. "Lack of funds," he said, "is the principal reason for Lilliput's faltering sea power. If only reasonable appropriations were made by the tricamerate, we could have some up-to-date ships. We could hire expert nautical architects to complete plans for new ships rapidly enough for us to get them under construction before they were outmoded by the scientific advances in naval warfare; we could employ enough more shipbuilders to complete a few ships before new treaty provisions or lack of modernity required their destruction."

"Admiral Spraygrees," I asked, considerably puzzled, "Do you mean to say that those ships being constructed are at the same time being destroyed simply because before they are completed they are no longer modern in design?"

"Exactly, Man Mountain, exactly! Before a single ship in those yards could be finished on the money now appropriated for shipbuilding, every last one of them would be out of date — unfit for modern naval fighting."

"But isn't the delay in their completion partially accounted for by the fact that they are being torn down as fast as they are being built?"

"Undoubtedly. But if it were not evident that a ship would be out of date before it could be finished, the Navy Department would not order it torn down. I tell you we need more money — a great deal more money to build an adequate navy."

"Why not," I asked, "employ constructively those men now tearing down ships along with those engaged in building ships? Why tear down at all? Would not that bring the desired results? Would you not get a modern navy built then?"

"But that would be impossible — you see, there are always ships becoming obsolete, consequently those men are always needed to scrap obsolete vessels. I tell you what we need is money — more money, a great deal more money! And the tricamerate won't give it to us. Bah!"

"Yes," put in the General, "and does the army get the money it needs? Right now we need an appropriation to train a corps of men and sea-gulls for sky-riding, and do we get it? No. The Scanezi have hundreds of trained gull riders who could fly into our territories and blow up our villages, while our government will not even provide for the maintenance of gulls, let alone for the maintenance and training of the men necessary to our national self-defense."

Before the General and the Admiral had convinced me that the defenses of Lilliput were dangerously weak, or that such weakness, if there were any, was due entirely to a lack of material appropriations, some naval officers appeared before us and, addressing me, inquired if I knew the whereabouts of Admiral Spraygrees, they not being able to see him from where they were halted on the ground. I immediately set the Admiral down before them. The usual formalities of naval salutes were exchanged, which to my mind were quite as vulgar as the Lilliputian army salutes, consisting mainly of suggestive noises, the idea of which is intimately associated with horses.

One of the officers delivered a message to the Admiral which he tore open and read with fixed attention.

"Oh, my!" he exclaimed when he had finished reading the missive, "I must hasten to have tea with Mrs. Wherding. She says that the Donkgop seems persistent in his intent to commission a sailor from the ranks to command a new diving boat. I must see here at once to enlist her aid with the Donkgop. Every naval officer from myself on down would be deeply humiliated by such an act of the executive. Imaging a common sailor — a man who never saw the inside of the Naval Academy at *Canndappletus* — being given command of a diving boat. The Donkgop needs better advisors. Just because a sailor invents a diving boat, is that any reason the common unlearned lout should be given a command in the Lilliputian Navy? Bah! I must go to tea —"

Still talking and waving his arms, he wheezed across the street, entered a scazpop waiting there, which, once the Admiral had seated himself and given orders to the driver, sputtered wildly down the street, skidding dangerously around the first corner and out of sight.

Thus were the General and I left alone. We proceeded along the edge of the navy yard, then came upon a broad drive skirting the wall around Mildendo and leading to one of the island's military reservations which the General had been kind enough to offer to show me. We soon arrived there, and the place was indeed an interesting one. The officers' and mens' quarters, as well as the arsenals, stables, and warehouses were of some hard transparent substance resembling glass, but really consisting of a secret amalgam of metals, principally transparent steel, so common in Lilliput. The General ordered out a company of infantry, and I was treated to quite a spectacle which demonstrated the efficacy of these buildings. Bullets from machine guns and rifles were rained upon the walls of one of the smaller structures with no apparent effect. Shots from several cannon had no more effect than fire from the smaller arms had had. Suddenly rays from a ray machine were flashed upon the walls, which quickly changed from a clear transparency to a milky opaqueness that deepened from white to blue, from blue to a deeper blue, and finally to a jet black as gradually the strength of the rays was increased. This change in the color appearance of the building I took to be an effect of the rays, but in this surmise I was wrong, as the General soon informed me, saying that each wall was double, there being a space between the outer and inner wall through which various liquids could be could be made to flow with the mere push of a button. These liquids were each impenetrable by some particular ray and had been developed as a defensive tool in ray warfare.

I was then entertained by a demonstration of some odd weapons in common use in the Lilliputian army, but totally unknown to me. For one demonstration General Ossdoc ordered a herd of perhaps thirty sheep driven to one end of the broad drill ground. We retired to the opposite end of the field at a considerable distance behind a deployed line of infantrymen. I was at a loss even to guess what was going to take place, especially since not a single man in the line appeared to have any weapons about his person, but the General soon began an explanation.

"These men," he said, "are equipped with our newest offensive weapons, *snickdids*, or in English, flying eggs. Each man has in the pockets of his uniform six snickdids like this one," and the General drew forth from his pocket a small metal object about the size of, and resembling, a sparrow egg. "The chemical contents of a snickdid, once a reaction is set up in it by a release of this pin," he went on, pointing to a pin-head like protuberance upon the surface of the egg, "acquire a strong, almost magnetic, affinity for flesh and blood. After the pin is pulled out there is an interval of time, just sufficient before the chemical reaction sets in, to allow a soldier to throw the missile at an enemy. He must take care to throw it quickly lest he be the one killed by its explosive attack upon his flesh, but his aim need not be accurate, for once the reaction has begun in a snickdid tossed in the general vicinity of an enemy, it will actually pursue him until its explosive force has blasted the life out of him."

At the commands of an officer three men in the line before us took snickdids from their pockets, pulled the pins, and threw them in a high arc toward the herd of sheep. A faint sizzling noise became audible as the missiles went through the air, followed by the sound of three nearly simultaneous explosions as they found their mark and slaughtered four or five sheep. The reverberation of the explosion had not died away when a confusion swept through the line of soldiers. Two of them began shouting some kind of warning to the others, then broke rank and started running across the drill field. The cause of the commotion was obvious almost at once, for a loud report broke the air and one of the fleeing men plunged headlong into the dust and lay there — a mutilated smoldering heap.

Naturally I was greatly shocked — indeed, considerably sickened — by this tragic occurrence. To see a man, even though he be a Lilliputian, suddenly blasted to pieces before your very eyes is, to say the least, an unpleasant and upsetting experience. Still stunned by what I had just witnessed I became gradually aware of General Ossdoc bouncing around in my coat pocket all the while imploring me to set him upon the ground. This I promptly did, and he shouted a terse command that echoed across the drill field. The soldiers, then entirely broken out of the line, quickly formed in close rank before their captain — all but the poor unfortunate victim of the snickdid. General Ossdoc, drawing himself up to his full stature and assuming the stern dignified bearing he so well and proudly wore, strutted across the field to face the captain and the troop. Perhaps, I should have asked permission to step upon the field, though at the moment no such thought entered my mind. Curiosity unrestrained led me to step out on the field far enough to be within earshot of what was being said between the General and the captain.

"*Captain Dampop*," said the General with emphasis and force that made his face red with the exertion, "can you explain to me how it is you have a company of dirty low down — cowards who break line and run away while fighting nothing more formidable than a bunch of sheep? Explain me that, will you? I command you — Explain me that!"

Captain Dampop was evidently nervous, for in executing the salute required by Lilliputian military usage from an inferior to a superior he lost his balance and sat down heavily. Rage caused the General to reel off a long vile oath, then, probably thinking better of it, he choked back another while his face turned purple. At last the flustered Captain had managed to deliver the salute. Even under the best of conditions the salute is difficult, requiring, as it does, that the soldier place his left cheek against his right knee, the right foot, of course, being lifted off the ground to enable him to perform the rite, while he at the same time emits with a puckered mouth that unpleasant noise which seems to be so firmly imbedded in the grain of so many Lilliputian ceremonies.

"Will — will you," the General sputtered again, "Will you explain to me why your command cannot even face a line of sheep?"

"Er — yes, **Nabsack**, (*a term of respect used by all Lilliputian soldiers in addressing a superior*) you see — that is, you see, a member of the ranks must have dropped a snickdid. By accident the pin came out. It was certain death to remain in line."

Only by dint of great effort did General Ossdoc smother the blind surge of wrath that furiously welled within him. His face went from purple to black. "Death! Death!" he blurted explosively. "Is death any reason for a Lilliputian soldier to break ranks? Bah! Pick up that carcass there and the whole company report to your barracks. Stay there in confinement until you receive further orders! Cowards! Rascals! Vermin!"

Growling these and other epithets the great Lilliputian commander spun on his heel and strode to where I was standing. He signaled me to replace him in my pocket.

"I must apologize Man Mountain Gulliver," said he. "I have never been so humiliated and angered in all my life. That such a thing could happen at all in the army of this great country — but in the sight of a foreigner — Oh, how could it be? Poor fellow — How — how —"

The old man faltered for lack of words to express himself. He was no longer angry — only sad. I looked down into his now drawn and haggard face and saw tears glistening in his eyes. Then, after a long interval of silence during which I was stirred by a number of mixed feelings — Pity for the "poor fellow", curiosity about him and his family, perplexity over some of the things the General had said, and a certain sadness arising from a vague, very vague, understanding of the import of the events I had just witnessed — I ventured to speak to my companion. "Who was the man who was killed?" I asked.

The General looked up at me, a puzzled expression playing across his face. "How should I know? What's that to me — the cowardly lout!"

I, in my turn, must have looked puzzled. "Didn't you know him or anything about him?" I persisted. "Poor fellow — What a terrible mishap!"

"Mishap — Bah! Is that any reason to break formation? Glory be and thanks there was one who did not run — who stood in line. But, poor fellow, he will now have to bear the bad name of having belonged to a company that broke line."

So that was the "poor fellow" alluded to by the General — a fellow, as it later developed in the *Scnakad* (*middle house of the Lilliputian tricamerate*), who was not aware that a snickdid had been dropped until he saw it explode. Poor fellow, indeed.

I was glad to meet the General's request to take him to the gates of Mildendo. Beyond a doubt I had missed many interesting military things the General had planned to show me, but it no longer mattered, for I had lost what little relish I had for such things. My friend addressed me only once on the way back to Mildendo.

"I probably will be unable to see you soon, friend Man Mountain," he said. "For the next thirty or forty moons, I will be busy compiling reports for the Donkgop and the tricamerate concerning the blunder you have this day witnessed in the Lilliputian army."

As I sat him down on the threshold of the eastern gate, I thanked him and bade him good-bye, then turned my steps toward the shore where my row-boat was beached. Whether my body or spirit were the more weary I could not have said. The vision of the tiny soldier's body, shattered and smoking, lying alone and all but forgotten — a bloody little pile on the broad expanse of a Lilliputian parade ground — weighed heavily upon my spirit, and my feet seemed all the more tired because of it.

Chapter XVI

Wherein the author presents the people of Lilliput the principle of the modern talkie; and wherein he makes a study of the legislative machinery of the State.

ONE FINE MORNING a few days after my excursion with General Ossdoc, while I was basking in the sunlight on the deck of the *Night-Hawk* and perusing a late Mildendo newspaper, I had just become engrossed in some flaming editorials concerning the activities of the **Pinks** in Mildendo when Nitpooperler Hirear came aboard. It seems that Pinks were people who, laboring under some foreign influence, were advocating doctrines subversive to the government of Lilliput. Further than that, I then had no knowledge of them, and, being interested as I then was, I would have made use of the opportunity to question Hirear about them but for the fact that he was intent upon other business. In his high official capacity as Nitpooperler over the Department of Gambling, Recreation, Amusement, and Public Works, he had come to have me make good a previous promise to present to the people of Lilliput the principle of talking pictures, so that the mechanism might be manufactured and put into use in Mildendo. With him he brought a corps of engineers, draughtsmen, technical experts, and workmen to carry out the plan. Doubtless the reader will remember that the motion picture projector which I had aboard the *Night-Hawk* was one of the old type designed for silent movies. While, of course, I had no technical knowledge of any mechanical device, let alone of those employed in the production of the sound cinema, I did have the ordinary layman's knowledge of the underlying principles — i.e., the recording of sound waves upon a film by means of first transposing them into light waves, and then recording the light waves upon a strip of the film. I also knew that the process was simply reversed when a picture was exhibited in the theatre. As sketchy and inadequate as my information was, Nitpooperler Hirear had long been of the opinion that such information would be sufficient to enable highly trained Lilliputian technicians to construct all of the mechanisms needed to produce talking pictures for Lilliput. In fact, he assured me that he was confident that Lilliput would greatly improve the technical quality of the process, "for," he said, "you have several times stated that Lilliputian photography is far in advance of photography in any other part of the world."

While the technicians set to work examining the moving picture machine to which I had given them free access, Nitpooperler Hirear and I remained on deck to enjoy the warm sunshine. The warmth of the golden fluid light combined with a stimulating salt tang in the sea air served to lift from my spirit the depression that had hung upon it ever since I had viewed the tragic death of the soldier. For a time the Nitpooperler and I had quite a gay conversation about this and that, interrupted only occasionally by an engineer who would appear on deck to ask me some question relating to the moving-picture machine. Thus it was, as it seems to have been so often in my life, that during the very rare moments when I was feeling somewhat satisfied with the world, and experiencing a modicum of human happiness, I was, at the same time, unwittingly sowing the seeds of future unhappiness and strife — unknowingly making a great mistake when, were things always as we think they are, I had some little reason to be proud for having done a good deed. Was the day not a beautiful one, and was I not making a splendid gift to Lilliput? Would any other person have seen a false step in making that gift? I think not, yet it was a great error — a colossal mistake, as the reader will see before this narrative draws to a close.

Meanwhile we talked — the Nitpooperler and I — about many things, the most of which were too trivial to be recounted here. But at last I got my companion launched on a more informative discussion. He had for some time been acquainted with my desire to learn all that I could concerning the lawmaking function in Lilliput and had once promised to introduce me to *Skrewky Noshort*, a well known figure, if not a great leader in the national tricamerate, saying on that occasion, "Skrewky can give you information bearing upon the inner workings of our government which even a governmental official like myself knows little or nothing about — not that I am exactly ignorant in regard to the workings of my government, but nobody could know as much as Skrewky, for he is strictly a specialist in knowing such things. Furthermore, he has a penchant which will serve your purpose admirably. I suppose there never lived a Lilliputian in which was better combined a desire to talk with the ability to do it. Skrewky Noshort can and will tell what he knows volubly, vigorously, and at length. For instance, although he was elected to the tricamerate from an outlying district, and consequently then little known throughout the rest of Lilliput, he has so often reiterated that he is **the Horseradish** in his own garden, with the brave innuendo cleverly brought out by his tone of voice and manner of delivery to the effect that he is **the Horseradish** in *any* garden, that he is now known far and wide under the grandiose title of THE HORSERADISH."

Although at the time it appeared to me that Nitpooperler Hirear was indulging in a bit of irony, such was not the case. He was really an admirer of THE HORSERADISH; however, in all fairness it must be said that there were persons in Lilliput who would have maintained that there had been some mistake made in the last two syllables of the nickname. Some would have limited it to one syllable, and others more liberal minded might have allowed two, but in either event the pronunciation would have been quite different, so that in its totality the complete cognomen would have designated something far more "horsey" than any mere garden vegetable. In view of the fact that the tricamerate was then in session, Nitpooperler Hirear promised to arrange a meeting between Skrewky Noshort and me as soon as might be. Thus again, through the kindness of my little friend, was I enabled to learn more interesting things about Lilliput.

The statute law of Lilliput, except for minor local ordinances passed by governing bodies in outlying towns and districts, is all ground out in the capitol building by the three houses of the tri-camerate. After meeting Skrewky Noshort, which it was my good fortune to do the third day after Hirear's visit to me, that corpulent fidgety-mannered little individual with a shake of his head tossed his mane-like hair out of his eyes, and, in his abrupt hurried way of speaking, invited me to view the proceedings in the tricamerate, very likely having been forewarned by Nitpooperler Hirear that such was the chief reason I wished to meet him.

"And," added Skrewky Noshort, "pick me up and hurry to the capitol for I have a speech to make about Garnite and Tomatocumber. I must conserve my energy, otherwise my voice may become a little weak on the sixth day of my oration, and I have planned to speak for seven days."

Although the capitol building of Lilliput bears very little resemblance to the great buildings of Mildendo, these latter being, as the reader will remember, chiefly tall steel zingpups, it is, nevertheless, an architectural gem. It is a long low building of seven stories, sky blue in color, and topped by a magnificent silver dome beautifully fluted. In it are many offices of the central government and the meeting halls of the **popweeze** (*the lower division of the tricamerate*), the **Scnakad** (*the middle division*), and a smaller hall housing the **paynetakit** (*the upper division*). I learned the locations of these halls and of various other offices in the great building by a series of inquiries, observations, and examinations, with an account of which I need not trouble the reader.

With Skrewky Noshort in my pocket, I proceeded toward the capitol as rapidly as was commensurate with safety, it always being necessary to exercise great caution both to avoid injury by a speeding scazpop in the mad whirling traffic and to avoid treading upon anyone. As I, following a broad winding path, neared the capitol, Skrewky, whom I had placed in my pocket, began to jump up and down and to thump my side. "Let me down!" he cried. "Let me down! Some fool in there may want to talk, and I have to beat him to it."

No sooner had I complied with his request than he was racing wildly toward the broad steps of the capitol, turning only to blurt back at me over his shoulder as he ran, "I'll send out a **fezerdick** to show you 'round."

I then understood that I had been presumptuous in expecting **The Horseradish** himself to serve as guide and do the showing "'round"; he was plainly too busy a man to waste his time in that way. The fact was, nevertheless, I had expected him to do it, and, when he had disappeared through the portals of the capitol, I was left at least mildly bewildered and without the slightest idea as to what a fezerdick could be. This deficiency in my knowledge was soon overcome, for within ten minutes of Noshort's disappearance into the capitol a diminutive man in queer attire emerged from the building and hastened to accost me.

"**Whangdompertit Esquerfle,** fezerdick super-especial to **Scnakador** Skrewky Noshort, at your service, Man Mountain, by the express order of THE HORSERADISH. What is your pleasure?"

So arrested was I by the accoutrements of this personage, I did not answer him at once, but stood fascinated by the details of his dress and ornaments. The fezerdick himself was a middle-aged man whose hair was just beginning to turn gray, and he wore a canary-yellow suit or uniform, which of itself was not even half as odd as most of the clothing worn by the male populace of Mildendo, but which was rendered more than odd in appearance by the variegated assortment of bric-a-brac appended to it. Dangling from his neck was a heavy gold chain bearing a gold clock reminiscent of the old time circus clown with his alarm clock for a watch hanging on a rope. The entire surface of his clothing had affixed to it an odd conglomeration of coins, medals, postage stamps, keys, pocket knives, razors, gold toothpicks, lottery tickets, paper moneys, watches, meal tickets, purchase orders, deeds, mortgages, suckorities, and dozens of other objects not readily identified. The little fellow made a jingling, flapping noise as he came near me, so numerous were the metallic and paper parts in his trappings.

At last remembering my manners, I ceased to stare at the fezerdick and returned his greeting, whereupon he remarked, "I understand, Man Mountain, that it is your desire to visit the tricamerate, and the Scnakador has commissioned me to serve as guide and answer you questions. Which branch of our government would you like to observe first?"

I replied, informing him that what I saw first made no particular difference, just so I might see the three divisions of the tricamerate in session, it being my purpose to make a thorough study of each.

My new acquaintance was a talkative little creature, so that I soon dropped the restraint that at first had kept me from making inquiries concerning the nature of his office and the peculiarity of his adornments, it being plain after a few moments that Whangdompertit liked to talk so well that one subject would do about as well as another.

A fezerdick he assured me was a favorite of one or more members of the tricamerate and was appointed to office in return for some favor tending to strengthen or increase the tricamerator's influence or political prestige. There were hundreds of fezerdicks in Mildendo, and many other hundreds in outlying provinces. What were their duties? Oh, they were many and sundry, such as designing new postage stamps, keeping accounts, spending the tax money on a multitude of activities, roads, bridges, sewer lines, sharpening the needles on sandburrs, creating weights and measures, planting trees, catching criminals, and thousands of other things. Indeed, fezerdicks controlled or at least had a strong finger in every pie in the nation. No business, public or private, existed that was not under their regulation and supervision. As a class they were powerful and important — practically the ruling class of the country, although ostensibly under the immediate direction of one or more tricamerators.

"We are," said Whangdompertit Esquerfle, undoubtedly speaking with honesty and frankness, "really *the* power in Lilliput. In the first place our office carries a reasonable stipend. But that is only a part — a small part. While we cannot go directly into the tricamerate and receive access to the treasury, we can, through our tricamerators, have them vote appropriations for the projects we wish to carry on. And who, Man Mountain, do you suppose spends that money? Right! Fezerdicks spend it. For instance, our mutual friend, THE HORSERADISH once tried to gain personal control over the spending of an appropriation in his district, but even he, the great HORSERADISH, had to relinquish his claim. Fezerdicks spend the money. Yes, indeed, *fezerdickery* is a great institution in our country and has been growing in strength and magnitude ever since the birth of the republic. Many Donkgops have professed a dislike for it and threatened to destroy it, but none have ever done more than that. The power of Donkgops really rests upon fezerdickery, because judicious fezerdick appointments not only bring votes for tricamerators, but also bring votes to the Donkgop candidate of the same party."

The queer custom of fezerdicks, requiring them to wear the trinkets already described, came about in the following manner, according to the information supplied me by my fezerdick companion: A few years after the founding of the republic one *Gant Sneebrew*, a newly appointed fezerdick, by means not entirely comprehensible to the populace, became very wealthy. While in the early days it was generally expected that a fezerdick would improve his fortune through the opportunities his office provided, there arose a general feeling throughout the country that the means whereby fezerdicks lined their pockets should be as well as possible known to the public, the theory being the same one already examined in connection with Lilliputian politics, namely that any practice, whatever it may be, if only it be well-known cannot be dishonest. In response to popular demand, the tricamerate passed a law requiring all fezerdicks to wear pinned to them for a period of three moons every gift received by them, thereby advertising the means whereby they attained affluence. The statute fell with terrific and tragic force upon Gant Sneebrew. In gold coin alone he had gifts in weight aggregating several times his own, to say nothing of a span of horses, three houses, a sailing yacht, a herd of cattle, two factories, one bank, and a fine saloon. What to do? He could not comply with the law, yet the breach of it carried heavy penalties. At last he hit upon the expedient of wearing upon his person for the required three moons an many of his small gifts as he could bear, then doffing these and donning others. This was as near as he could come to obeying the mandate of the law, yet, as to the property he retained without having first displayed it upon his person, he was breaking the law. The dilemma he faced was settled tragically. One dark rainy night he slipped into a mud puddle head first and his burden of gold coins affixed to his coat held him there. The next morning the poor fellow was found dead. He had drowned. During the two years preceding his demise Gant Sneebrew had become almost as popular as he had been previously notorious. His courageous and honest effort to obey the law had become known, and he was quite generally admired. His untimely death focused the attention of the tricamerate upon the harshness of the law he had so nobly tried to observe, and several amendments to it were passed, removing patent defects. The wearing of a deed to real property or the bill of sale to live stock, carriages, farm machinery and other large objects of personal property was made a sufficient compliance with the **Fezerdick Publicity Act**, and gold coin only to an amount equal to one-fourth the weight of the wearer, along with deposit receipts for the remainder, was also declared a sufficient compliance with the Act. Whangdompertit Esquerfle assured me that these timely changes in the law have prevented any other sad occurrence similar to the death of Gant Sneebrew.

So much for fezerdickery. Now to acquaint the reader with some of the things I learned about the tricamerate. First, I looked in upon the popweeze. My friend the fezerdick had made his way through the building and ascended to the roof, where he pointed out a skylight admirably suited to my needs. By aid of the same periscope which had theretofore served me so well in Lilliput, I was able to look down upon the several hundred dignitaries there assembled. When I first peered down upon the meeting, everything was quiet except for the droning voice of a speaker I could barely hear. The members were lounging about in various attitudes of silent inattention in their overstuffed seats, which ran in semi-circular rows around the hall in such a way as to face toward a dais at one end upon which were the speaker and several officers of the popweeze. Behind the speaker was a figure wearing a black mask and a wide flowing black robe. In his hands he bore a long pointed stick or pike with which, at irregular intervals, he prodded the speaker, using no little energy in the process. For a long time, as I viewed this strange procedure and strained my ears trying to understand what the *popweezer* was saying, I was unable to determine whether the queer figure in black was interfering with the speech or merely prompting or prodding the speaker on. At last it seemed that each time the figure in black performed the duty of his strange office, the voice of the speaker became somewhat louder and clearer, so it was a fair conjecture that the prodding was designed to help rather than to hinder. This surmise was correct according to Whangdompertit Esquerfle. The black robed figure was a *paynetakitor*, or a member of the paynetakit, the third great division of the Lilliputian legislature. Paynetakitors spend nearly all of their time prodding popweezers and Scnakadors, such being the sole purpose for the existence of their office.

"But how comes it," I asked of the fezerdick, "that popweezers and Scnakadors need prodding? Will they not perform their work without it?"

"Oh, yes — yes, indeed. They would perform their work all right, but likely not to the satisfaction of certain paynetakitors and those whom they represent."

"Whom do the paynetakitors represent, and whom do the popweezers and Scnakadors represent?"

"Scnakadors and popweezers represent those whom the paynetakitors represent, of course," my little guide answered.

"And whom do the paynetakitors represent?" I asked again.

"That," replied Esquerfle, "is a matter of deep uncertainty. Many are those who would like to know just whom or what a paynetakitor represents. Indeed, many a fine paynetakitor would like to know just whom or what some other fine paynetakitor represents. Information of this particular kind can be, and frequently is of great value. The fact is, Man Mountain, that an enterprising fezerdick gifted with sharp ears and a power of observation can, and frequently does, swell his fortune by garnering such information and yielding it in those quarters from whence has come the highest bid. This wide field offers fezerdickery some of its most fruitful opportunities; this kind of work is gratifyingly lucrative, though often dangerous. Once a paynetakitor has caught a fezerdick spying on him, the fezerdick's life is of little worth, for by fair means or foul, the paynetakitor will see to it that the fezerdick forfeits his life. Owing to this great danger, and my own lack of any aptitude for the work, I personally do not take part in any activity in this branch of the service."

Whether the fault lay in my poor comprehension or in a real lack

of clarity in the words of Whangdompertit, I failed utterly to understand them. "Paynetakitors represent somebody, but nobody know
whom?" I puzzled. "Please, my good friend Esquerfle, tell me more.
How do paynetakitors attain their office? Why does the Lilliputian
government have a paynetakit?"

The good little fezerdick smiled, probably at my lively show of
curiosity in questioning so rapidly, then he expounded fully and at
length the matters about which I had inquired.

Originally, so Esquerfle told me, the paynetakit was not a branch
of the tricamerate at all, and even now is not directly on the government payroll. Following the organization of the tricamerate (which
was then call the *dudecker* — a word for which there is no English
equivalent but meaning approximately — *a place for big talk*, there
being some elusive connotations) after the successful revolt against
the monarch, the paynetakit was unknown, but it came to pass that
men wanting certain legislation passed would either go to the capitol or send someone to corner members of the legislature to implore
them to pass legislation which the implorer thought would benefit
their country or themselves. As time went on, more and more men
imploring passage of laws found their way into Mildendo when the
dudecker was in session, until each season saw swarms of them in
the halls of the great capitol building. Popweezers and Scnakadors
were buttonholed at every turn; some were threatened — one actually disappeared and was never heard from again. Then came the
great war of the *estibelobs*, as those numerous implorers at the capitol were called previous to their evolution into the modern paynetakit. Violent quarrels and bitter feuds broke out among the estibelobs. Men knifed and shot each other down on sight; blood flowed in
the halls of the capitol; the business of the dudecker could not go on
at all, such was the terrible tumult and strife going on in its very corridors. In some manner never explained, two or three Scnakadors,
along with the Donkgop, managed to get into one of the offices of
the capitol, whereupon it was there decided to call out the army to
restore order among the estibelobs. But before the troops arrived,
the tumultuous crowds had been warned of their coming. A convincing speaker had gained their attention and announced a plan for
organizing the paynetakit into a well planned and powerful branch
of the government, the plan had been adopted, and the corridors
were deserted. From that day to this the paynetakit has maintained
its vigorous control over the tricamerate, steadily wielding greater

and greater power. Oddly enough, with all the organized strength of the paynetakit, the individual members bitterly hate many of their fellow members; thus comes it that they wear black masks and black robes. They cannot recognize bodily and facial characteristics of enemies, so feuds and the venting of bitter hatreds are avoided. In some few matters wherein the paynetakitors are all agreed, they work in mighty concert, prodding the Scnakad and popweeze into action to the benefit of those whom the paynetakitors represent — who, by the way, I learned, were commercial firms, merchants, manufacturers, bankers, et cetera — in short, the wealthy class. Since the constituents of the paynetakitors have conflicting interests , their representatives naturally heat up at the point of friction.

How it could be that a dignitary such as a Scnakador or a popweezer would allow himself to be prodded and picked by paynetakitors lay beyond the power of my reason to penetrate, but Whangdompertit states that any Scnakador or popweezer who does not submit to such domination cannot hope to retain his office, even if by chance he might once attain it. Furthermore, to run counter to the paynetakit is not only political suicide, but may be economic suicide, as well. One who refuses to submit to the prodding of the pike affronts the powers behind the man who wields the pike, and those powers can swallow up a man's property and deny him a means of livelihood. Esquerfle told a story to illustrate the point.

> For a long time after the first organization of the paynetakit, there were many tricamerators who threatened to break the clutch of the paynetakit. Most of these old fellows were simply being borne up by a well-earned reputation and past popularity. Their threats were chiefly talk, and were for the most part disregarded. But along came *Skaywan Horbo* — a man of a different ilk. A popular figure among working men, he was elected to the Scnakad by them, and this was achieved in spite of the fact that he spent not even one sou for votes! The opposition offered a fortune, but *Skaywan Horbo* won! This was something to make the country sit up and take notice. Here was a man to be reckoned with. Steadfastly he refused to allow any paynetakitor to touch him with a pike. One after another they tried. None succeeded. One even got his head bashed in with his own pike as a reward for his insolence. This was a mistake, for the ire of the paynetakit was aroused, and three days later Horbo was arrested for horsestealing, and his accuser's horse was found in his, Horbo's, barn. On the fourth day he was sued for stealing another man's wife, and the upshot of it all was that Skaywan Horbo, what with criminal charges and property forfeitures, one after another, was soon totally bereft of worldly goods, and had been sentenced to a life term in prison. There

were a few vague murmurs concerning the justice behind Horbo's rapid descent, but the thick shadow of the paynetakit muffled their sound. It was more strongly intrenched in the Lilliputian government than ever, and never since the days of Skaywan Horbo has one arisen to question the right of a paynetakitor to wield the pike.

★   ★   ★

Although I peered into the popweeze on several occasions I never saw or heard anything of great interest transpiring there. Usually some speaker droned on and on while most of the popweezers dozed or snored. A bit of life did manifest itself once for a few moments when someone introduced a resolution to censure a certain *Stang Swarly*, an officer having something to do with the regulation of mails and communications. The proponent of the censure complained that Swarly had authorized such a variety of stamps to be designed and printed that it was becoming difficult for a Lilliputian to know whether he was getting a genuine and legal stamp or not when he wanted to make a purchase of some. Hot replies came from the floor, some shouting that the new stamps were highly artistic, and that Swarly had done a great service to the nation. Several others joined in the vociferous hubbub until an officer on the dais hammered loudly on a desk with a hammer, and remarked: "Your speaker does not know anybody in this assembly who knows art from asininity, and anyway, you bellowing dotards all send your mail by frank privilege. What's it to you how stamps look since you don't have to buy any?" This seemed to quiet the popweeze. One belated fellow shouted: "The glue on them stamps tastes better than it used to!" The officer hammered, all noise but the buzzing drone of a speaker ceased, and soon the popweezers were again nearly all asleep.

Fortunately for me at the time of my visit, the Scnakad was far livelier a place than the popweeze had been; and I was also fortunate in being able to see and hear what was going on there. In general appearances, the meeting hall of the Scnakad resembled that of the popweeze, but was smaller, better lighted, and had numerous cubby-holes opening off the main hall. The popweeze may have had its counterpart of these cubby-holes, but I saw none there. In the Scnakad however, these cubby-holes were much used in a manner and mode with which the reader will soon be better acquainted.

Some kind of a trial seemed to be in progress when I first peered into the Scnakad. An advocate was asking of a man, who seemed to be a witness: "Did you see anybody stick pins in the *Stangl-Hinstool* suckorities?"

The man, who seemed to be the witness, replied, "Yes — I did not see somebody sticking pins, but when the water ran out of those suckorities I was surprised to suddenly find I was all wet."

"You were all wet?" queried the advocate.

"Yes," replied the witness.

"Why?" asked the advocate, his eyes beaming as though he were about to elicit something important.

"Water — water — water, wet," the witness answered as though puzzled at what the advocate might be driving. "Water wet me," he replied.

Then the advocate, with much satisfaction at having performed some miracle invisible to me, turned to the officer on the dais, "I move to have that stricken from the record as a conclusion of the witness. He only knew he was all wet, he didn't know water wet him, for he didn't see the water wet."

"Wetter wrike wit wout," ruled the officer, and the witness, motioning weakly to an attendant, pointed to a pitcher of water on the table, then pointed to his throat and muttered feebly, "Wroat wis werey wey — wasser, wrick!"

Whangdompertit Esquerfle, it turned out, knew much more about the Scnakad than he did about the popweeze. This was probably attributable to his closer associations with members of the former body, especially with Skrewky Noshort. As we listened to the proceedings he informed me that the Stangl-Hinstool investigation to uncover fraud in the great Stangl-Hinstool suckorities business had been going on with some interruptions for thirty-three moons, and at least, so Skrewky had told him, was not even well started.

The Scnakad spends most of its time investigating, and so little did I understand of the proceedings that I tired of listening in on them. My fezerdick friend kept saying that I would soon see the spectacle of a vote on proposed laws, but this pleasure was denied me for seven days. Each day I peered down upon the Scnakad, while waiting for a vote, I amused myself by observing what was going on in the cubby-holes along the wall. Many of them were at such angles from the skylight as to be hidden from me; but there were those in which I could perceive what was taking place. In one cubby-hole sat three old men assiduously picking over thousands upon thousands of papers, fitting some together, tossing others aside, trying, discarding, etc., very much as persons do in attempting to fit together a difficult jig-saw puzzle. Indeed, this is very nearly what they were doing. Esquerfle said that the old men's committee was trying to piece together a composite bill embodying in it the desires of all the paynetakitors, the citizens who had troubled to write, the Donkgop, ninety-two popweezers, the army, the navy, four-hundred eighty-six postmasters, and Jaaypie Ganhorg. The poor old men looked weary — oh, so weary that I grew weary watching them and turned my periscope toward another cubby-hole. It was considerably larger than the first, but in it old men were at work, and the work was similar. They were sorting over pieces of paper, selecting pieces from a great flat heap in one corner, putting one here, one there, and another in a third place along the wall where hundreds of stacks of paper were being piled up.

"And what are these old men doing, kind Fezerdick?" I asked.

"Who? They? — Those old greybeards in hole Number Three?" he was forced to ask, since he, unlike me with my longer vision, could not see into the cubby-hole from the skylight.

"Yes, those in the third hole from the main door," I answered.

"Why, those old fellows I know well. I visit them often. They are busy classifying and compiling statutes preparatory to publication. They are just now finishing those passed by the fifth to the last tricamerate."

I peered into the next cubby-hole which at first appeared to be almost wholly filled with nothing but paper, chiefly rubbish. But lo and behold in a moment there was a faint rustle, a miniature landslide occurred in the pile of paper, and the tiny head of a little old man appeared in a breach, only to be smothered with a fresh avalanche of paper dropping from a hole in the ceiling.

"Those papers in Number Four," explained Whangdompertit, "are decrees and executive orders of the Donkgop. They are surely getting the old boys down."

★   ★   ★

About eleven o'clock one night Whangdompertit came rushing aboard the **Night-Hawk** to inform me that the Scnakad was just about ready to vote on a huge number of proposed laws. He let me know that if I wished to be present for the event I would have to hurry.

Never in all my stay in Lilliput did I get such a disappointment as I got in watching the vote casting in the Scnakad. Whangdompertit had led me to expect something without any other warrant than the rarity of a Scnakad vote. Rare as it is, it is nevertheless dull. A speaker droned along just as the one had done in the popweeze. All of the Scnakadors lounged around inattentive, asleep, bored, indifferent, or all four, while the speech went on. After the speech was finished the proponent of a bill called out — "Push my button and I'll push yours." The paynetakitors prodded their victims first awake, then up to the wall where there is a long row of electric switches, and where each one pushed a button or did not push it according to the behest of his paynetakitor, few of them seeming to know how they were voting, nor for what, but in this way a new law was passed or rejected — I never knew which.

Chapter XVII

Home and family life in Lilliput — recreation and
amusement — a children's party.

ORKADAY LIFE IN LILLIPUT is much the same as it is in other
W parts of the world, but as I continued to dwell in this mighty
little country, and talk with people from all walks of life, I learned
a few things about the home and recreational life of the average
Lilliputian, some of which may interest the reader. That recreation
and amusement in Lilliput is a serious matter is well attested to by
the fact it is classified along with public works in the Department
of Gambling, Recreation, Amusement, and Public Works, under the
stewardship of the illustrious Nitpooperler Hirear. Gambling is perhaps the most common of all Lilliputian amusements, especially in
Mildendo. It is indulged in by every person young or old who has
the wherewithal and the requisite intelligence to understand a game
of chance. I have seen children not above the primary school grades
seated in the middle of the sidewalk playing a game of chance by
means of a spinning wheel and a complicated system of numbers
around its circumference. They risked their toys, rings, bits of clothing, lunch tickets, and one even risked his watch. I was surprised
to discover that the one who risked his watch could not tell time,
although he could read all of the complicated figures on the wheel.

Daily there great fortunes change hands by the mere spin of a
wheel, flip of a card, outcome of a wager, or in some of a thousand
other ways through which devotees may woo the favor of Lady Luck.
Gambling houses flourish throughout Mildendo and are openly patronized by all citizens alike. Of course, there are classes of them;
some cater chiefly to the more wealthy and run games for high
stakes, thus by that very reason exclude the poorer people. But no
man with anything to risk need search far in Mildendo for a place in
which to risk it, and there are always plenty of takers. The most popular game of chance in Mildendo, aside from the popular flea-hops
(a kind of a flea jumping contest upon which much money is wa-
gered), is a game played with cards. (And by way of digression it is
interesting to note that Lilliputian cards, although indigenous to the

country, are remarkably like those known throughout the world at large. A Lilliputian deck of playing cards contains four suits known as Reds, Blacks, Greens, and Yellows, instead of hearts, clubs, spades, and diamonds. Each suit has fifteen, instead of thirteen, cards which are known by name rather than number.) The game mentioned is played by four persons, and is called something like *moronsnidge*. (The exact word may have escaped me.) The players sit around a table, and the cards are all dealt out. In the gambling halls and men's clubs, there is a certain grim seriousness about the playing, but when played by women or in mixed groups in the home (and one-third of every woman's time is spent playing moronsnidge) a certain levity in the demeanor of the players is to be noticed. To start off the game a player says: "Umph — umph — two-reds." Or maybe the remark will be: "Oh, I have all the mice in the deck. Why can't I get some eagles. Umph — umph — three yellows." (Mice and eagles are names of cards in each suit.) I have listened to several of these games, and the *umph, umph* seems to be a definite part of it. Following the opening remark, if women are playing, one of them will remark: "*Skerenzie Tootsiehot* has dyed her hair, and I hear she wants a divorce." This will be followed by a great deal of talk after which, if the opportunity presents itself, the person who made the original remark will repeat: "Umph — umph — ump: Four greens." Then all of the players will peer into her eyes in an effort to guess whether she really meant four greens or three reds (it seems to make some difference) and to see if they can see the reflection of her hand of cards glittering in her eyeballs. This rite having been performed, some other person will say, "Umph — umph — Let's see — umph — five yellows," whereupon some woman will say, "The *Skiteets* have a new scazpop with pink upholstery — and, do you know, I just heard Mr. Skiteet has not been drinking enough lately? They say his wife is furious about it."

Then another woman will lay her cards face down upon the table and exclaim: "But did you hear about Mrs. Skiteet! You know, they say her husband was driven to it. He's always been jealous, you know, and Mr. Skiteet declared in front of **Mrs. Peebrosk**, who told **Miss Totedirrt**, who told me, that he would absolutely stop drinking and gambling if his wife did not stop seeing that young professor from the university. Everybody has seen Skiteet's wife and Professor Mudelpate together. They say she has made a fool of herself over him — and isn't he good looking?"

"Yes, he is good looking, but who would think of leaving Skoy

Skiteet with all of his civic honors, high winnings at billiards, and excellent disposition, for a poor young professor, however good looking?"

When a game of moronsnidge being played by mixed company has progressed about to this point, some male player invariably, as though feigning anger, bites his cards in two and pulls his own hair. Of course, never having learned the game, I could never understand the full significance of this act, which quite oddly seemed to be a part of the game when played by mixed company, and seemed to be a performance indulged in by men only.

There are many other games played with cards by a few people, as well as numerous games played without cards, but of these I never really learned anything, since whatever they are, none are even one-twentieth as popular as moronsnidge.

It may be of passing interest to the reader to know something of the problems I faced in getting the little information I have about life in a Lilliputian home. The dwelling houses of these folks, except for some large hostelries in mid-Mildendo, are low one or two story affairs, and it was impossible for me to get any adequate idea of how life went on in one by observation. While the physical impediments to such observation might have been overcome, the psychological factors were insurmountable. In the first place, nobody wanted me peeking in upon their private lives, and, had any family been kind enough to grant me the privilege, the very known fact of my presence outside the dwelling would have altered the usual routine of the household. I was able to see and hear moronsnidge played at a garden party in one of the Mildendo parks, but most of my other information about the happenings in an ordinary Lilliputian household was attained as a result of a happy inspiration. To ask one of my friends to depict for me what went on in a household was no solution to the problem I had before me. Let the reader put himself in the position of being asked: What happens in an average American home? Could he give an answer readily, fairly? I thought that I could not do so, therefore I concluded it would be just as difficult for Nitpooperler Hirear or any of my small friends to give me a fair unprejudiced depiction of daily life in a Lilliputian home.

The inspiration came to me when I saw and overheard a child on the beach tell a man, presumably her father, that he was an "ugly old man and your nose is too long."

Small children tell the truth! That was my inspiration. I would give a party for the children, and get what information I could about their home-life by bribery — ice-cream, candy, etc.

With a certain uneasiness of conscience owing to my unrevealed ulterior motive, I broached the idea to Nitpooperler Hirear, saying that, in appreciation of all the splendid favors the Lilliputian people had done me, I wished to reciprocate at least in some small way, and that I thought a party given for the children of Mildendo might answer this purpose. The Nitpooperler agreed with me readily, and since a children's party came under the head of Amusement, it fell within the scope of his office, so he offered all the facilities of his department to carry out the project. By order of Nitpooperler Hirear, fifty workmen were transferred from a new sewer construction job to the job of making arrangements for the party. Immediately they set to work issuing two-thousand five-hundred hand written invitations, gathering tables and chairs, setting up play houses, and planning a program. Lest my purpose be defeated I had to take a hand in planning the program, and, after some insistence on my part, it was decided that for a period of about twenty minutes during the party every child would be asked to play "house" and "grownup". This game had the double advantage of being universally popular with children and of being an admirable means to uncover intimate details of Lilliputian home life about which I was exceedingly curious.

At last the day for the party arrived with all preparations made. The setting for the gala event was just outside the city walls in the same spot where banquets already described in this journal had been held. Tables, chairs, play houses, swings, slides, and other paraphernalia were set up in a suitable manner, and colored bunting and crepe paper was much in evidence. To avoid even the possibility of my bringing tragedy into the juvenile festivities I had resolved to take a seat several paces removed from the site of the party and there remain until every child had retreated at the conclusion of the affair through the great gate in the Mildendo wall.

Early in the afternoon the great gate opened and the procession, a bedlam of noise — blare of trumpets, yells, squalls, howls, squeals, and gay, excited laughter — and a riot of color — began to pour through the gate. Nitpooperler Hirear, gaudy in a pied suit, led the parade tooting a horn so loudly as to risk bursting his lungs, and was followed by two-hundred fifty waiters and nurses, the need of whose services can well be imagined. Following them was the wriggling, pushing, shoving, noisy stream — boys and girls — Mildendo's hope for the future. Upon seeing me, a horde of children swarmed over me. They had to be captured and admonished by mothers and nurses to stay away, lest some be injured by falling or some inadvertent movement of mine. Another horde, equally as numerous, raised their scared voices to a nerve rasping crescendo of howling squeals in fear of me. By expending much energy in repetitious assurance, explaining that I would not move until the party was over and all the children led home, the Nitpooperler finally succeeded in reducing the great wail to a few isolated squeaks.

There was considerable more confusion during the subsequent interval absorbed in a debate among Nitpooperler Hirear's Committee on Arrangements, one faction contending that it would be better to feed the children before starting the games, since such method would tend toward greater cooperation among them, and the other faction contending that once the children at a party had been fed, the party itself, as far as they were concerned, would be over, since those who were not actually ill from over-eating would be sated to the point of no longer having any real interest in anything but home and bed. The discussion arrived at no conclusion, for while it was in progress some of the waiters began to serve the ice-cream and cake. Bedlam again broke loose; one-thousand tiny voices set up the howl that he, the shouter, should be served ahead of little Honksnort, or *Chizzlewit*, or *Diddledump*, etc. because his daddy (the shouter's) had more suckorities than Honksnort's, Chizzlewit's, or Diddledump's, etc. or his daddy had better luck at gambling than Honksnort's, Chizzlewit's, or Diddledump's, etc. One little girl, whose voice rose shrilly above the rest, informed the assemblage that her mother's name was *Mrs. Tangeytea*, that her mother was the best moronsnidge player in Mildendo, that her mother was a lady, that she (the daughter) was a lady, that she wanted some more ice-cream, and that she wanted it now.

A dangerous riot was averted only by the belated cooperative efforts of the adults present. Mothers, nurses, committee members, and onlookers set to serving ice-cream and cake, thus soothing away the surging wrath of young Mildendo. Soon everybody's temper had been sweetened by a liberal application of ice-cream and cake, not only to those internal portions of childish anatomy where sweets are most satisfying, but also to all of those external portions where its application seems to be inevitable.

For a time I feared that this precipitate gorging of my young guests would weaken their propensities for "playing house", and thereby upset the most cherished of my plans. However, as it turned out, this fear was not very well founded, for not long after the cake and ice-cream had disappeared, Nitpooperler Hirear, acting as a Master of Ceremonies and rising to heights the like of which I had hardly deemed him capable, got the game of "playing house" under way. So many "households" were quickly organized that I could not possibly follow the activities of all; but a few caught my immediate interest.

At one of the smaller tables where three little girls and two little boys had just partaken of their refreshments the "household" suggested by the Nitpooperler was organized as nearly as I can remember somewhat as follows:

A little girl, whose name was **Zee Ezoyoi** (I believe), said, speaking to the largest of the two boys, "You be the daddy, and I'll be the mamma," and then turning to the other three children, "You'll be our three babies."

"I won't be a baby," was the immediate retort of one of the little girls. "Anyway I'm bigger'n you, an' I wanna be mamma."

Zee must have expected this for she parried without hesitation, "All mammas aren't big. Mammas make soup. You can't make soup, can you?"

"I don't wanna make soup. My mamma doesn't make soup. Cooks make soup."

"Oh — won't that be fun! You can be the cook. See? You can use this dish and spoon and start stirring right now." In this way did Mamma Zee acquire a cook who soon was stirring merrily.

"Aw, gee, I don't wanna be a baby. Babies is dumb." complained the little boy. "They're awful dumb."

"You know very well, **Zapear Huzzlebee**, you can be awful dumb if you want. An' you aren't very big either."

"Well, I'm bigger'n a baby, I don't wanna be a baby."

"Zapear Huzzlebee, you are a baby an' you've got to be the baby. Any family ought to have anyway two babies. My daddy says so."

"Aw, gee, I don't wanna be a baby — Boo-hoo-hoo — Why do I gotta be a baby — Boo-hoo — Couldn't I be a scazpop driver? Boo-hoo —"

"Of course, dear. You can play you're mamma's little scazpop driver. Now play lak you're cleaning the scazpop to take mamma to market this afternoon."

Again were tears cleared away by "Mamma" Zee, and Zapear was soon lost in his role — busily intent upon the pantomime of shining a scazpop.

The third little girl who had been assigned the role of a baby assented with reservations.

"I'll be a baby, but babies aren't dumb as Zapear says. My daddy says that babies are mighty wise. He says my little brother knows even too bad-word much. He says my little brother knows when he is coming home all tired before he gets within a block of our house, for he always begins yowling, and never lets up until my daddy goes to the club to get some rest. I'll be a baby but I won't be dumb — I'll bawl."

And bawl she did loudly, continuously, and most realistically.

Turning to the one she had appointed "daddy", Mamma Zee swept into the role she had assumed, "*Jawge Mizzlit*, I heard you were seen having lunch with a certain young lady today — How long do you expect me to put up with your chasing hussies down town? You know —"

Jawge Mizzlit did not fall into his part readily enough to utter any brilliant lines extemporaneously, though he did manage an "Aw, gee," before Zee interrupted.

"You needn't tell me it was your cousin from *Schlizpot*, or a business acquaintance, or your partner's best client, or, or — I know it was that secretary from the office across the hall from yours."

Zee paused, evidently more from lack of breath than lack of words, and this time Jawge edged in a sentence, still not entirely in keeping with his character.

"Aw, gee, I don't take no girls to lunch, but I sure would like some more ice-cream an' cake."

"All right, dear. Dinner is almost ready. *Dinnaw* has been busy in the kitchen all afternoon fixing it. It will be served as soon as you have changed your clothes."

"What ya mean — changed clothes?"

"Changed to your clean dinner clothes, Jawge."

"Aw, *utznay*. My dad takes off his shoes, and sometimes his shirt to eat dinner."

"Little Zapear, won't you go with daddy and lay out his clean clothes for him while he shines his goatee?"

"I'm not Little Zapear. I'm the scazpop driver. And your car is ready, Madam. Will you be going to tea at Mrs. Skiwok's, or meeting Mr. Zwaxibrow at the Casino?"

"I'll have you know that I do not answer my servants' unnecessary questions. I'll tell you where I am going when I am ready to go."

This little drama ended at this point, for Jawge suggested, and all but Zee agreed, that it was a dumb game.

"All right," said Zee, "I'll go and be the mamma in another family."

In the midst of the raucous confusion of many "households", my attention was next arrested by a shrill wailing above the other sounds. It was the sound of real crying. An adult Lilliputian woman rushed up to a small boy who was crying and shouted almost as shrilly as he cried, "What's the matter, sonny boy?"

"*Sizzy Luie* hit me with a dish," he blubbered, pointing to a little girl.

"Why, Sizzy Luie, did you do that?" the woman asked, the tone of her voice betraying deep resentment.

"Sure, I did. We was playin' house, an — he was the daddy, an' he wouldn't quit readin' the newspaper an' empty the garbage when I told him. I heard my mamma say you do that to daddy when he won' empty the garbage when you say."

The woman snatched the little boy and whisked him away so quickly his tiny heels clicked in mid-air. For one small fellow with a bump on his head the party was over. He was going home.

I overheard one other bit of conversation before an incident occurred which cut the party somewhat shorter than it had been planned.

A rather sad faced little boy who still sat at the table where he had finished his ice-cream and cake apparently had taken no part in the game of "playing house".

"It's no fun playing house," I heard him say. "That game's *ski-washy*. Even a real house's not fun, when yer old woman an' ole man leaves ya alone all day, 'cause they've gotta work. People is crabby in houses — 'cept fire houses. Firemen in fire houses drink a lot an' is jolly, an' don't do nuthin'. Ya gotta work in family houses."

"Aw, you do not," piped up another little boy. "You can play in family houses and have a good time."

"Maybe in yours — not mine. My ole woman an' my old man is crabby. I like fire houses."

This conversation was interrupted by a great commotion in an-other quarter. Shouts of "I want some more ice-cream, too" burst from first one throat, then twenty, forty, one-hundred, a thousand

— Some waiter, evidently more highly endowed with kindness than mentality, had given to some child the last remaining dish of ice-cream, and a second child had witnessed the act. Even with the great faith I then had in Nitpooperler Hirear's ability to control these children, I must confess that I had my doubts. The very heavens must have heard the screaming of these Lilliputian boys and girls.

From somewhere among the paraphernalia brought along for the service of the party the resourceful Nitpooperler produced a whistle which could be heard above the yelling. Gradually quiet began to descend, and when everything was silent enough to permit his voice to be heard, the Nitpooperler produced the trump card which turned the trick and saved the day. Unbeknown to me, he arranged to have a bag of candy passed out to each child as it left the party. This fact he announced, and the children lined up single file to receive their present. In a few moments each one had a bag of candy and had disappeared from the scene of the fray through the great gate of Mildendo.

The party was over.

Chapter XVIII

Lilliputian religion, or lack thereof, and the author's efforts to introduce Christianity upon the island; Onk Watwil again.

WHILE I WOULD HAVE LIKED to learn more about Lilliputian family life, no ready means for making a study of it seemed to present itself. The children's party had been only moderately successful with reference to such purpose, and in view of the actual danger to life and limb occasioned by the none-too-gentle conduct of my diminutive guests, I must confess experiencing a great sense of relief when it was over. Had not another matter weighed heavily upon my conscience I might in time have been able to devise a method through which I could have become thoroughly familiar with the Lilliputian home as an institution. As the reader will recall, I had been from time to time disturbed by my own lethargy in carrying out, as best I might, the noble project of my poor departed comrade, Glykus Spaddle, namely to bring to Lilliput the great message of the Christian religion. What a fertile field there was for it there! And with what great zeal poor Spaddle could have undertaken the task of converting the islanders! But I — what could I do? The knottiness of that problem was not the least of those things which had so long deterred me from the undertaking.

Of all the places in the world known to man, Lilliput is the most utterly devoid of any concepts which might, even by a long stretch of the imagination, be characterized as religious. In the days of my great and beloved ancestor, Lemuel Gulliver, the concept of a Divine Providence was a basic one in Lilliputian life. I remember that he wrote, "... the disbelief of a Divine Providence renders a man incapable of holding any public station; for since kings avow themselves to be the deputies of Providence the Lilliputians think nothing can be more absurd than for a prince to employ such men as disown the authority under which he acts." With the overthrow of the old monarchy, this concept of a Divine Providence seems to have vanished along with the kings who owed so much to it. Nowhere in Lilliput did I see or hear anything which suggested even remotely that anyone there believed in a Divine Providence, or any other divinity, for that matter. I cannot truly assert that Lilliputians are either atheist, agnostic, heathen, or pagan; they are simply devoid of any religious precepts. Laws they have, and customs, and even a queer system of ethics and morality.

In answer to a question which I put to Nitpooperler Wickdomp Ooick concerning the Lilliputians' ancient belief in Divine Providence, he stared at me a moment as though not grasping the meaning of what I had asked.

"Oh, yes," he replied finally, "Sand in the eyes of the common man — dust from the feet of kings —"

If there is an educated man in Lilliput, that man is Wickdomp Ooick, so the reader may well imagine how much thought the general populace gives to Divine Providence when such a man as he had difficulty in remembering that belief in a higher Being was once almost universal in Lilliputian thought. The Nitpooperler's answer to me was calm and without feeling. He spoke as though repeating from memory some line he had read in a book long, long ago. Lilliput was truly without a religion.

While I had always been a Christian, and had been brought up on the Protestant religious doctrine as a boy, I could not help feeling my inadequacy in attempting to do the things which I knew Spaddle, could he have told me so, would have wanted me to do. Eloquence, oratory, persuasion, indoctrination, and all that sort of thing had always been beyond my horizon. My efforts to convince others of the truth of my beliefs had never been exactly successful. To say the least, my efforts in such wise had never proved convincing. Why had I gone to Spoop Sanitorium — that abominable place? Why? Because I had failed to convince others — to convince them that there was a Lilliput — to convince them that some one could go there — to convince them that I was going there. And yet, here I was in Lilliput, and had been for many weeks. No, it was not my doubts in the truth of Christianity that made me falter; it was the grave doubts I had in my own persuasive powers. In this realization I could not escape a reflection on the strangeness of this world. Some men who know truth cannot utter it convincingly; others, who know no truth at all, can so sway the world with falsehood that it drinks it in as truth! But yet I reflected, "Perhaps I am fortunate in coming to a virgin sod to sow my grains of truth; perhaps that is God's way of making it easy for me to succeed. In my own opinionated land, where every mind clings to some doctrine as it does to some organ of the body with which it is born, I could not with my meagre endowments hope to succeed, but here in Lilliput, where even scholars have lost all concept of religion, maybe I can easily make an imprint upon the unmarred wax." So I resolved to try.

A few days after the children's party, when the Nitpooperlers Hi-rear and Ooick were basking in the sunshine with me on the deck of the **Night-Hawk**, our conversation was proceeding lazily from point to point — in fact, without any point — I took it upon myself to speak of Spaddle and his intended mission to Lilliput. My listeners' attention was aroused at once. Being thus encouraged, I recounted briefly for them the manner of Spaddle's death, and explained that in point of honor I felt obliged to do whatever I could to acquaint the people of Lilliput with the teachings of Christianity.

The word *Christianity* greatly puzzled my friends. "Christianity — Christianity —" they both repeated as though saying something very unfamiliar.

"Oh, yes, indeed," said Nitpooperler Wickdomp Ooick, "Chris-tianity — Christian — we've always had it in our school books, but never knew its meaning. In a few of our old English textbooks based upon your great ancestor's letters the word has been used as being synonymous with Man Mountain, meaning a large man like yourself, but modern scholarship has rejected that meaning as inadequate. It simply does not fit squarely with certain uses of the word in Lemuel Gulliver's letters."

Such a rendering of the word was, of course, inadequate. I has-tened to outline for my friends its true meaning, pointing out in so doing that the word *Christian* did not apply to all large people like myself, but applied chiefly only to those who lived in Europe or America, and that it did not apply to all people in those parts of the world, but only to those who believed in and followed the teachings of Jesus Christ.

"And the teachings of Jesus Christ — what are they?" Nitpoo-perler Ooick was quick to inquire, and in answer to his question, I explained that they were many and could not be recounted briefly, but that if I could get the permission of the Lilliputian government I would be very glad to give a series of lectures upon the subject be-fore an assemblage of all the Lilliputians who could be persuaded to attend.

"That, Man Mountain Gulliver, might be arranged," said Nitpooperler Hirear. "But how is any governmental authority to be in a proper position to grant your request without knowing beforehand something about the subject concerning which you are to speak?"

"Perhaps," I suggested, "Such permission is not necessary. I mentioned it only because it is my earnest desire to obtain a permit if it be needed."

Neither Nitpooperler Hirear nor Nitpooperler Ooick knew whether or not a permit would be needed, but suggested that legal advice be sought upon the point. They suggested that I see a lawyer, or at least consult with the Donkgop, who, being not only a lawyer by profession, but also being by reason of his office in a position to be familiar with such things, would most likely give me a sound answer at once.

"In any event," Nitpooperler Hirear went on, "before anyone can say whether or not a permit is needed, that person must know something concerning that about which you are to speak. Some things are forbidden to be uttered; some things are not. To which class do your proposed lectures belong? Would anyone know the answer to that without knowing what you are going to talk about?"

Feeling at the moment that this was something of a dilemma, I thoughtlessly blurted out, "In my country free speech is allowed."

My friends looked at me in such a way that I regretted the trace of ill-temper which I betrayed in my tone. Nitpooperler Hirear's reply was something of a relief, for his answer showed that his eyebrows had been raised more through his own misunderstanding than because of my bad manners. We were at the moment speaking English and he had fallen into the confusion of homonymy.

"I presume," said he, "that all speech of any consequence in any country is aloud, since whispered speech has the not-to-be-overlooked deficiency of being inaudible."

"I intended no joke," I replied smilingly. "I meant that in my country free speech is allowed — permitted; that is, people are allowed to express themselves freely —" then quickly apprehending that the manifold meaning of my last word might lead to further misunderstanding, I hastened to add — "at will; this is, my people are permitted to express themselves at will."

"Oh," remarked Ooick.

"Absurd," commented Hirear.

Taking immediate advantage of my opportunity to turn the conversation into channels more nearly befitting my purpose, I proposed outlining to these two friends some of the tenets of Christianity to the end that they, once they were in possession of such information, might then obtain for me the official permit to hold the public meetings I wished to hold. To this they assented without hesitation, being as always ever ready to grant me a favor.

Where to start was a problem, so for want of a better plan I began with the nativity of Christ, related what I could remember of His early life, of His casting the money-changers out of the temple, of His changing water into wine, of His healing the man who had lain thirty-eight years infirm, of His feeding five-thousand with five loaves, of His walking upon the water, of His giving sight to the man who was born blind, of the raising of Lazarus, of the Last Supper, of the Passion, and the Resurrection. My hearers listened with evident interest. Questions, some of them embarrassing, were asked when I had finished my recital.

"Do all people in your land follow the teachings of this man?" Nitpooperler Hirear inquired.

"All save a very few profess to believe in them," I countered.

"Offhand I see no evil in the doctrines of Christ as you have related them to us," Wickdomp Ooick volunteered. "I, for one, will be glad to approach the Donkgop to obtain a permit for you to carry the message to our people."

"And I will accompany you on that mission," the kindly Hirear offered. "I must be going," he added quickly noting how near the afternoon sun approached the horizon. "Will you accompany me, Nitpooperler Ooick?"

"Yes," and he pinched Hirear's ear in a token of gratitude.

Soon their shining water scazpops, which had lain fast to the *Night-Hawk* since early morning, were spinning rapidly toward the shore, and leaving in their wake a fine spray glistening brightly in the slanting rays of the western sun. I watched them until I saw them land upon the beach, then turned and went into the cabin. From among some things which had belonged to Spaddle I picked up a Bible and sat down to compose some lectures and sermons in order that I might be prepared in the event that my friends obtained the permit for me to address the populace, which I had little doubt they would.

Putting Christian doctrine into the Lilliputian language was no easy task, and it brought me to a fuller realization of the difficulties which must have beset those early bearers of the light who sat themselves down to render into the language of their fellow men the teachings of the Master, which then could be found only in Hebrew, Greek, and later in Latin. In spite of the difficulty, I worked far into the night and at last, after elaborating upon the story of Christ as I had told it to the Nitpooperlers in the afternoon, produced what I then thought was a fairly presentable text for my first lecture. The following morning, being alone upon the *Night-Hawk* and no one having appeared to disturb my solitude, I set to work again and produced a sermon in which were embodied some of the greatest teachings of the Lord. This I planned to use for a second address, providing I was successful in the first.

*   *   *

The following day, late in the afternoon, Nitpooperler Hirear came aboard the *Night-Hawk*, bearing with him a legal document purporting to be a permit granting me the right to address public assemblages upon the subject of Christianity. It was signed by Donk-gop Medid Wherding, and countersigned by Nitpooperlers Hirear, Ooick, Flebrow, Garnite, Gravinap, Scantak (the successor of the unfortunate Bittzzora), and Tomatocumber, as well as General Ossdoc, Admiral Spraygrees, and the Chief Magistrate of Mildendo, it being, as Hirear explained, uncertain under whose authority the granting of such a permit fell.

I was, of course, delighted, and I thanked the Nitpooperler by pinching his ear, at the same time requesting that upon his returning to shore he dispatch me a messenger whom I could trust to carry copy to the printers for the printing of hand bills announcing my first lectures on the day after the morrow, to see that such hand bills were distributed, and to oversee the making of seating arrangements for my audience upon the beach outside the gate of Mildendo. This he promised to do. Departing, he wished me the best of good fortune in my undertaking, and expressed the wish that my utterances bring a wealth of good into the hearts of the Lilliputian people.

*   *   *

The messenger sent by Nitpooperler Hirear came aboard the *Night-Hawk* just as it was growing dark. After giving him a five dollar gold piece as earnest money, of which he made no complaint despite the fact it weighed down rather heavily in his small satchel,

I gave him his directions and handed him a copy for the hand bills which read:

On the 73rd anniversary
of the second Donkgop's
encounter with the great cockroach,
your visitor, Man Mountain Gulliver,
will address the people of Lilliput
upon the subject
— CHRISTIANITY —
outside the great gate
on Mildendo Beach soon after breakfast.

The LIGHT of my world to YOU.
COME ONE! COME ALL!!
STAY ALL!!!

      ★   ★   ★

The morning of the day for my first talk arrived. The crowd over-flowed the seating facilities provided on Mildendo Beach, and many were compelled to seat themselves upon the sands. Never having in all my life made a success as a public speaker, I naturally enough was not without those qualms which beset even an experienced speaker to say nothing of one as inexperienced as I. The thought that I might acquit myself as I had at the banquet held to welcome me to Lilliput made me sick with fear. What if I did? Impossible in a meeting of this kind — yet, only too possible! I would rather die! But there was the crowd waiting; I had invited them there; I had to give them what I had offered.

When it was all over I was surprised that I could have felt any uneasiness in the beginning. Once I had begun speaking my appre-hensions left me. I spoke before that vast throng of Lilliputians for more than one hour and a half without the slightest nervousness and without a single thing occurring to interrupt me. It was a success — decidedly. When I had concluded, the multitude cheered me with the most raucous of Lilliputian cheers — a breach of Christian deco-rum which I, in my then state of high elation, resolved to correct before I was through preaching sermons to these people, but which, notwithstanding its incongruity at a Christian meeting, was then very pleasing to me for it assured me that I had not failed. I left the beach and rowed to the *Night-Hawk* with a strange joy in my heart that I never felt before.

The next week at the same time and place, I preached to a throng even larger than the one of the week before. Taking the Golden Rule as my chief text, I elaborated upon it, illustrated it, went through the ten commandments and their origin, and showed how they exemplified the Golden Rule; I talked of Genesis, of Adam and Eve, of Cain and Abel, of Sodom and Gomorrah, of Noah and his ark, of the Gospels, of Heaven and Hell — in short, I preached long, taking this time more than three hours. Again the applause — the Lilliputian cheers, I had forgotten to instruct my flock in the elements of decorum at a solemn Christian meeting. Oh, well, that would come later. I was becoming accustomed to the reverberating sounds of Lilliputian cheering. Again I rowed out to the *Night-Hawk* happy in the thought that I had done well. Why, in time I might become a minister even in the United States. Why hadn't I thought of it before?

On the evening of my second success I had a caller — a little man I had not seen for a long while — none other than the non-volitionist healer whose release from prison I had once obtained through the services of Attorney Buzknut. His name, by the way, was *Zucow Hockdog*, and he had come to inform me of something at which I was first inclined to scoff at as being insignificant, but which later I began to view with some misgiving, seeing as I finally did, that Zucow Hockdog took the matter quite seriously and was the very soul of sincerity in his desire to promote my welfare. The reader will recall that the cavalry officer, Onk Watwil, had, soon after my arrival upon the shores of Lilliput, conceived a dislike for me. We had gotten off to a bad start and several circumstances had conspired against my winning his friendship. First was the incident of his horse getting its feet stuck in a discarded wad of my chewing gum which caused the officer to incur the pain of a bad fall; then came the incident of his fall into the toilet bowl, which, although attributable in nowise to any fault of mine, did, nevertheless, occur aboard the *Night-Hawk*; then his jealousy concerning my supposed improper relations with his wife, Mezarra Watwil — all conspired against his becoming truly friendly to me.

Zucow Hockdog came to inform me that Onk Watwil was going about Mildendo in a high state of patriotic frenzied ecstasy, trying to stir up the passions of various and sundry folk against me. Having imbibed fully as much as the Lilliputian law required and considerably more than the law anywhere else would have tolerated, he was going about, so Hockdog informed me, stating, "Here is this foreign cesspool and garbage incinerator (referring to me) telling our people not to covet another's wife, while the big vile smelling hypocrite has stolen mine. He says to us, 'Do unto others as ye would have them do unto you,' thus inciting all manner of strife, iniquity, and vice. Should you, the people of Lilliput, who loll in sloth on the beach of Mildendo drinking in his falsehoods, do as he bids you do, privates would command generals, employers would be on the dole, horses would ride men, children chastise parents, criminals sentence judges, Donkgops elect people, jailers be jailed, wards become guardians, and frogs grow on warts. Oh, men of Mildendo as you value your lives, as you cherish the traditions of this great nation, stop up your ears — stop up your ears — stop up your nose — pull down this cheese whose foreign stench pollutes the current of our free air — pull down the creature whose words incite riot, and bloodshed, and threaten the foundations of our great government — Pull down, I say, this awful Pink, whose ruddy doctrines reek and stink — Pull down this hateful foreign hulk — Come, Patriots, we'll have a drink."

This tirade Zucow had obtained verbatim. Others, he said, had been even worse, and Watwil was really getting Mildendo into quite a hubbub. While I felt no fear for myself, I did realize that history might in a way repeat itself, and that if Watwil did succeed in rousing a mob to storm the **Night-Hawk**, it would not do for Hockdog to be found aboard. He, as a traitor, would fare worse than I, therefore I urged him to go ashore, taking every precaution not to be seen. As I have said, I did not fear for myself, but I did fear for my loyal friend who had risked so much to return a small favor. Thanking him hurriedly with a vigorous pinch upon the ear I let him down in a basket to his waiting water scazpop, and returned to the cabin. Following the wise precept of Safety First, I locked and barred the door before turning into bed, where I spent a restless night, notwithstanding my lack of fear.

Chapter XIX

*The author receives a letter and some **Kurst** newspapers*
— things turn pink — more of Onk Watwil.

EARLY NEXT MORNING I was awakened from a troubled dozing by
a rapping on the door of my cabin. Springing out of bed, I
shouted, "Who is it? Who's there?"

"A messenger," was the reply.

Cautiously I unbolted and unlocked the door, taking care not to
expose myself when opening it very slightly, and peeping through the
small crack. Outside I saw a young Lilliputian boy in a messenger's
uniform. If anything, he was even more cautious than I was, for
when I opened the door and he saw me peer out, he sprang back,
startled at the sight of my huge bulk. His action must have been one
purely of reflexive avoidance, for quickly he gathered courage and
stated that a gentleman had sent him to deliver a letter and some
day-after-the-morrow's morning papers. These he thrust through the
crack in the door, then hurried across the deck, clambered over the
rail, caught hold of a dangling hawser, and soon was spinning along
in a water scazpop bound for the shore.

The letter was from Hockdog, and after a few minutes lost in
searching for my magnifying glass I was able to read it. It stated:

> Man Mountain Gulliver:
>
> I am sending with bearer several Mildendo papers, which will
> confirm all that I told you last evening. Anything may happen. You
> can rely on me. Be careful.
>
> Your grateful servant,
>
> *Z.H.*

The first of the newspapers which I unfolded was the Kurst
News, and I am able to reproduce for the reader some of the items
I read there (minus the weird column twisting and type blurring
characteristic of Lilliputian newspapers in general) because they almost burned themselves into my memory, so greatly did they affect
me. Captioned with tall headline reading: **MAN MOUNTAIN GUL-
LIVER'S LECTURES INCITE RIOTS** — was the following article:

Mildendo — *(The day after Gulliver's second lecture.)* Late last evening, rioting broke out at the bakery located on the corner of Cat and Rat streets. Several hundred men, some of whom said they were hungry and were standing near the bakery to smell the pie, began shouting, "Give us some pie," whereupon the proprietor appeared and demanded they go away because they were interfering with his business. Somebody threw a stone and a general scuffle ensued, which was broken up only by the appearance of a squadron of police. Several of the men who were clubbed over the head and taken to jail admitted they had heard Gulliver's lecture in the afternoon.

WOMAN KILLS HUSBAND
Admits Gulliver to Blame

Mildendo — Late last night, a comely young woman who gave her name as Mrs. Ha Cha-Cha, was taken into custody for stabbing to death a man said to be her husband. The man's body was found lying stabbed through the neck with an ice pick in a kitchen of a house in **Kittitit Road**. The woman, taken by police from the porch of the same house where she stood screaming, after some questioning at headquarters, confessed the killing, but stated that she was only applying the Golden Rule, since her husband at many times would have liked to kill her. She admitted that she heard Gulliver's lecture in the afternoon.

COMMANDER WATWIL URGES
WAR OF EXTERMINATION
AGAINST MAN MOUNTAIN

Mildendo — Last night before a large group of persons assembled at the **Patriots' Public Drinking Palace**, Commander Onk Watwil, High Officer in Mildendo's Finest Cavalry Troop, advocated war to the death against Man Mountain Gulliver. The Commander asserted that Gulliver had set afloat subversive influences throughout Lilliput, which, if not halted at once by the most drastic means, would throw the country into a civil war. He further stated that there was nothing either good or new in the utterances of Gulliver. They were the same things a few long-haired, disgruntled, pink Blefuscudians had been uttering covertly in Mildendo for some time.

SWEET SHOP PROPRIETOR JAILED

Mildendo — Last night *Sagzt Flozzipup*, proprietor of a sweet shop on Ox-Cart street, was taken into custody by police and booked at the jail on suspicion of having sold pink ice-cream. Flozzipup stated to Kurst News reporters that either the arresting officer was color blind or some of Gulliver's confederates had slipped pink ice-cream into his freezers unbeknown to him.

SCNAKAD PROBE INTO
GULLIVER SCANDAL LOOMS

Mildendo — Faced last night with reliable information that an official permit had been issued to Man Mountain Gulliver to spread his outrageously subversive doctrines as he has recently done on two occasions, *Scnakador Hottzilip* stated that he would call for an immediate Scnakad investigation of the matter.

PROSECUTOR BLAHSQUAAKY
MAY SEEK INDICTMENT OF GULLIVER

Mildendo — In a brief statement issued last night, *Prosecutor Blahsquaaky* made it known that it was his opinion that, even though a permit to lecture had been granted Gulliver, such a permit was mute and squashy under Lilliputian law, there being no officer empowered to issue such a permit. This fact the prosecutor said, rendered Man Mountain Gulliver subject to criminal indictment, and that he would probably issue and file the writ forthwith.

LITTLE GIRL SETS HOUSE ON FIRE

Mildendo — Last night little *Zizzo Xnot* struck a match and lit the curtains in her parents home on Wool street. The house burned to the ground. When questioned as to why she did it, little Zizzo said that she liked to see pink flames. Her parents admitted that Zizzo had attended Gulliver's afternoon lecture with them.

**EPIDEMIC OF 'PINKEYE'
BREAKS OUT IN NORTHERN
SECTION OF CITY**

Mildendo — Late today it was observed that the ravaging epidemic of 'pinkeye' which swept into the northern portion of Mildendo was rapidly spreading. Several score new patients were rushed to the Mildendo Hospital for treatment. When they were questioned by a Kurst News representative, most of the new patients treated at the hospital stated that they had attended one or both of the recent lectures given by Man Mountain Gulliver.

The reader may well imagine how chagrined I was by these newspaper articles. "Pink", as used in the Kurst News, referred to a political organization of scant numbers and unpopular principles in Mildendo. On one or two occasions, I had heard Nitpooperler Hirear make brief and uncomplimentary remarks anent "Pink" agitators and "Pink" doctrines, and upon being questioned he informed me that the "Pinks" were a subversive group of lazy louts who would not work and whose only steadfast belief was the righteousness of robbery and anarchy. Naturally I was troubled. For the life of me I could not see by any stretch of the imagination how any sane person could associate me or my lectures with anarchy. Turning to another page in the newspaper I read the following:

**SAVANT SAYS GULLIVER'S GABBLE
ANCIENT DESPOTISM IN DISGUISE**

Mildendo Goosaree — *Professor Snoopdeap* of Mildendo University said yesterday that the "Divinity" to which Gulliver has alluded in his lectures is none other that the "Divine Providence" used by the ancient despots of Lilliput to delude their subjects, who were, in olden days, held in virtual slavery upon this island. He made a strong plea before the students in one of his classes to beware of falling into delusive snares which would deprive them of the hard won liberties of their forefathers, and denounced those among them who had been giving too much credence to the dangerous utterances of the gigantic foreigner.

GENERAL OSSDOC SOUNDS TOCSIN

Mildendo — General Ossdoc, in an exclusive interview with Kurst News representatives last evening, stated that, although he had conceived the greatest respect for Man Mountain Gulliver, he did see the danger in his recent utterances. "While I cannot minimize the greatness of character with which his ancestor, Lemuel Gulliver, was endowed, that very fact should cause us to scrutinize carefully the facts surrounding the present visit of a giant to our shores. He may be an agent of Blefuscudian 'Pinks' who, knowing the respect we have for the great Lemuel, seek to throw us off guard by sending here another Gulliver. Our world is going through difficult and uneasy times. The Scanezi are watching us with the eyes of a vulture. Who knows but what they have sent the giant here to undermine our morale — possibly to do us actual physical harm? I do not assert these things — I ask them."

In spite of all these disheartening articles, I could not bring myself to believe that a people only yesterday so friendly to me were actually becoming distrustful and hostile toward me. It did not seem possible. Especially the statements in the last article seemed impossible. They were so utterly absurd, and the General had been so warm in his show of friendship toward me. I hardly need assert that I did not know a Blefuscudian, "Pink" or otherwise, from a Lilliputian, and, so far from being an agent of the Scanezi, I had never even seen a Scanezi. Thrusting the paper aside I sat back to think the whole matter over.

At the outset, I resolved to go about my business and await developments, taking only precautions that common sense demanded in the light of the situation. For instance, I would not go ashore until I received some assurance of safety, and I would not deliver my third lecture the following week unless the atmosphere had definitely cleared. I further determined that at all cost I would not fall into hostile Lilliputian hands, but would do nothing to arouse hostility against me. If given the opportunity, I would try to convince all Lilliput of my true and sincere friendship; I would submit to no trial on any charge should any be preferred. I would injure no Lilliputian, but if attacked would beware of the paralytic ray and Lilliputian firearms. If necessary I would fire a few warning shots with a rifle.

These resolutions having been formulated, I remained idle in the cabin till early afternoon, then taking up courage, unbarred the door and went out upon the deck. Slowly and with caution I made a tour of inspection to satisfy myself that there were no lurking Lilliputians aboard, then sat down upon a pile of furled sail. No one came to molest my solitude, and neither scazpop nor ship was to be seen on the shining golden plaque of water lying between the *Night-Hawk* and the shore. The sun went down and I remained there through the twilight watching the reflector rays flash like flaming rockets as one by one they burst into brilliancy in the sky over Mildendo. While the lack of visitors was not necessarily an indication of hostility toward me, there having been many days when no visitors came aboard the *Night-Hawk*, it seemed, nevertheless, to corroborate the evidence of unfriendliness contained in the Kurst News.

Just after darkness had descended I was startled out of my quiet meditation by the sound of a voice directly at my elbow. Startled is not exactly the right word. In fact, I was deeply shaken by the sudden appearance, without any warning whatsoever, of a Lilliputian. He had approached the opposite side of the *Night-Hawk* in a small, silent boat, had by some means never known to me scaled the side of the ship, and noiselessly come to within my very reach without my being aware of his presence. He was in the uniform of a Donkgop's aide and by this token I knew he had come from the Donkgop.

"To Gulliver a message," were the words that startled me, and he handed me a letter. When I had in some measure regained my composure I retired to the cabin where I might read the letter by aid of a light and my magnifying glass. It read:

Hot Day – 9th Anniversary after Hot Hot Day
Mildendo on the Island of Lilliput in Mid-Ocean

To Gulliver Greeting — and to him Greeting:

Confusion and doubt having arisen concerning, pertaining to, and with reference to the legality, propriety, desirability, virtue, necessity, convenience, political expedience, and economic aptness of your lectures, you are hereby requested to squash any and all of those devised, planned, or contemplated for the future, all previous permits, orders, injunctions, or licenses to the contrariwise or likewise notwithstanding and stand-with-notting. Your reference to divinity approaches treason, and is my face "pink"!

Yours — The Donkgop

Medid Wherding

Donkgop of Lilliput

Before dismissing the messenger who had brought me this unpleasant missive, I inquired as to the means by which he had come aboard the **Night-Hawk**. His reply was civil enough, but entirely noncommittal. "The aides of the Donkgop," he said, "have certain initiative and certain resources." With saying that he raced to the starboard rail, and bounded over. Before I reached the place where he had disappeared, he was in his boat and bound for shore, so I am still in the dark as to how he went up and down the sheer side of a ship with no apparent mechanical help. He may have been a "human fly", or still more likely, he may have been equipped with some small mechanical contrivance which I did not see. I never ceased to marvel at the ingenuity of the Lilliputians. With them anything is not beyond possible accomplishment, and the less any particular accomplishment is expected, the more likely it is to be accomplished.

That night I retired to a barred and shuttered cabin in a more uneasy frame of mind than ever. Sleep seemed out of the question, yet so necessary. Bad dreams troubled the little sleep I had. What would the morrow bring? This question, which weighed heavily on my mind, began receiving answers with the coming of the dawn.

Zucow Hockdog came aboard before daylight and called to me at the cabin door, which I opened to admit him at once. He brought more newspapers with him, and as he entered the door he glanced back furtively as though he was fearful lest somebody had followed him. "Man Mountain Gulliver," said he, "your very life is imperiled. Not only have **Articles of Impeachment** charging you with many crimes been drawn and your arrest ordered, but large numbers of people in Mildendo have been roused to such a fury by the items in the Kurst News that some attempt may be made to take your life without recourse to the law. I recommend your immediate departure before some harm befalls you. While I am willing to do anything within my power to help you, I believe there is nothing I can do at present. If I should be seen with you now, my own life would be almost certainly forfeited. The frenzy of a Mildendo mob is a fearful thing for even so great and mighty a creature as you are. I must —"

Hockdog's discourse was broken by the unmistakable sound of

many scurrying feet upon the deck. His face blanched, and for a moment I stood as though frozen solid with — with (yes, I must confess
it) fear. The continued sounds were such as to leave no doubt that
a large party of Lilliputians had boarded the **Night-Hawk**. I came to
my senses at once with the sudden realization that they might set the
ship afire. Quickly picking up Hockdog, I hid him in a cracker-box
which I placed on a high shelf, then made my way to a port-hole and
peered out cautiously. In the dim light of the dawn I saw perhaps
seventy-five Lilliputians scurrying hither and thither, nosing in and
around coiled ropes and furled sails as though searching for something. Among them I finally discerned one whom I knew — none
other than my avowed enemy, Onk Watwil. I observed that he was
in a very drunken and disheveled condition. He reeled around curs-
ing incoherently in such a way that it was evident he scarcely knew
what he was doing. This circumstance was a fortunate one. It provided me with an inspiration. Stealthily I tiptoed to the door, silently
removed the bar and released the lock, then going back to the port-
hole, watched the movements of Watwil until he approached near
the door. The opportune moment having arrived, I sprang to the
door, rushed out, seized the dazed little fellow by the nape of the
neck, jerked him into the cabin, and locked the door behind me. As
quick as I had been, I was not able to escape a painful slash across my
right forearm from Watwil's sabre, which he had drawn with lightning quickness the very instant I touched him. Once I had him in the
cabin I disarmed him and sat him down none too gently upon the top
of a table. This experience, which must have been quite shocking,
seemed to sober him somewhat. He sat staring up at me, his face
tense with anger but with steady eyes.

"Watwil," I said, "I want only friendly relations with you and
with the people of Lilliput. But conditions being such as they are,
your being guilty of invading my ship with the drunken rabble, and
self-preservation being to me, as to you, a first law, I have taken you
as a hostage. Your safety — your very life depends upon my safety,"
and to the end that I might put into execution my expressed design,
I took a stout cord from a cabinet drawer and forcibly bound my
hostage hand and foot.

A great commotion had arisen on the deck, to quiet which I
placed Watwil before the port-hole and directed him to order all Lilliputians ashore for his own safety. This he did with none too much
resolution and emphasis, so I bellowed to the mob that I would kill

Watwil unless every Lilliputian aboard went ashore without further delay. Gradually the riotous noise died down, and the rabble, realizing that I meant business, slowly and reluctantly left the ship. As soon as I was reasonably satisfied that all had departed, I sat Watwil again on the table, and, addressing him in a tone of voice vibrant with the indignation I deeply felt, asked him the purpose of his unbidden visit to my ship.

"That, Man Mountain Gulliver, is a thing I need not answer; yet, since it is a thing of which I am not ashamed, I will answer, even though in speaking to you I speak to a pig — all the greater pig for your greater size. I came here to perform a service to my country. I came here, pig, to butcher you — to cut your lying throat, and roast your lardy carcass in your own pig-sty."

"An admirable purpose, and a real undertaking," I commented in my most sarcastic tone, "but one that might have been more efficiently executed had you come less dazed by the fumes of strong drink."

"The comfort you feel in having me at your mercy shall be of short duration. Whether or not you kill me is a matter of small import, and of no ultimate import to you, for, whether I live or die, before another darkness falls on Lilliput, you shall be dead, and your carcass dismembered and destroyed. My country is awake and knows the manner of treatment best suited for traitors and 'Pinks'. You would die were you a hundred — a thousand times your size."

One could not help admiring the courage with which these words were spoken. That Onk Watwil was a brave man was past denying. Here he sat, helplessly bound at the mercy of a man forty times his size — a man who could have popped his neck more easily than a poultry-man wrings a chicken's. How I regretted the train of events and misunderstandings which led to this unhappy situation. I regretted having to keep Watwil a prisoner, yet, that my life was in grave peril was now beyond any doubt. I tossed him from the table onto a bed where he would be more comfortable, and set forth. I had work to do — to prepare to defend myself, and, in the event that no reconciliation with the Lilliputians was possible, to be prepared to weigh anchor and put to sea.

Chapter XX

Still more of Onk Watwil; Articles of Impeachment; the Navy employed; the author departs.

MY FIRST CONCERN was to see that the firearms aboard were loaded and ready for use. Two rifles and a shotgun were set in order and loaded. In addition I placed an automatic and a pistol in my pockets. Next I descended to the engine-room, refueled the motors, and after disengaging the gears leading to the screw shaft, tested the engines. I had great difficulty in getting it started owing to the weakness of the storage batteries which had run down considerably during their long period of disuse. Once I had the engines running, I set the generators to going and left them, in spite of the fact that there was very little fuel aboard, for I could not well run the risk of being unable to start the engine on a moment's notice. Although the *Night-Hawk* was still well provisioned with enough food to last one man for two or three years if necessary, there was a scarcity of water aboard. While this might lead to hardship if I had to set sail, I had, in that event, no intention of trying to navigate the *Night-Hawk* further than some port in Australia or New Zealand, and once there to dispose of her. Besides being nothing much of a sailor myself, the *Night-Hawk* was too large a craft for one person to man successfully very long. When I had finished in the engine room, I made a complete tour around the deck, drawing up all dangling chains and ropes. I then approached the cabin to see after my prisoner. Just as I placed by hand upon the latch, I remembered that I should arrange the anchor so that I could cut it loose quickly if necessary, and as I shoved open the door, I turned back to attend to the matter. Just at that instant, the loud report of a gun boomed from the cabin and a charge of shot splintered the deck directly behind my heels. When I turned around I saw Watwil through the cabin door stretched out unconscious against the wall with my shotgun lying on the floor before him. He had managed, trussed up though he was, to get my gun from a peg on the wall, where he had seen me place it, then lay in wait to assassinate me. No doubt the weight of the weapon had saved my life. The combined circumstances of his small stature and his being

tied as he was, made it impossible for him to raise the gun sufficiently to shoot me, but he had made the attempt, and in so doing
the violent repercussion had flung him against the wall and knocked
him senseless. Acting almost instinctively and without thought, as
one does in such emergencies, I rushed to Watwil, plucked him up
by the belt, and hung him on a coat-hook screwed into the wall.
I had no more than finished with my unconscious would-be murderer than I saw one of the largest battleships of the Lilliputian fleet
steaming out of Sizez Harbor, round a jutting point, and head toward the **Night-Hawk**. Whether to lock myself in the cabin or to
occupy some position on the deck was a question which threw me
into a momentary quandary. As the man-of-war drew nearer I chose
the latter course, for although it put me in some danger of hostile
gun-fire and the paralytic ray, it would afford me some opportunity
to ward off any boarding party which might try to set fire to the ship.
Then too, if flight became necessary, I needed unimpeded access to
the engine-room, which could not be had from the cabin. Taking a
rifle and the shotgun with me, I crept along the deck to a vantage
point behind a coiled cable and remained secreted there until the
battleship came within hearing distance of my voice, whereupon I
fired a shot into the air to attract attention, and shouted a warning
to approach no nearer. The ship slackened its speed but kept right on
coming. I shouted another warning, but still the ship came toward
me, and on the deck I could see a group of sailors whipping around
the paralytic ray projector to turn it in my direction. The effects
of that horrible machine were something I dared not risk, therefore
lying against the cable coil, I took careful aim with my rifle, and
fortunately (I say fortunately, for I am a very poor marksman) the
bullet sped true. It smashed the lens and reflectors of the machine
to bits, and served effectively to bring the dreadnought to a full stop.
Shouting again, I informed the enemy of my willingness to parley,
but with no more than two men who should come aboard alone and
unarmed, the ship to remain where it had halted. Following this, the
sailors within my line of vision remained stationary at their posts, evidently awaiting orders, while two or three officers moved about on
the deck and seemed to be holding an animated conference among
themselves. At last I heard echoing across the expanse of water between a shout from the throat of somebody, who must at some time
have had considerable training as a politician, which signified assent
to my proposal, and, in a few minutes, a pea-pod motor boat con-

taining two men was lowered. Rapidly it sped toward me, and as it drew along beside the **Night-Hawk**, I recognized Nitpooperler Hirear. The other man I did not know. Even then, in spite of all that had happened since I last saw him, I still had complete confidence in the honor and integrity of Nitpooperler Hirear. He had been the best friend I had had in Lilliput, and I felt that friendship would continue if it were possible for him to continue it and not incur the opprobrium of a traitor among his people. Trusting him as I did, I left the protective cover of the coiled cable, and let down the basket to hoist the emissaries aboard. Hirear's greeting was courteous though reserved and matter-of-fact. He introduced his companion, *Skyresh Bagumsock*, at the same time informing me that he was a police officer commissioned to serve me with **Articles of Impeachment** and effect my arrest. Both were polite enough not to insist that I submit to a formal Lilliputian salutation.

"Nitpooperler Hirear," I pleaded, "can't all this mess be settled in some amiable manner? I have not wittingly done any wrong, and have in all things been governed by the best of motives. During my stay upon your shores, I have had in my heart only the warmest affection for the people of Lilliput, and have never at any time acted with malice or anything but the best of intentions. If I have failed and committed some wrong, it has been occasioned through pitfalls latent in your intricate society — pitfalls such as a stranger could not in all justice be expected to see and avoid. A few short days ago even you and the learned Wickdomp Ooick were of the opinion that my lectures were not only legal, but might prove to be a positive force for good in Lilliputian life. Is there no way to right myself without standing criminal trial? Is it possible that a man can be tried criminally for an act officially sanctioned by the highest officials in the land?"

Nitpooperler Hirear looked up into my face and his words softened into something like an expression of his old friendliness. "All you say is true, Man Mountain, but there is nothing I can do about it, however much I might like to. The legality of your permit to preach has been called into question by legal proceedings, and there is nothing I can do to stop them. Only your trial can authoritatively determine the legality of the permit. But the utterance of 'Pink' doctrine is not the only crime with which you stand charged, nor the only one with which you will be charged, seeing that you have only this morning forcibly detained the person of Onk Watwil and have committed an overt act of war in firing upon the Lilliputian navy. No, Gulliver, I see no way of raising you again in the esteem of the people. You have gone beyond the pale of the law. Read him the **Articles**, Officer Bagumsock." The officer began reading:

ARTICLES OF IMPEACHMENT
AGAINST ARTHUR C. GULLIVER

Being a summation of his high crimes, misdemeanors, and contraventions against and in violation of the laws of Lilliput.

To the defendant, Arthur C. Gulliver.

GREETING — and to him GREETING, GREETING:

You, Man Mountain, *Quinbus Flestrin II*, otherwise known as Arthur C. Gulliver, are hereby and herewith commanded by the sovereign authority of the Island of Lilliput to submit yourself to arrest and trial for the high crimes, misdemeanors, and contraventions against and in violation of the laws of Lilliput, which high crimes, misdemeanors, and contraventions are hereinafter set forth in these articles to wit, and to witter:

ARTICLE I

The sovereign authority of the Island of Lilliput alleges that the defendant aforesaid has introduced upon the Island of Lilliput a schipidtpot which produces moving pictures upon a sheet, and which is calculated to, and in fact, does lower and debase the morals and integrity of the Lilliputian people, contrary to statute prohibiting schipidtpot fabricated immorality;

ARTICLE II

That the said defendant aforementioned has uttered Pink doctrines subversive to the government of the Island of Lilliput;

ARTICLE III

That said Pink doctrines so uttered by the aforesaid defendant have incited riots and violence in the city of Mildendo;

ARTICLE IV

That said Pink doctrines so uttered by the said defendant have contributed to the delinquency of minors;

ARTICLE V

That said Pink doctrines so uttered by the defendant afore-mentioned have incited children to commit arson;

ARTICLE VI

That said Pink doctrines so uttered by the said defendant aforementioned have incited men and women to murder;

ARTICLE VII

That the said defendant has obtained unlawfully naval and military secrets;

ARTICLE VIII

And lastly, that the defendant has repeatedly violated the Lilli-putian drinking laws by failure to consume his portion daily —

WHEREFORE the sovereign authority of the Island of Lilli-put demands that the body of the said defendant be dismem-bered and consumed by evaporation.

When the officer had finished reading the **Articles** he paused to breathe deeply, then added, "To these **Articles** will be added those covering your acts of this morning — kidnapping and direct treason. Do you submit yourself to arrest?"

"I do not," I answered promptly. "With all the love I bear for the people of Lilliput, I would not enjoy being dismembered and evaporated by them."

"Oh, that shall be done to you whether you enjoy it or not. The Skorks of Mildendo always get their man," — and eyeing the bulk of me towering above him he finished with the afterthought — "even though they have to call in the army and navy."

"They didn't get Lemuel," I answered, then once more pleaded with the Nitpooperler, "Is there no way out of this? It is all so regret-table."

"Regrettable, indeed," he replied, "but I see no way out except to stand trial."

"In that case, goodbye. I am taking the way I see out, and I'm taking Watwil with me as an earnest that no Lilliputian craft will follow me. Into the basket, gentlemen, and I will lower you."

Skyresh Bagumsock hesitated but a moment. A movement as though I intended to pick up the shot-gun was all that was needed to make him see the wisdom of getting into the basket along with the Nitpooperler. I lowered them to their waiting motor boat and they sped away toward the dreadnought.

After hauling the anchor, I set the rudder in such a way as to cause the *Night-Hawk* to swing in a narrow arc of one-hundred eighty degrees, made my way to the engine-room, engaged the screw in gear, and accelerated the motors to full speed. Beginning to move very slowly the *Night-Hawk* gained momentum very rapidly, so that before the complete turn had been maneuvered she was going fast enough to cause a sharp lurch to the starboard. When I came on deck again, the compass showed her heading east-northeast by east. Unleashing the helm, I spun it around to level her off and left the shores of Lilliput fast receding behind me. Through my spyglass I watched the dreadnought off the stern. No sooner had Nitpooperler Hirear and Skyresh Bagumsock clambered aboard than she started full steam ahead in pursuit. A small shell fired from her forward gun burst and ricocheted along the forward deck and sent splinters flying. Without returning the fire I crouched down prayerfully hoping that none of their missiles would strike me. More shells were fired, some of which burst with a frightful boom against the stern just above the water line.

It was at this juncture that I heard a voice near me shouting. "Gulliver! Gulliver! Gulliver!" Staggering along the deck and using the cabin wall for support was Zucow Hockdog gazing about every which-where, looking for me, and shouting my name. In the rapid sequence of events which had taken place that morning I had completely and perhaps ungratefully forgotten the one remaining Lilliputian friend I had. I answered his call whereupon, spying me, he reeled dazedly over to where I lay near the wheel. He had a cruel bump on his forehead caused, as he told me, by a fall in the cracker box when it slipped from the shelf in the cabin as the *Night-Hawk* lurched in negotiating her right-about turn.

"You aren't going to take me away from Lilliput, are you?" he pleaded, his face white from the shock of his recent fall and nostalgic tears running down his cheeks at the thought of leaving his beloved island.

"What can I do now?" I asked. "How can I return you now? And would you not be in danger of imprisonment, or even death if you returned?"

"Death in Lilliput is better than life elsewhere," he answered. "Please, Gulliver take me back. Oh, how I wish I were not here!"

For once in his life the non-volitionist must have gained control over the elements of his science, for at that moment the **Night-Hawk** made a sharp dip, and, the sea washing over the port rail forward, washed him through a scupper. Notwithstanding the shrapnel still bursting all around, I could not allow my friend to drown. As fast as I possibly could I obtained a lifeline and tossed it overboard near where I had seen Hockdog disappear. In spite of the fact that I had not an opportunity to stop the **Night-Hawk**, the life-preserver landed within the reach of the bobbing little Zucow. When I began to draw in the lifeline he protested frantically, even going so far as to stand upright on the narrow cork rim buoying him up and make signs indicating that he wanted me to release the line. Finally I understood. He, knowing that those aboard the dreadnought had seen through their powerful telescopes what was taking place aboard my fleeing craft, wished to remain on the life-preserver until picked up by his own countrymen. I complied with his wish and dropped the line.

Although I would have liked nothing better than to take a Lilliputian back to the United States with me I could not find it in my heart to take Zucow by force after seeing his tears and realizing how dearly he loved his native country. Nostalgia would have eaten his soul away in no time. True, I still had Onk Watwil aboard. For a few moments I debated whether to take him along with me or set him adrift on a life-preserver to be rescued as Hockdog would be. I decided to follow the latter course for three reasons. First, Watwil, being an avowed enemy, gave little promise of ever becoming friendly or companionable; secondly, I thought of Mezarra, his wife, and could not find it in myself to make her a virtual, if not soon an actual widow; thirdly, Onk Watwil was a cunning and crafty little fellow who had fallen short of killing me that very morning only by the intervention of Providence. Taking him down from the hook on the wall and holding him at arms length by his belt, I cut his bonds and tossed him into the sea along with a life-preserver. This act of mine proved to be a valuable stratagem. The pursuers having to halt twice to rescue first Hockdog then Watwil permitted me to outdistance them completely. Soon the island of Lilliput was no longer in view and I had lost sight of the tiny man-of-war. I was alone at sea.

Steering a course which I had roughly calculated would bring me to the northwest coast of Australia or at least upon some of the islands of the East Indian Archipelago I kept on going unswervingly. With mingled emotions I sailed away from Lilliput. Disappointment — at having been compelled to leave so soon before having completed the extensive research I had planned and without having collected the articles I had hoped to carry home with me to place in a museum, was lightened only by the joyous relief of having escaped with my life. A week before I would not even have dreamed that the Lilliputian people could turn against me — that they would force me to flee for my life. What a volatile little folk they are. I could not escape the reflection that the good opinion of man the world over is a thing far too ephemeral to accept as the foundation upon which to rear security. Social ties are flimsy, and social passion harsh. Love that is spoken of as eternal, and honor well deserved can, like a whiff of smoke on a far horizon, blow away *so* fast.

Until nearly dawn the following morning I continued to steer straight east by north, at which time I became so weary of the watch that I shut off the engines and dropped anchor. I had to have some sleep. Therefore, leaving a strong lamp burning on the mizzentruck, and making sure that both port and starboard lights were burning, I retreated to the cabin and was soon deep in a sleep from which I did not awaken until late in the afternoon, at which time I resumed my voyage.

By way of coming quickly to an unpleasant part of my story, I wish only to preface it with the remark that misfortune at sea seemed to be a spectre always haunting me. It came without warning the third night out while I was again sleeping in the cabin. I was aware only of a sudden and violent lurching of the **Night-Hawk**. Nautical instruments slid off the table, dishes came clattering and crashing out of cupboards onto the floor, a mast came smashing down upon the deck. For a brief instant the **Night-Hawk** seemed to right herself, then lurched even more violently in the opposite direction. More dishes crashed down upon the floor, and I distinctly heard the anchor chain clang with an odd ringing sound as one of its links parted, leaving the anchor to sink to the bottom of the sea. It was as though a giant god Neptune, or two of them, had reached up from the floor of the ocean, grasped the hull of the vessel in both hands, and was shaking her like a child trying to shake coins out of a toy bank. Every timber in her hulk quivered and trembled, creaked and moaned, cracked and split; then the furies of hell bore down upon her. Amid an indescribable din of shrieking and howling, splitting of timbers, and crashing of spars, I found myself floating in a lashing sea, in utter darkness, surrounded by all manner of wreckage and debris against which swirling currents flung me unmercifully. By queer freak of chance and the intervention of Providence, I found myself clinging to a capsized lifeboat, and there I clung till morning, while the water around me gradually became calm again.

When morning came, I felt half dead from remaining submerged in the water so long. My hands were numb and my strength ebbing, but I managed with great effort to right the boat and get in. It was, of course, almost full of water, but the air tanks were unbroken, and therefore it floated well. Hour after hour I laboriously and painfully bailed water with my hands until I had the boat nearly empty.

By that time I realized that a typhoon had literally smashed the **Night-Hawk** to bits, and, strangely enough, the first clear thought about the disaster was not connected with my own precarious predicament, but was the despairing thought that the last vestige of anything to show that I had been to Lilliput was lost — utterly and irretrievably lost.

How long I drifted in the Pacific Ocean in that open boat suffering exposure and deprivation I shall never know, but some days afterward, when I had been reduced to a pitiful state of emaciation and delirium, I was rescued and taken aboard the **S. S. Standard Bearer** bound out of Bombay for San Francisco.

Epilogue

In which the author ends the account of his life up to the present and sets down a few of his reflections

WHILE I CANNOT DENY that Providence has been bountiful with me in more than one respect — in carrying me through many perils to ultimate safety, in preserving me whole in body and (from my viewpoint) in mind, and in permitting me a glimpse into a part of the world no living man, save the natives there, has ever seen — yet, I cannot forego the observation that I, like one unnamed but better known, have been marked by Melancholy for her own.

Entirely alone in this world of man I sit on a high pinnacle, caressed only by the cold currents of my own solitude, the ugly worms of futility and despair gnawing out my heart. What does it avail me to know the truth when I am the only one who knows it? What good does it do for me to batter out my brains on the solid wall of man's stupid incredulity? In this, Fate has been cruel. She has led me down the rainbow, but refused the pot of gold — the ultimate proof of where I have been. I came home empty-handed, and, therefore, because of truth uttered but uncorroborated, empty-headed in the eyes of my fellow men.

Two weeks after my rescue, the **S. S. Standard Bearer** docked in San Francisco, and Captain George Wilhelm, who had showed me every kindness during the voyage, turned me over to the police, having concluded, as do all others, that my statements concerning Lilliput were proof positive of mental aberration. So here I now am, and likely to be for some time, returned as a fugitive to my starting point — Spoop Sanitorium.

As the saying goes — "While there is life, there is hope;" and, although I am despondent to the point of death, I shall not lose all hope. Perhaps some day I again shall sail beyond the sunset and return bearing my vindication and my proofs.

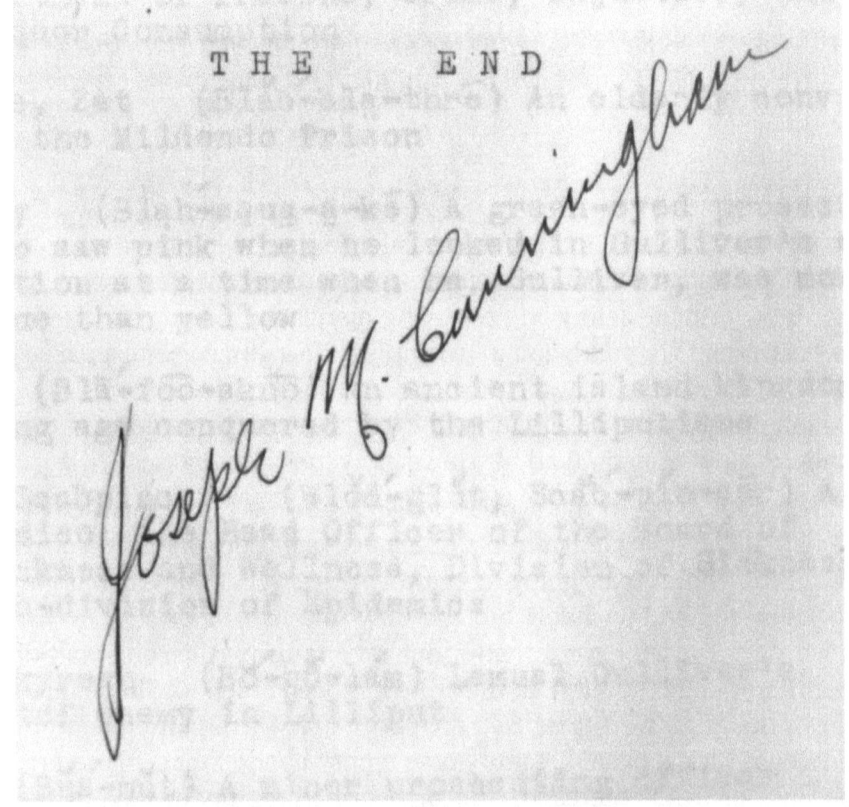

THE　　END

Joseph M. Cunningham

Glossary

Ammzstyo, Stonk [ăm-mēz'-tyō]
A modern Lilliputian poet; author of **Skonkup Schklel.**

Ampspamps, Stinglot [ămps'-pămps]
A famous Lilliputian mathematician.

Bagumsock, Skyresh [băg'-ŭm-sŏck]
A highly respected police officer on the Mildendo force.

bakdsemis [bākd'-sĕm-ēs]
Professors of a science composed largely of psychology.

Banzatti, Stickeo [băn-zăt'-tē]
The name of a certain condemned criminal in the Mildendo Prison.

bibancrib [bĭb'-ăn-crĭb]
A Lilliputian institution devoted to the education of youth; roughly — very roughly — a secondary school.

Bittzzora, Barrister [bĭtzz'-zō-rä]
A Nitpooperler, and an unfortunate one; the Head of the Department of Prisons, Crime, Injustice, and Liquor Consumption.

Blabblathre, Zat [blăb'-blạ-thrē]
An elderly convict in the Mildendo Prison.

Blahsquaaky, Prosecutor [blạh'-squạh-ạ-kē]
A green-eyed prosecutor who saw pink when he looked in Gulliver's direction at a time when he, Gulliver, was more blue than yellow.

Blefuscu [blā'-foo-skoo]
An ancient island kingdom long ago conquered by the Lilliputians.

Blodglut, Scabpincer [blŏd'-glŭt, scăb'-pĭn-çēr]
A medico; the Head Officer of the Board of Sickness and Wellness, Division of Sickness, Subdivision of Epidemics.

Bolgolam, Skyresh [bō'-gō-lăm]
Lemuel Gulliver's chief enemy in Lilliput.

Buzknut [bŭz'-nŭt]
A minor prosecuting officer who concentrates on raking in the booty.

Canndappletus [cănn-dăpp'-lĕ-tŭs]
Seat of the Lilliputian Naval Academy.

Chalbrig [chăl'-brĭg]
A petty naval officer.

Chizzlewit [chĭz'-ĕl-wĭt]
A very common Lilliputian name.

Cornhuski [cōrn-hŭs'-kē]
The title of a poem by Snarle Kandrug.

Corziltah [cōr-zĭl'-ta̱]
The name of a farmer's wife who lived in the region of Kerwilly.

Cracklfire, Zerro Zero [crăck'-ĕl-fī-ēr]
A popular Mildendo columnist whose lengthy column seldom gets anywhere, though a little of it goes a long way.

crinkplunk [crĭnk'-plŭnk]
A family institution in rural Lilliput patronized by the whole family for diverse and sundry purposes; an outbuilding adorned chiefly with star and crescent-shaped apertures.

Custonk [cŭs'-tŏnk]
An old section of Mildendo.

Dampop, Captain [dăm'-pŏp]
An army officer rebuked by General Ossdoc for having fled from an exploding snickdid.

Degrethre [dē-grē'-thrē]
A Lilliputian police captain; the title of his office.

Diddledump [dĭd'-dĕl-dŭmp]
A common first name in Lilliput.

Dinnaw [dĭn'-na̤]
A given name.

disthedons [dĭs-thē'-dōns]
Those adhering to the doctrines of the distheismdon; those who believe that everybody does what pleases him best, or that women do what they please, while men do the best they can.

distheismdon [dĭs-thē'-ĭsm-dŏn]
(See disthedons.)

donjon [dŭn'-jŭn]
Some region, place, or building in Mildendo prated about by Cracklfire.

Donkgop [dŏnk'-gŏp]
He is the IT — the chief executive of Lilliput — an elective office, the powers appertaining to which make monarchs appear as pikers.

dudecker [doo'-dĕck-ẽr]
The early Lilliputian legislature before the paynetakit became part of it and the tricamerate evolved.

Esquerfle, Whangdompertit [ĕs'-kẽr-flē, whăng-dŏm'-pẽr-tĭt]
Skrewky Noshort's chief fezerdick.

estibelobs [ĕs-tēb'-ĕl-ŏbs]
Literally — implorers; they evolved into the paynetakit.

Ezoyoi, Zee [ēz-zō'-yo͞e]
The name of a little girl.

fezerdick [fĕz'-ẽr-dĭck]
An appointive officer, appointed throught the influence of a tricamerator; one who practices fezerdickery.

fezerdickery [fĕz'-ẽr-dĭck-ẽr-ē]
Any of various practices designed to draw in the booty.

Flebrow, Nitpooperler [flē'-brŏ̤w]
High Civil Officer of Elections and Politics.

Flestrin II, Quinbus [flĕs'-trĭn, kwĭn'-bŭs]
A name sometimes applied to Gulliver by the Lilliputians; Lemuel Gulliver had been called Quinbus Flestrin.

Flimnap [flĭm'-năp]
High Treasurer under the Lilliputian Emperor in the days of Lemuel Gulliver.

Flozzipup, Sagzt [flŏz'-zĭ-pŭp, săg'-skŭt]
The name of a Mildendo sweet-shop proprietor.

Fluzez, Whillila [floo'-zēe, whĭl-lī'-lạ]
A girl friend of Mezzara Watwil.

Fuzzlebeanz, Blaptrap [fŭz'-zĕl-bēns, blăp'-trăp]
An attorney engaged by Gulliver after his injury by the scazpop.

Ganhorg, Jaaypie [găn'-hōrg, jā'-pī]
A wealthy Lilliputian banker and industrialist; a get-goer without peer.

Garnite, Nitpooperler [gạr'-nīt]
Head of the Bureau of Garbage Disposal, Onion Culture, and Sandburr Conservation.

Gohing, Twan [gō'-hĭng, twăn]
High Lilliputian Attorney — advisor to the Donkgop and to the tricamerate.

Goosaree, Mildendo [goo'-sạr-ē]
A university in Mildendo.

Grafnix [grăf'-nĭx]
High, or Top Magistrate.

Gravinap, Nitpooperler [gră'-vĭ-năp]
High Officer of Health, Happiness, Disease, and Mortality.

Gue, Golbasto Momarem Evlame Gurdilo Shefin Mully Ully
[goo, gōl-băs'-tō (mō-mạr'-ĕm or mō'-măr-ĕm) ē-vl'ạ-mē gŭr-dĭl'-ō shĕ'-fĭn mŭl'-lē ŭl'-lē] The last king of Lilliput.

Hirear, Nitpooperler Oxmut [hī'-rear, ŏx'-mŭt]
Head of the Department of Gambling, Recreation, Amusement, and Public Works.

Hockdog, Zucow [hŏck'-dŏg, zōō'-kow]
The non-volitionist healer who was very kind to Gulliver.

Honksnort [hŏnk'-snōrt]
The name of a pupil in primary school.

Horbo, Skaywan [hōr'-bō, skā'-wăn]
A once-popular Scnakador whose downfall was brought about by his defiance of the paynetakit.

Hordapyl, Scordut [hōrd'-ä-pīl, skōr'-dŭt]
A rich farmer of Skaldit kire.

Hottzilip, Scnakador [hŏtt'-zĭ-lĭp]
The Scnakador who threatened a Scnakad investigation into the alleged spreading of pink doctrines by Gulliver.

Huzzlebee, Zapear [hŭz'-zĕl-bē, zăp'-ear]
The name of a little boy who came to Gulliver's party.

ix nertz oink blutz [ĭx nẽrtz oink blōōts]
De minimis non curat lex (the law does not consider trifles).

Jizpip [gĭz'-pĭp]
The name of a little girl in primary school.

Kandrug, Snarle [kăn'-drōōg, snärl]
A modern Lilliputian poet; author of **Cornhuski**, such as it is.

Kerwilly [kẽr'-wĭl-lē]
A cross-roads country village in Lilliput.

Kittitit Road [kĭtt'-ĭ-tĭt]
A residence street in Mildendo.

Kladanks [klă'-dănks]
A Lilliputian actor of note.

Kurst News kẽrst
A popular daily newspaper in Mildendo.

Looddlyn [lōōd'-lĭn]
The name of a large theatre in Mildendo.

Luie, Sizzy [loo'-ē, sĭz'-zē]
The name of a child at Gulliver's party.

Mildendo [mĭl-dĕn'-dō]
The largest city in Lilliput and its capital.

Mizzlit, Jawge [mĭzz'-lĭt]
The name of a Lilliputian boy at Gulliver's party.

moronsnidge [mŏr'-ōn-snĭdge]
A mild, though persistent form of Lilliputian insanity thinly disguised as a card game.

Nabsack [năb'-săck]
A term of respect used by an inferior when addressing a superior in the Lilliputian army.

Naills, Sticck [nāls, stĭk]
The master-builder of crinkplunk fame.

Nitpoopo [nĭt-poo'-pō]
Literally – footlickers; the Nitpooperlers collectively; a Board or Cabinet consisting of the Heads of the more important departments of the Lilliputian government.

nitzbutz [nĭts'-boots]
Scofflaw, or drinking-law violator (both singular and plural).

Noshort, Skrewky [nō'-shōrt, skroo'-kē]
A certain Scnakador of long wind and robust constitution; the HORSERADISH.

Olvedts, Randew [ōl'-vĕts, răn'-doo]
The author of Lilliput's drinking-law; a great patriot and honorary Skork, D.T.

Ooick, Wickdomp [ōick, wĭck'-dŏmp]
Nitpooperler of Education, Labor, and Cockroach Extermination.

Orflatz, Manzupe [ōr'-flăts, măn'-zoo-pē]
Chief engineer on the project of building the first zingpup.

Ossdoc, General [ōss'-dŏc]
A member of the Nitpoopo, and the High Commander of the Lilliputian Army.

Pash, Spogden [păsh, spŏg'-děn]
A modern Lilliputian versifier who experiences so much trouble with the language as he finds it that he makes up most of his language as he goes along.

paynetakit [pān'-tāk-ĭt]
The upper house of the tricamerate; it came into existence when the estibelobs got organized.

paynetakitor [pān-tā'-kĭ-tōr]
A member of the paynetakit.

Peebrosk, Mrs. [pē'-brŏsk]
Something of a gossip about town, and decidedly a subject for gossip.

pink [pĭnk]
Something invisible to others which a Lilliputian seeing red, or wearing rose glasses, perceives in an object, person, or idea when the same does not correspond to his prejudice, or when it lies beyond his comprehension.

popweeze [pŏp'-wēz]
The lower house of the tricamerate.

popweezer [pŏp'-wē-zẽr]
A member of the popweeze.

quink [kwĭnk]
A Lilliputian unit of linear measurement — 208 feet, 6.1821 inches.

ruquat [rōō'-kwăt]
A drinking vessel; a goblet.

Saavecassh, Woostow [sāv'-căsh, wōō'-stŏw]
A condemned criminal whose execution Gulliver witnessed at the Mildendo Prison.

scandunk [scăn'-dŭnk]
A Lilliputian unit of linear measurement, approximately 2.2 inches.

Scanezi [scăn-nē'-zē]
A small Island people near Lilliput feared by the Lilliputians.

Scantak, Barrister [scăn'-tăk]
Successor to Bittzzora; Head of the Department of Prisons, Crime, Injustice, and Liquor Consumption.

scatchmanmond [scătch'-măn-mŏnd]
An ancient Lilliputian indoor game invented by a lunatic to while away his time when convalescing from a severe sunstroke.

Schlizpot [schlĭz'-pŏt]
A town in Lilliput; they do not even drink beer there — they drink saki.

scazpop [scăz'-pŏp]
Common vehicle – hollow sphere.

schrunk [shrŭnk]
Lilliputian unit of currency worth approximately very little.

schipidtpot [schĭ-pĭd'-pŏt]
Any machine or mechanism.

Scnakad [scnă'-kăd]
The middle house of the Lilliputian legislature.

Scnakador [scnă-kă'-dōr]
A member of the Scnakad.

scramblivity [scrăm'-blĭ-vĭ-tē]
A modern theory of education characterized chiefly by a breakdown in distinctions in subject matters.

shari [shăr'-ē]
A Lesbian.

Sizez Harbor [sī'-zĕz]
The Naval base of the Lilliputian navy.

Skaldit kire [skăl'-dĭt kīr]
A political subdivision somewhat like a county.

Skeetut [skē'-tŭt]
Official residence of the Donkgop.

Skiteet, Skoy (Mr. and Mrs) [skĭ'-tēēt, skōy]
A family for a long while the subject of much Mildendo gossip.

skiwashy [skī-wäsh'-ē]
A juvenile slang term denoting something not pleasing or good.

Skonkup Schklel [stŏnk'ŭp sh-klĕl']
Sea Suds — the title of a poem by Ammzstyo.

Skork [skōrk]
Something of a hundred-per-center — an honored officer in the
law enforcement service – very patriotic, and usually drunk.

Skreekwow [skrēk'-wŏw]
The name of a certain child in primary school.

Skuztop, Skad [skŭz'-tŏp, skăd]
A rich Lilliputian scazpop manufacturer.

slaginzebob [slă'-gĭn-zē-bŏb]
A profane word having vile connotations, but no definite meaning.

Slisepaarts, Healer [slīs'-parts]
The name of a certain member of the "cutter" school of the
healing profession.

Sneebrew, Gant [snē'-brŏw]
The name of a fezerdick famous in the history of the early Lilliputian republic.

snickdid [snick'-dĭd]
Literally – a flying egg; a small bomb-like offensive weapon
used in the Lilliputian army.

Snoopdeap, Professor [snōōp'-dēp]
A professor in the Mildendo Goosaree.

Spraygrees, Admiral [sprā'-grēs]
A member of the Nitpoopo, and High Commander of the Lilliputian Navy.

sprugswel [sprōōg'-swĕl]
The chief executive in a town — a mayor.

Squeesegraft, Chief [skwēz'-grăft]
The Chief of the Mounted Police.

Staidorf [stā'-dōrf]
A famous Mildendo hotel.

Stang Lob [stăng lŏb]
The principal street in the city of Mildendo.

Stangl-Hinstool [stăng'-ĕl hĭn'-stōōl]
An industrial concern which floated many suckorities that sank the holders thereof.

suckorities [sŭk-kōr'-ĭ-tēs]
Rubber balloon-like objects which serve as the chief article of trade and commerce in Mildendo; originally they were symbolical of, and evidence of the holder's interest in some business enterprise; of late the holders thereof.

Swaff, Flink [swăf, flĭnk]
The special prosecutor in the Bittzzora trial.

swak [swăk]
A profane word.

Swarly, Stang [swar'-lē, stăng]
An officer having something to do with the Lilliputian mail, and a great deal to do with politics.

Sympson, Richard
Lemuel Gulliver's cousin, and a vandal, if there ever was one, for he destroyed the part of **Gulliver's Travels** which set forth the directions for reaching Lilliput.

Tangeytea, Mrs. [tăng'-ē-tē]
A Lilliputian woman reputed to be an expert moronsnidge player.

thgbainbut [thĭg-bān'-bŭt]
A kind of Lilliputian brandy.

Tilutug, Scar [tĭ-lōō'-tŭg, scăr]
The name of a student in the Mildendo Goosaree.

Tomatocumber, Nitpooperler [tō-mā'-tō-cŭm'-bēr]
High Officer in the Department of Money, Change, Cash, and Corruption.

Tootsiehot, Skerenzie [tōōt'-sē-hŏt, skĕr'-ĕn-zē]
Mildendo woman often mentioned in loose gossip.

Totedirrt, Miss [tōt'-dĕrt]
The champion gossip of Mildendo.

tricamerate [trī-căm'-ĕr-āt]
The Lilliputian legislature.

tricamerator [trī-căm'-ĕr-ā-tōr]
A member of the tricamerate.

utznay [ŭts'-nā]
A juvenile slang word expressive of scorn or indifference.

Waaxwroth, Sat [wăx'-wrŏth, săt]
An inmate of the Mildendo Prison convicted of murder.

Wardorg, Scance [wạr'-dōrg, scănce]
A famous Lilliputian lawyer who defended Bittzzora.

Watwil, Mezarra [wŏt'-wĭl, mĕz'-ăr-ă]
The wife of Onk Watwil, the calvalry officer.

Watwil, Onk [wŏt'-wĭl, ŏnk]
A cavalry officer who becomes Arthur Gulliver's chief enemy in Lilliput.

Wauskivilli [wạ'-skĭ-vĭl-lĭ]
A Lilliputian city, exceeded in size only by Mildendo.

Wherding, Medid [whēr'-dĭng, mē'-dĭd]
The latest Donkgop of Lilliput.

Whingdid, Madluuk [whĭng'-dĭd, măd'-lŭk]
The name of a convict in the Mildendo Prison.

Xnot, Zizzo [znŏt, zĭ'-zō]
A little girl who set a house afire.

Zachpedst [zăch'-pĕdst]
A profane word.

zangnuts [zăng'-nŭts]
Mirror or reflector, rays of which supply out-of-door lighting in Lilliput.

zingpup [zĭng'-pŭps]
Literally — a moon scratcher; a tall building.

Zinpan, Scan [zĭn'-păn, scăn]
A Lilliputian architect who created the first zingpup.

zishawshawws [zĭsh'-aw-shaws]
A generic legal term meaning whereas, wherefore, said, aforesaid, etc.

Afterword

About the author, Joseph Martin Cunningham.

MY FATHER, Joseph Martin Cunningham, was born in 1904 near Raton, New Mexico Territory, and grew up on a ranch near Springer. He was named after his grandfather, Dr. Joseph Martin Cunningham (1846-1922) – osteopathic physician and surgeon, President of the San Miguel National Bank in 1892, and the second Mayor of East Las Vegas, New Mexico. His father, Charles C. Cunningham (1885-1921), was killed while my father was still in high school.

Joe, my father, attended the University of California at Berkeley studying law. However, because of serious illness, he completed his degree in teaching instead of law. Although I understand he later passed the bar exam, he never practiced law professionally. He did write an introductory guide to constitutional law in the form of a question and answer dialog. I remember seeing the manuscript many times in my youth, but the manuscript has since been lost.

He moved to Los Angeles and taught English for 33 years at Thomas Alva Edison Junior High School on Hooper Avenue in Watts. He married his first wife, Kay Johnson, also from New Mexico, who gave birth to my sister, Tanya Louise, in June, 1930.

During the early thirties my father was actively writing poetry, short stories, and a play.

By 1942, Joe, Kay, and Tanya were living in the first house I remember on Melbourne Avenue. Kay ran as the Republican candidate for the 56th District of the State Assembly, which included the Los Feliz district of Los Angeles. She narrowly lost the election to Ernest E. Debs.

Sometime after that my father and Kay were divorced. He married my mother, Carmelita Victoria Woodworth (1906-1969), in November, 1944, and I was born in August, 1948. They separated before I started Kindergarten, although they never divorced, and I was raised by my father.

Joe used to love to tell stories and extemporaneously made up bedtime stories for me. Sometimes he would read me poetry: John

Masefield's *Sea Fever*, Alfred Noyes's *The Highwayman*, Robert Service's *The Cremation of Sam McGee*, and other humorous poems. He loved to pun and to make up what he called "Terse Verses", usually just two rhyming words in startling juxtaposition. The old saw, "I'm a poet / and don't know it", and haiku are positively garrulous compared with these.

He died in the Spring of 1970 at Queen of Angels Hospital in Los Angeles, the hospital where I had been born in the Summer of 1948.

★   ★   ★

For more discussion of references in the novel, its relation to other utopian literature, and my memories of my father, follow my blog, **The Estibelob Wars**, on www.newlilliput.com.

Barry W. Cunningham
Cleveland Heights, Ohio
May, 2010

This book was typeset with LaTeX 2.09 using TeXnicCenter 1.0. Its primary font is Bitstream Charter.

Cover photograph and design by Barry Cunningham.

The large scale map of Australasia is from the Library of Congress, Geography and Map Division (http://hdl.loc.gov/loc.gmd/g8950.ct000506). It was drawn by John Pinkerton and published in 1818. A detail from this map, with a notation, possibly in Arthur C. Gulliver's own hand, appears near the front of this book.

The microminiature reproductions of the map *The Kingdoms of Lilliput and Blefuscu* from **Gulliver's Travels** is part of miniature map portfolio **Gulliver's Maps** produced by Bo Press Miniature Books (bopressminiaturebooks.com).

Joseph M. Cunningham's signature at the end is scanned from the original typewritten manuscript of the book.

Back cover photograph shows Joseph Martin Cunningham and Barry Cunningham at Barry's 6th birthday party, August 9, 1954.

www.ingramcontent.com/pod-product-compliance
Lightning Source LLC
Chambersburg PA
CBHW030514020726
47494CB00004B/1096